MOTHER KNOWS BEST

ALSO AVAILABLE BY KIRA PEIKOFF

Die Again Tomorrow

No Time to Die

Living Proof

MOTHER KNOWS BEST

A Novel of Suspense

KIRA PEIKOFF

NEW YORK

This is a work of fiction. All of the names, characters, organizations, places and events portrayed in this novel are either products of the author's imagination or are used fictitiously. Any resemblance to real or actual events, locales, or persons, living or dead, is entirely coincidental.

Published in the United States by Crooked Lane Books, an imprint of The Quick Brown Fox & Company LLC.

Crooked Lane Books and its logo are trademarks of The Quick Brown Fox & Company LLC.

Library of Congress Catalog-in-Publication data available upon request.

ISBN (hardcover): 978-1-64385-040-5
ISBN (ePub): 978-1-64385-041-2

Cover design by Melanie Sun
Book design by Jennifer Canzone

Printed in the United States.

www.crookedlanebooks.com

Crooked Lane Books
34 West 27th St., 10th Floor
New York, NY 10001

First Edition: September 2019

10 9 8 7 6 5 4 3 2 1

For Zachary,
who made me a mother

Now you are mine
From your feet to your hair so golden and fine,
And your crumpled finger-tips . . . mine completely,
Wholly and sweetly;
Mine with kisses deep to smother,
No one so near to you now as your mother!
Others may hear your words of beauty,
But your precious silence is mine alone;
Here in my arms I have enrolled you,
Away from the grasping world I fold you,
Flesh of my flesh and bone of my bone!

—Lucy Maud Montgomery, *The Mother*

PART ONE

CLAIRE

An hour into our drive, Abby's announcement startles us.

"I have a surprise for you, Mommy."

"Oh?" I crane my neck to see her grinning in the back seat. She has the same coy dimple as Colton, the brother she never met. "What kind of surprise?"

"A *big* one." Her cell vibrates then, sucking her attention into its dragnet. For once, I'm thankful; she doesn't notice my sharp inhale.

But my husband does. He takes one hand off the wheel to rest it on my thigh. As we speed down the West Side Highway, I stare out the window at the gloomy gray Hudson. I despise nothing more than surprises, but my daughter is a black box of mischief, brimming with secrets and delight.

While she's lost in her phone, I peek again at her face. Her eyes are cool blue, like glacier ice; her nose is spattered with freckles; her creamy skin is not yet pimpled by puberty. It's impossible to tell that my beautiful girl is the first of her kind.

Even she doesn't know.

The only thorn in the comfort of her appearance is her hair. It's the color of a shiny penny, though no one in the family is a redhead. I'll never forget the time a stranger joked, *Are you sure she's yours?*

She catches me staring and closes her phone. "How much longer?"

"Five minutes," Michael says, turning off at 79th Street and Riverside Drive.

We exchange puzzled looks. This trip to the Natural History Museum, our annual ritual on her brother's birthday, means little to her. He passed away a few years before she was born.

Michael never met Colton either, but he savors my tradition because it's the one day each year we allow ourselves to act like the regular family we've never been. Once a year, I'm willing to take the risk. The odds of disaster are so low.

The rest of the time we avoid the city. God forbid we wind up caught on camera, then splashed across social media. I view the outdoors the way others view blizzards—as dicey exposure to the elements, requiring us to cover up. Better to hunker down and lie low.

But someone out there will never give up searching. Someone who's long out of prison, whose name I can't bear to utter or think.

J looms over every school pickup and drop-off, as I stay behind the wheel of my Accord, declining to chat with the other moms. If one recognizes me and the media pick up the scent, the police will come knocking—

And J won't be far behind.

As we cross Broadway toward the museum, J lives in the recesses of my brain like a bloody knife buried deep underground.

Abby knows nothing about J. One day, we'll have to sit down with her. Tell her the truth. But not on Colton's birthday. Today he would have been twenty-one.

Michael parallel parks on a side street near the museum, and my throat constricts. Visiting my son's favorite place brings me so much closer to him than visiting his grave.

As soon as the car stops, Abby jumps out.

"Wait!" I yell, but she's already zipping past a row of yellow tulips planted along the sidewalk.

"Hurry up!" She beckons me impatiently. "It's almost time!"

"Time for what?" I ask Michael.

He shrugs. "No idea."

As we step out of the car into the cool spring morning, I tug the brim of my baseball cap down low over my eyes. It's a Yankees hat I ordered online to blend in with the city people, even though I couldn't name a single player on the team.

The city's energy is a jolt after our rural town upstate. Pedestrians, joggers, and dog-walkers vie for sidewalk space between rows of half-bare trees. Across the street, a group of protesters is huddled in front of a grocery store holding signs that read SAY NO TO GMOs and QUIT TRYING TO GET IN MY GENES. A few yards ahead of us, Abby pauses to ogle them—not much activism happens in our sleepy town—and Michael quickly shuttles me past.

"It's okay," he mutters. "No one's looking."

My nervous side glances have become a tic. But he's right. Nobody sees us, nobody cares. Do people still remember scandals over a decade old? To be safe, we walk faster and stare forward like normal people who aren't living in fear.

Today is about Colton, I remind myself.

I wonder whether Abby's surprise involves a tribute to him. After all these years of her whining about the long drive to the city and the "boring" museum, maybe she's decided to finally participate in honoring his memory. But I have no idea what her gesture might be, or why it would involve a schedule.

What was she typing into her phone?

When I catch up to ask her, she smiles. "You'll see."

Then she skips ahead. The museum looms large, its magnificent glass and steel dominating the entire city block. Walking the path reminds me of the final month of Colton's life, when I pushed his wheelchair from our apartment to the museum for the last time. I try to tamp down the guilt, but it still twists knots in my stomach.

Michael telegraphs his support by squeezing my hand: *It wasn't your fault.*

When we reach the bottom of the museum's legendary steps, my eyes are stinging. I lean against the railing.

"I just need a minute."

Abby hops up beside me.

"So Mom, remember when we did that spit test in biology a few months ago?" She rises onto her tiptoes with a strange excitement.

"Not right now, honey."

"Okay, but you do remember?"

I sigh. "Of course." The entire fifth-grade class participated in a genetic experiment through the company MapMyDNA. All the kids spit into a tube and received a report of their inherited traits, like whether they had detached earlobes or could taste bitter flavors. We felt cornered into letting her participate. It was easier than answering the questions that would follow, but the test came and went without a hitch.

"What about it?" I ask.

"Well, me and my friends created profiles so we could compare our reports."

"You never told me that!"

My sudden harshness makes her scowl.

"It's not that big a deal, *jeez*. But guess what, I have two hundred and thirteen distant cousins!"

My back stiffens. In the corner of my eye, I notice Michael frown.

"So get this," she continues, oblivious. "I got a message from someone who shares thirty-seven genes with me, and we started talking, and it turns out she's a cousin you lost touch with!"

I grip the railing to keep my balance. "Did you say thirty-seven?"

"Mom doesn't have any long-lost cousins," Michael snaps. "And since when do you have permission to talk to strangers online?"

"Yes, you do," Abby says to me, ignoring him. She jumps off the railing to look me in the eye. "I know for a *fact*, 'cause DNA doesn't lie!"

My knees turn liquid. Michael's arm shoots out behind me.

"Mom's not feeling so hot," he says. "Maybe we should go."

"But I promised her she could meet us today! It was going to be a family reunion in Colton's honor."

I hear myself gasp. "What? Where?"

She points up the dozens of stairs to the museum's glass doors.

The time it takes me to turn my head stretches out to the length of her lifetime, all eleven years flattened down to one irrevocable glance.

All the way up on the top step, a young woman with sleek red hair stands watching us. She's wearing a skintight black dress that shows off her cleavage and her confidence. Anyone else might call her beautiful, but all I can see is the hardness in her gaze, the smile that is both triumphant and chilling.

It is J.

Noises cease. Hours unfold in the space of seconds.

For some indeterminate period, I simply stare. I'm capable of nothing else. My mind is on lockdown, my reflexes on standby. I'm trapped in her gaze as though she has me by the neck.

Though she's at least fifty steps away, I can sense the victory in her smirk:

Gotcha.

In this numb state, I am severed from time and space. I find myself tumbling back years, to the last time we saw each other. It was at a wine bar only a few blocks away, the meeting that set our lives on a collision course. Back then, her beauty evoked Renoir—the ginger curls tumbling over her large breasts, the fair skin, the full pout. But unlike the soft eyes of those painted women, hers were weapons; their intelligence cut through you like an act of violence, an intrusion into your soul.

They hook me again now. It's how I recognize her, because she has transformed. Gone are her long curls, her round cheeks, her ample curves. She's still young, still fifteen years younger than me, but her body has grown hard and lean. Her hair is cut close to her chin, and her face, despite her smile, projects a bitterness that terrifies me.

Over the years, I've fantasized about fighting her if she ever came near Abby—pushing her off a cliff, drowning her in our pool. But now I see that's a joke. If I punched her in the stomach, my knuckles would probably bruise.

"Mom!" Abby cries, breaking my trance. "Are you okay?"

I pull her instinctively against my chest, the way I used to when she was a baby and the world was still actively searching for us.

Michael folds us both into his arms. He's blocking us from her sight, protecting us however he can. His eyes are wide. His shock compounds mine.

Abby squirms away from us. "What's *wrong*?"

I've never felt more unprepared to answer her. I'm about to open my mouth when something at the edge of my vision catches my eye.

A little boy is playing on the top step amid all the tourists who are waiting in line. I shift to get a better look at him, and immediately sink to the cold concrete; a scream erupts from my throat.

He's Colton in the flesh.

I am gripped by a panic and longing so intense I can't move. Michael tries to lift me off the ground, Abby says a few words I don't hear.

He's eight years old again, the age he died, but now he's smiling and skipping in circles around a group of other children—I know that straw-colored hair, that perky nose, the shape of those eyes, almond like mine. I have missed him, dreamed of him, ached for him for thirteen years, bargained with a God I don't believe in, if I could only see him one more time . . .

My sight goes opaque behind a curtain of tears, and just like that, he's gone. I claw at my eyes, but it's no use. He's vanished. I lunge toward the stairs, I will find him—*to hell with J*—but Michael yanks me back, shouting, "What are you doing?"

"Let me go!" I smack his chest, but he's stronger, he holds me down, and I whiplash back in time again to the dark days when my son's silhouette teased me in the shadows.

Michael's voice obliterates the memory. "You're hyperventilating. Breathe."

My head is throbbing. A sour liquid climbs up my throat.

"Did you see him?" I choke out. "Over there?"

"Him?" Michael peers up at the stairs in confusion. J is still there, smirking at us beside a stone column, but I blank her out, searching for my boy.

"Colton." As soon as I say his name, I know I'm losing it. Michael's horror tells me as much.

"But he was right there . . ." I trail off, staring at the spot where he was laughing and running like the healthiest boy in the world. Of course it wasn't really him. Colton could never run. Colton is *dead.* The word still shatters me.

Abby backs away from me. "Mom, you're freaking out."

"I swear to God I saw him." The tears are falling fast. "That boy . . ."

"Honey," Michael says gently, "you're having a panic attack. Let's get out of here."

He ushers me and Abby away from the museum, away from J's disturbing stare. I want to argue, negotiate, plead with him to believe me, but I know he never will. The worst part is, I know he never should.

"We just got here!" Abby stops. "What about your cousin?"

"There is no cousin," he retorts. "We're going home. Your mother needs to lie down."

"But I talked to someone who knew her."

"You talked to a *stranger* who tried to meet you," he says, as we march down the sidewalk toward our car. My legs cooperate somehow, even though my mind is back on the steps, on that boy—my boy.

"From now on," Michael is telling her, "you're forbidden from talking to anyone on that website. I'm canceling your profile as soon as we get home."

"But she shared my DNA!"

"So what? Don't you have over two hundred 'cousins'?"

"Well, yeah . . ."

"It means nothing. Understood?" He says it to me as much as to her. My eyes have rebelled against my mind. It's not the first time.

"It means nothing," he repeats, in my direction.

"I heard you before," Abby grumbles.

"Then let it go."

Our car is in sight a block away. He peeks over his shoulder, walking briskly, though no one is following us. I check, too. She's not there. He unlocks the car with the key fob. Its horn bleeps, the headlights flicker. We're going to get away scot-free. Like nothing even happened.

He takes me by the hand. "Okay?"

I slide into the passenger seat, dazed. Abby climbs in the back seat. He slams his door and peels away from the curb. I pick up on his nervous energy, the speed with which he swerves onto the street.

I press my nose to the window, as if my late son is about to come waltzing around the block. Michael puts his hand on my thigh.

"Did you bring your Xanax?"

His question is rhetorical; I always carry a bottle in my purse for emergencies. I scoop out a little white pill and stick it under my tongue for fast relief. Sure enough, within a few minutes, my pulse begins to slow.

He clears his throat. "So no one was there, right?"

After a brief hesitation, I nod.

It's settled, then: I've reconciled with reality, and we will not be telling Abby about J. She's still too young, her universe too innocent. Her experience of danger is limited to falling off a horse.

In an hour and a half, we will arrive at our house in the woods and attempt to burrow back into our inconspicuous life, where Michael makes blueberry pancakes on Sundays, Abby rides her bike down our empty street, and I keep counting my lucky stars for another day, another month, another year of peace from the world.

But after today, I know this much: nothing will ever be the same.

ABBY

ONE MONTH LATER

My mom has been acting super weird lately. I mean, don't get me wrong, she's always been weird. She stays in the house most of the time, except for school drop-off and pickup, and she doesn't come to stuff that all the other moms go to, like bake sales and soccer games. It sucks when people ask where she is. I usually pretend she's sick or out of town. This year, I started telling everyone she has a rare disease that makes her allergic to sunlight. But I know the other kids don't believe me. They still talk behind my back, especially this one mean girl named Sydney. According to my best friend Riley, they have all these theories, like that she's a witch or a secret agent. I wish it was something that exciting.

The truth is kind of embarrassing: she has serious anxiety issues. My dad told me it's called agoraphobia, and it's extremely hard to cure. I don't get what's so scary about going outside. I hate when she misses my games, even though she makes us go all the way into the city once a year for Colton's birthday. The one exception is for him. *Never* for me. But this year was such a bust that I don't know if we will ever go to the city again. Ever since that day of her meltdown, she's been acting even weirder than usual.

Before, she kept busy around the house while I was at school and Dad was at work. She would go swimming in our pool, and garden in our backyard, which is this big meadow surrounded by trees. Our veggie patch has kale, zucchini, red peppers, snap peas, cucumbers, and cherry tomatoes. Every day after school, we would go out to pick stuff for salads. Then, while I did my homework at the kitchen counter, she made dinner—lasagna or tacos or coconut chicken soup. When Dad was finished with his work, we would all eat together. Life at home was pretty normal, except for her not going anywhere.

But since that day at the museum, she's been acting different. We've started eating frozen dinners or ordering in because she doesn't feel like cooking. The flowers are wilting and the vegetable garden is drying up. When she picks me up from school, her hair is all frizzy and she's wearing sweatpants and a hoodie, with the hood up. Even though it's May and the weather is perfect, her pretty dresses are stuck in her closet.

I keep asking if she's okay, and she always tells me she is *fine, just tired*, or that she's coming down with something. She's been staying in bed a lot, and it freaks me out. I don't know what's wrong, but it feels bigger than a cold.

Tonight, after we all take our seats around our dining room table, I try to pretend everything is normal. Our pizza has just been delivered, and I help myself to a slice of pepperoni while talking about the sleepover Riley invited me to this weekend.

"We're going to watch an R-rated movie," I announce proudly. "The scary one with the clown."

I wait for them to flip, but instead, they barely seem to hear me.

Mom is sticking her fork into a garden salad made of white iceberg lettuce, which she never eats because it has "no nutritional value." Dad is silently watching her.

"The clown that eats kids," I add. "When Riley's brother saw it, he slept on their parents' floor for a week."

Dad sighs. "Abs, you know you're not allowed to watch that stuff."

"But Riley is!" I shove my pizza in my mouth, and the hot cheesy oil drips down my chin. "Her parents are *cool*."

"Well, you're stuck with us squares." He hands me a napkin.

I wipe my lips. "Squares?"

"Old-people slang for nerds."

I give him a sassy smile. "Only squares say *square*."

"Touché."

Dad and I often tease each other, and Mom is our audience. But tonight, she's staring down at her plate as she eats the yucky lettuce. It's no use asking if she's okay. Her answer is always the same.

Dad clears his throat. He catches my eye, and we trade a glance that she doesn't see. The way his lips press together, it seems like an apology.

"I have an idea," he says. "Let's each share one good thing about our day. Honey," he says to her, "do you want to go first?"

Her face is pale. "Well, I got to take a nice nap earlier."

"Anything else?"

"Oh, just stuff around the house." She shrugs as though we can't see right through her. "The usual."

"Right."

She touches her neck. "I might be getting a sore throat."

I can't help rolling my eyes, but she doesn't notice. It's like she doesn't even see me. I put my elbow on the table and reach across her to grab another slice out of the cardboard box. She doesn't bother to scold my bad manners.

"My turn," I say.

Dad gives me his attention. "Let's hear it."

"We got a cool new art teacher." Mom and I love arts and crafts projects, so I expect this to interest her.

"That's nice," she says, looking both at me and through me. It gives me the creeps.

"What are you working on?" Dad asks.

"She's going to show us how to make mandalas." I turn to Mom hopefully. "I could bring one home for us to do together."

I see the twitch in the corner of her mouth—the effort to show delight. "Sure."

"I remember making those once," Dad says quickly. "My dad showed me how."

His dad is long gone, same as my other three grandparents. I'm sad I never got to meet any of them. The Burke family line ends with me. Sometimes I get jealous of the other kids who go visit their relatives over summer break and play with their cousins. Riley thinks it's strange that I have no family besides my parents. I guess it is. I don't know anyone else with such a small family. More than anything else, I wish I had a brother or sister, but Mom won't have another kid no matter how much I beg her.

I squint at her. "Why did you become such a freaking zombie?"

"Abigail!" Dad snaps his fingers. "That's not how you speak to your mother!"

I expect her to come down on me too, but she sighs like she can't be bothered, which pisses me off more.

"What is *wrong* with you?" I demand. "Are you, like, dead inside?"

Dad jumps to his feet, pointing at the stairs. "Go to your room right now."

I bite off a huge mouthful of pizza. "I'm not done."

"You certainly are." He comes around the table and yanks my chair out.

"But I'm the only one being honest!" I glare at her. "Ever since that day in the city, you've been different and I'm sick of it."

She sighs again. "I already told you, I get panic attacks around Colton's birthday. It's a hard time of year."

"But it's been almost a month!"

"Enough." Dad puts his hand on my shoulder and steers me toward the stairs. "Go to your room."

"Wait," she calls. We both turn around.

"I'm sorry, sweetheart. I know I haven't been myself." Her eyes glaze over and I feel my heart squeeze. I want to run and hug her, but I don't. She usually gets sad for a few days or a week around Colton's birthday. Not for this long. She also gets spooked at the littlest things these days—a dog barking, me opening her door. I feel like there's something bigger going on, something she won't admit.

I know what's bothering me and I can't let it go.

"What about your cousin?" I ask. "Was she there that day or not?"

Her whole face darkens. "How many times do I have to tell you? I don't have any cousins."

"But—"

"No buts!" Dad interrupts. "You were chatted up by a sicko. A stranger. This is exactly why you're not allowed on social media!"

"There's no one your family lost touch with?" I ask, ignoring him.

"No!" she shouts. "I'm not going to answer this again."

"*Fine*, jeez." I'm never going to get anywhere, so I stomp up the stairs and slam my door. I've given her enough chances, and she shuts me down every time.

When my parents canceled my profile on the MapMyDNA site, they made it impossible for me to contact the mysterious woman who shares my genes. But I still remember our messages because I took a screenshot of the whole conversation and emailed it to Riley with the headline OMG get this. . . .

A few weeks before the museum, a random chat bubble popped up from someone whose screen name was JH0502: Hi, you showed up as a close relative. Want to connect?

I accepted out of curiosity, and we exchanged DNA maps so we could see how we were related. The site said we shared thirty-seven genes and that we were connected through our "maternal haplogroups" or something like that. We talked in the chat window for a bit. She told me she was a distant cousin of my mom who fell out of touch, and she asked if I had a brother. I explained about Colton and told her we were driving to the city from Garrison to honor his upcoming birthday. When she said she lived in NYC, I invited her to meet up with us. We agreed it would be fun to make it a surprise family reunion.

But then my mom's panic attack ruined the whole thing, and we never got to meet her, and now I can't even message her anymore.

I sit at my desk, thinking of the one line of our conversation that still bothers me:

Do you by any chance have a brother?

If mom doesn't have a long-lost cousin, how could the stranger have known?

My heart is racing as I open my laptop.

I know my mother is lying. And I'm not going to let her get away with it.

CLAIRE: BEFORE

TEN MONTHS TO GO

One pink line. That's all there ever is.

This time, this test stick, will be number twelve. I know because Ethan and I started trying again exactly one year ago, back when we skipped a Yankees game to stay in bed all day.

At least, he believes we're trying. I don't have the heart to tell him no, there is no way in hell I will test fate again. But he is far beyond willing. He's desperate.

Please, he begged me. *We deserve another chance.*

It was his brutal mix of pain and desire, fueled by the fantasy of what had never been, that made me give in. In a moment of weakness, I nodded. That simple concession, I've come to realize, was crueler than a slap in the face. Now, every month, I find myself caught in the same charade, wasting money on pregnancy tests, feigning hope and disappointment.

I hear him pacing outside the bathroom while I sit on the toilet, my underwear circling my ankles, the latest test in hand. He might be in suspense, but I already know the answer.

I proceed with the monthly ritual anyway: Unwrap the pink plastic to insert a fresh tip into the test stick. Hover awkwardly over the miniature cup. Perform the delicate task of peeing into it without spraying my hand—by now, I'm an expert.

Then I insert the stick into the pee and wait. The three-minute countdown begins.

I wish his anxious footsteps outside the door still charmed me. When we were first married, I used to think his earnestness to have a child was flattering. Most of my friends in those days were dragging their feet on kids, though my greatest dream had always been motherhood. I considered myself lucky to find an older man who was ready for the real deal. When we met, he was an esteemed forty-year-old professor of public health and bioethics, already the director of his department at Columbia University, and I a bright-eyed twenty-five-year-old journalism grad student who literally bumped into him in the 116th Street subway station.

Fast-forward to the birth of our son, who came out jaundiced and shuddering, with a wail to rival the bleakest human suffering. And then came Colton's eight-year struggle with mitochondrial disease, against which he never really stood a chance, thanks to his defective genes.

My defective genes. Too late, I learned that the crucial energy-producing parts of my DNA carry a code for faulty wiring. My own invisible flaw became my immutable legacy, magnified and unfixable in every one of his cells.

Now, three years after his death, Ethan craves another child. A second chance. As if my screwed-up genes might respect the agony of the past and erase their faults this time around. To me, the facts are grim: a future child of mine will definitely inherit my abnormal mitochondria. This variety of DNA is always passed from mother to child, virtually unchanged.

But Ethan, stubborn optimist that he is, remains hopeful, because the child's clinical picture could range from asymptomatic—like me—to severe, like Colton, or anywhere in between. My own grandmother was healthy, but my mother suffered bouts of mysterious muscle weakness and breathing difficulties until her death from pneumonia at age forty-eight, when I was only a sophomore in high school. The effect of the damaged mitochondria is random and impossible to predict.

It's worth a try, Ethan urged me. *You could always get prenatal testing, and if it's bad . . .*

But I can't bear to set myself up for another loss.

Nor can I stand to crush his hopes of being a father again. He was such a good dad, affectionate and playful, never showing Colton the fear that consumed us as his illness progressed. After his death, I wasn't sure I would survive. Even now, my mind flees from the black hole of those memories. Too much darkness remains. Things I would never admit to my closest friends.

But Ethan kept my secrets, kept my shame, and dragged us both up despite the gravitational force of our grief.

"I can't go back to that place," I told him when he started talking about trying again. "You know I can't."

"You won't," he promised me. "You've come such a long way. And I have faith that this time will be different. You'll see."

In a burst of hope last year, he painted Colton's old bedroom a pale yellow with a trim of cartoon zoo animals, as though an adorable wall would coax a healthy child into being. To christen our "new start," we made love on the plush carpet. These days, our cleaning lady is the only one who goes in there. We don't even venture down the hall.

"Claire?" he calls, knocking on the bathroom door. "It's been three minutes."

I swallow hard. He uses my name only when he's on edge.

"Hang on."

But he's right. Three minutes are up, and the display on the stick still shows just one line. I'm buying myself time before I must disappoint him again.

I also have a certain unfortunate chore to complete. It's four o'clock on the dot. I pull up my underwear and reach under the bathroom cabinet for my box of tampons that is never empty. It's a box I ran through last year but didn't throw out; I know Ethan will never look inside.

I retrieve my pink disc of birth control pills, pop one of the white tablets under my tongue, and snap it closed. Then I return the box to the cabinet, take a deep breath, and open the door.

The moment he sees my face, the crease between his eyes deepens. He pushes a lock of graying blond hair off his forehead, sighing, without the consolation of a shrug.

We're way past the pretense of better-luck-next-time remarks.

I yearn to feel his sturdy arms tighten around me. But we're past that, too. I'm not sure he has any comfort left to offer. He stares at the floor. It's never gotten this bad, to the point that he won't even look at me.

I've half-heartedly suggested adoption. But he's adamant that we first try in vitro fertilization, no matter how exorbitant the cost or uncomfortable the procedure. We can't keep going like this. The natural route—ovulation tracking, charting my basal body temperature, timing sex to the hour—isn't working. I let him believe it's because of my age, which at thirty-nine seems reason enough. Eventually, I figure, he'll give up and opt for adoption. But deep down, as selfish as it is, I don't want someone else's baby either if there's any chance we can have a healthy child of our own.

One who will thrive past age eight, who will make it to double digits, to the vexing teenage years and beyond—and who will carry a little spark of Colton along the way. I can imagine no greater gift than to bring Colton's sibling into the world. But not if he or she is doomed from the start.

To secure the baby's freedom from mitochondrial disease, I would do anything.

Even if it means secretly betraying my husband's deepest convictions.

I can see the distance in his eyes, the disappointment tearing him away from me. My heart hammers, because what I'm about to say marks the turning point. There will be no going back.

I imagine myself in the future flashing back to this very moment, explaining that I had to lie to save our marriage, that total secrecy was required to protect us both. By then, with the baby in his arms, he'll be overwhelmed with gratitude; he'll empathize with the pain of my choice, and thank me for having the courage to push forward alone. We'll gaze at our sleeping child together, amazed at the life that a genius doctor has made possible. How could he possibly be mad at me then?

"I've decided to give IVF a try," I blurt out.

His head snaps up. "You will?"

"I know how much it means to have our own baby."

I'm amazed to see his eyes grow wet. Ethan never cries. He must be closer to the breaking point than I realized. It only strengthens my resolve.

"I can't believe it," he says. "I thought you were going to give up."

"I'll give it one shot. As long as . . ." I pause to underscore the importance of what I'm about to request.

"What?"

"You let me choose the doctor."

"What difference does it make?"

I hold his gaze without flinching. "I want to see Robert Nash."

He rolls his eyes. "Very funny."

"I'm serious. He has one of the highest success rates of any fertility doctor in the country."

I don't add my other reason. The *real* reason I want to meet the maverick Dr. Nash, whose boundary-breaking research has endeared him to patients but amassed him many critics. Ethan himself, who sits on the President's Bioethics Committee advising the federal government about new medical technology, dealt him a scathing blow in the press a few years ago. After Nash announced his success in silencing a gene associated with deafness in embryos, Ethan wrote a scornful op-ed that shot to the number-one most-read story in the *New York Times*. Ethan wrote passionately of the dangers of manipulating human life: the slippery slope of designer babies, the possibility of introducing unknown harms, and the arrogance of eradicating diversity in the gene pool. "Could one person's disability be another person's desired state?" he wrote. "We should be so suspicious of medical interventions that marginalize legitimate ways of being in the world." A few months later, the FDA came down hard with new restrictions against editing the genes of human embryos, and Nash has declined to publicize his work ever since.

But if the online chatter I came across is true . . .

"Seriously?" Ethan is shaking his head. "That guy is an asshole."

I suppress my irritation. Ethan's influential beliefs about the hazards of biotechnology are a sore spot between us, the kindling for many dinner arguments that until now have been only theoretical.

"Actually," I say, "he's kind of a big deal for fertility patients."

"You know he must hate me, right? I mean, how could he not?"

I flick my wrist. "It's not like he'll recognize you." Ethan's camera shy; he turned down a national talk show after his article went viral. The result is that only his name carries significance, not his face. And we can easily change the former.

Still, he makes no effort to hide his discomfort. "Can't we go to *anyone* else?"

"I already scheduled the appointment, since I was pretty sure this cycle was a bust." I slide my palms into his, interlacing our fingers. "And I guess it's our lucky day after all, because he's normally booked six weeks out, but he had a cancellation."

Ethan hesitates. "For when?"

"Tomorrow. We're seeing him at nine AM sharp."

ABBY: NOW

I'm about to lock my bedroom door when I hear my parents arguing. They're still in the dining room. I crack open the door and poke my ear out.

Dad's voice floats up the stairs. "But she can't *do* anything. How could she?"

Then they must start whispering, because I can't hear any more.

I bet they're talking about me. They don't want me to figure out the truth about Mom's cousin. They think I'm going to drop it because I have no other choice.

But they're wrong. I can do something, and I will. It's so unfair how they still treat me like I'm a baby. Like, I stopped believing in Santa forever ago, but Mom still insists on pretending he stuffs my stocking every year, and Dad shrugs because he can't stop her. She also thinks I've never seen an R-rated movie, and that I'm not on any social media because "it's not safe to talk to people online," even though I have fifty-six followers on Instagram—almost the whole fifth grade. I can only check it secretly on my laptop because she won't let me have a smartphone like everyone else. I know she has serious anxiety problems, but I'm too old for the mom filter.

While my parents are still downstairs, I set my plan into motion.

I can't log on to MapMyDNA anymore since they canceled my account and installed this stupid Net Nanny software on my computer.

But Riley can log on.

I text my best friend on my lame flip phone what I need her to do:

Hey, will u order me a new MapMyDNA kit and bring it to school? Will pay u back. DON'T tell anyone!!

She texts back a row of surprised emojis. What r u up to?!

Tell u tomorrow.;)

The kit has a special Q-tip you use to swab your cheek and collect some saliva. You mail it back so the lab can study your DNA. Then they email you a report, for $99 plus tax and shipping. Luckily, I have $145 saved up from my allowance.

Tomorrow, I'll tell Riley I'm going to test my mom to find out exactly how she and the stranger named JH0502 are related, because DNA doesn't lie. If they *are* cousins, she'll have to tell me the truth. And then maybe she'll see that I don't want to be treated like a baby anymore.

The only problem is, how am I going to get her saliva?

CLAIRE: BEFORE

When Ethan and I arrive at the clinic, on the first floor of a brick building on Central Park West, he stops outside the door.

A plaque reads in gold script: Dr. Robert Nash, MD, PhD.

"I don't know," he mutters. "I have a bad feeling about this."

I rub his back. "Just relax. We won't tell him who you are."

Or else he'll never trust me.

I remind Ethan that I booked the appointment under my maiden name—Glasser instead of Abrams—so there will be no reason for hostility.

"Still," he says irritably, "you should have let me pick the doctor. I could have gotten us in to the top guy at Columbia."

"That's okay."

"But you know this is my area."

I snort, pushing open the door. "When you grow a uterus, you can pick the doctor."

The waiting room looks more like a spa than a doctor's office: white leather couches, a glass pitcher of water and lemon slices, a piano concerto piping in through the speakers. There's one other patient waiting—a woman in her early forties, not visibly pregnant, who keeps glancing up from her phone to stare at the inner door.

I shiver with excitement as I pretend to read through *Fit Pregnancy* magazine. My mind is so far away that I don't notice Ethan offering me a conciliatory smile.

"That could be you soon," he says, pointing to the spread on "What Not to Eat During Your First Trimester."

"I hope so."

A few minutes later, a nurse appears in the doorway and calls me by the name I haven't used in over a decade. "Mrs. Glasser? Come on back."

We follow her past a row of exam rooms to an empty, wood-paneled office. Leather club chairs await us in front of a wide cherry oak desk.

"The doctor will be in shortly," the nurse says, closing the door. My curiosity takes over and I wander around the office, while Ethan sits and escapes into his phone. Several framed diplomas from NYU and Harvard hang on the wall in shiny black frames.

"Top schools," I remark.

Ethan gives the credentials a cursory glance. "Great."

My gaze sweeps over the gleaming surface of the desk, the new Mac desktop with double monitors, and the matching cherry shelves lined with heavy medical tomes like *Clinical Gynecologic Endocrinology* and *Development of Pre-implantation Embryos.*

"He doesn't have any family photos," I note.

As a journalist for the pop science magazine *Mindset*, I'm fascinated by people whose work requires strict boundaries. My job is to break those down, probe deeper, unearth any relevant knowledge and illuminate it for the masses. The trick to a good interview is to gain the trust of the person behind the uniform, whether doctor or researcher or CEO, by finding some element of human connection. But some subjects prove much harder to access than others. Especially those with something to hide.

"Claire." Ethan sighs. "Sit down before he finds you snooping."

I plop into the stiff leather seat a few seconds before the door opens.

Dr. Nash is taller and younger than I expected—about my age—and undeniably more striking. His features are hard and symmetrical, lending him a certain gruffness despite his neutral expression. At the same time, his unruly black hair gives the opposite impression—that he can be unrestrained, even playful.

When Ethan and I stand to shake his hand, he dwarfs my husband, who stands a respectable five foot ten. By Ethan's thin smile, I can tell he is none too pleased to look up at the man he once minimized.

We exchange introductions. Unlike other doctors who shuffle between paperwork and their computer while patients talk, Nash folds his hands on his desk and smiles politely. His gray eyes seem astute enough to see through my pretense, though I know that's impossible.

"So," he says, "how can I help you?"

I glance at Ethan, noticing the stamps of our tragedy in his creased forehead and receding hairline. He nods for me to explain.

"Well." I nervously clear my throat. "We want a baby, but we need to use an egg donor."

My pace slows over the word *egg*. If Nash notices, he doesn't show it.

"You never told me that," Ethan interjects. "I thought you wanted to try yourself." His tone betrays a hint of indignation, tempered for the doctor's sake.

"I've been thinking, and . . . and I feel like it's too risky."

"How so?" Nash asks.

I explain briefly about Colton. The faster the saga, the less likely I am to break down. It's like skidding over a lake of brittle ice.

Nash grows solemn. "I'm so sorry." To Ethan, he says, "I think your wife is making a wise decision not to roll the dice again with her own eggs. We have no way to predict how significantly her next child would be affected until he or she is born."

Exactly, I think.

Ethan furrows his brow. "But I thought you wanted our own child?"

I do, I want to shout. *Of course I do!*

Instead, I say, "I want a healthy child more. And it's one or the other." Innocently, I look at Nash. "Right?"

There's no slight pursing of his lips, no widening of his eyelids. After years of interviewing, I'm attuned to micro-expressions, but Nash seems even more practiced at neutrality. His expression remains placid.

"I'm afraid so."

Ethan leans forward. "But what about doing PGD before implantation of the blastocyst? Since a trophectoderm biopsy can pinpoint genetic abnormalities, you can screen out the most severely affected ones, can't you?"

I feel myself stiffen. It's so *Ethan* to negotiate, even if it means inadvertently revealing who he is.

"Spoken like an expert." Nash eyes him curiously. "What is it that you do, Mr. Glasser?"

I know Ethan must be thinking, *It's* Dr. *Abrams, director of the bioethics program at Columbia*. But he says, "Oh, I'm a teacher." He pauses. "High school bio."

I release my hostage breath. "And I'm a writer." Not that it matters, but I feel compelled to gloss over his fib. I fiddle with one of my gold hoop earrings.

"Your question is valid," Nash says. "But mitochondrial disease is not a straightforward genetic problem. Mutation levels don't necessarily correspond to severity of disease, so even if we did try to select for any embryos with lower levels of faulty DNA, there's no guarantee the child would be healthier. Or healthy at all."

It takes all my self-control not to blurt out my next thought: *But you can get around that, can't you?*

Nash stands, smoothing out his white coat, and gestures for us to follow him. "Let's take a look at you, shall we?"

I nod. "Sure." As he and Ethan walk out of the office ahead of me, an idea strikes. I unlatch my earring and drop it quietly on the floor.

Then I trail them into an exam room and hop up onto the chair's starchy paper sheet. Ethan sits on a stool while Nash reviews the chart I filled out in advance with my medical history. As he starts to discuss the process of choosing an egg donor, I touch my earlobe and gasp.

"Shit, my earring," I interrupt. "I'm so sorry, it must have fallen off. I'll be right back."

I hurry down the hallway back to his office and shut the door. I open his desk drawers and find a stack of Post-its and pens. Scribbling hastily, I write on a neon yellow pad:

I know your secret. Let me tell you mine. Meet me tonight at 9, the Stone Rose Lounge. I think we can help each other.
(Thanks to Jillian.)
Claire Glasser

I leave the pad on his keyboard and return to the exam room, where Ethan is doing his best to ignore Nash by replying to an email on his phone. I make a show of putting my earring back on.

"Found it!" I chirp. "Now, where were we?"

ABBY: NOW

The week after my text about the new spit test, Riley shows up to first period with an extra bulky backpack. Across the room, she grins at me and flashes a thumbs-up.

Our desks used to be side by side, but we chatted nonstop, so our homeroom teacher moved us as far away from each other as possible. Now it's even more fun because we spend the day passing notes instead. We'll walk past each other's desks and drop folded squares into the other person's lap when the teachers aren't looking. They rotate every period while we stay in the same classroom. But if we want to be extra careful, we'll go over to our cubbies, where our backpacks sit in labeled bins, and we'll zip a note into the other person's bag. Pretty much the whole fifth grade uses this method to pass notes because we're less likely to get caught than doing it out in the open. (It's how my crush Tyler told me he liked me: he stuffed a note into my bag with two blank boxes and the question, *Do you like me? Yes or no, check one.* I checked yes, and now we sit together at lunch sometimes.)

Today, as class begins, Riley pushes back her chair. While the morning announcement comes on—permission slips due for the upcoming field trip, yearbooks available next week—she heads toward the supply cabinet, passing my desk.

I pretend to concentrate on my notebook. Mrs. Miller, the art teacher, is sketching at the whiteboard with her back to the class, so she doesn't see Riley's fist open over my lap. I catch the folded square and open it under my desk:

Got the kit! Meet me in the bathroom at lunch.

As she walks away, I mouth, *You're the best.*

That's when I notice Sydney, to my left, giving me a dirty look. Ugh. She and I do *not* get along. It started when I didn't invite her to my birthday party last year after I found out she called me a dork behind my back. Then she spread a horrible rumor about my mom, saying she hides inside because she has a flesh-eating bacteria. The principal made her apologize, but we still aren't cool. The latest thing is that she asked Tyler to hang out after school, but he said no to go to my soccer game. She's been really pissed at me since then.

Anyway, I have bigger things to worry about. Like, how am I going to get my mom to spit into a tube? I think of what Mr. Harrison, our science teacher, taught us about the scientific method: *ask a question, do background research, create a hypothesis, test your hypothesis, analyze your data, and draw a conclusion*. But if your whole experiment is a secret, how are you supposed to pull it off in the first place?

Our next period is science class. I decide to raise my hand and find out.

Mr. Harrison, a big scruffy teddy bear of a guy, calls on me in the middle of his lecture about the heliocentric theory. "Yes, Abigail?"

I try to ask my question in a way that won't make him suspicious. "So, you know how everyone was supposed to think the sun was the center of the universe?"

"Yes?"

"Well, how did Copernicus and those other astronomers prove it wasn't?"

Mr. Harrison raises his bushy eyebrows. "You mean, with what kind of telescopes?"

"No, like, how did they get away with it?"

"The short answer is they didn't. Does anyone know what happened to Galileo, for example?"

The boy next to me raises his hand. "Didn't he get arrested?"

"Worse." Mr. Harrison becomes very serious. "He was convicted of heresy by the church and sentenced to house arrest for the last nine *years* of his life." His gaze returns to me. "Does that answer your question?"

So much for encouragement. "Um, I guess so."

Riley raises her hand with a sparkle in her eye. "But it was worth it, right? Even though he got in big trouble?"

"Oh, yes." Mr. Harrison gives us a slow, wise nod. "In fact, I would argue that the pursuit of truth even at grave personal cost is the definition of heroism."

Across the classroom, she flashes me a smile.

Okay, I think. *That's more like it.*

CLAIRE: BEFORE

The Stone Rose Lounge is a swanky fourth-floor bar with circular leather booths walled in by a sheet of glass that overlooks Central Park South. Waiters wearing bow ties breeze over marble floors carrying nineteen-dollar cocktails to titans of finance and fashion, people whose idea of a perfect night surely doesn't involve tiny hands or toothless smiles.

I don't belong here. Ethan and I rarely go out for date nights anymore. Concentrating on a movie or getting dressed up takes too much effort, and feels too hollow. Posing among these carefree strangers now seems like a betrayal of Colton, as though their cheeriness undermines my loss.

But this meeting, if Nash even shows up, is the furthest thing from entertainment. I sit up straighter, touching the diamond studs I unearthed from my jewelry box. I'm determined to establish my credibility as someone trustworthy and rational, even though I still feel like an impostor of my old self.

Then again, eighteen months off my antidepressants, I'm still getting dressed every morning, still writing monthly features for the magazine. My colleagues think I've recovered admirably. But they don't know the half of it.

Sipping my outrageously priced merlot, I cringe about fibbing to Ethan. He thinks I'm grabbing a drink with my editor. That way, if he decides to locate me on Find Friends, he won't be surprised to see me at a bar. Our shared GPS-tracking app is a bit stalker-ish, but it does come in handy as reassurance when one of us travels or can't be reached.

I adjust my low-cut silk blouse, making sure it doesn't reveal too much cleavage. There's a fine line between attractive and slutty. A pinch of the former probably couldn't hurt, but the latter might doom me from the start.

My heart sinks when I glance at my phone. 9:18 PM.

He's not coming. It's obvious. I peel my gaze away from the entrance and try not to look so desperate.

He must think I'm a creep. In fact, he's probably laughing about my stupid note with his wife right now, if he has one. And she's probably rolling her eyes at my earnest handwriting, invoking our mutual "secrets." *God*, how pathetic.

But I've been so swept up! Given the source of the rumor, it seemed plausible. I ponder where I could have gone wrong.

About five years ago, when Colton's illness accelerated to its final stages, I received an invite from the hospital staff to join a private online support group called Mighty Mito Moms. The women offered comfort, understood my devastation, and answered questions about everything from cleaning a feeding tube to managing a low-blood-sugar meltdown. The group also feverishly sought news of cutting-edge research into mitochondrial diseases. As sophisticated as grad students after years of coping with their children's illnesses, the moms scoffed at overhyped words like *cure* and *breakthrough*.

So when a trusted member called JohnsMom111 recently started a new thread titled "Legit Development in NY Lab—Could Be BIG," I paid attention.

JohnsMom111 had met a postdoc named Jillian who worked in Nash's lab. I wasn't surprised by this connection, since the moms were well networked with innovative scientists across the U.S. This Jillian had confided a tip about Nash's current project in order to secure private funding from the moms' wealthy donor circle. But the project was under wraps, so details were spare.

All we learned was that Nash had allegedly managed to create a healthy egg for women who carry mitochondrial diseases. In other words, we could give birth to our own genetic children—safely—with a slight caveat. Word is that he's figured out how to stitch together two women's DNA—the healthy nucleus from a woman like me, and the healthy mitochondria from a donor woman to make up for the former's deficit. This is theoretically possible because mitochondrial DNA is found *outside* a cell's nucleus.

If the nucleus is like a big, important mansion, housing almost all the cell's DNA, then the mitochondrial DNA is like a little gas station in the backyard. The station may be tiny, but its energy powers the entire lot. In some cases, however, the gas station is prone to catching on fire, which threatens to wipe out the whole property.

Nash's idea is to rescue the mansion from the burning property by airlifting it onto somebody else's safe property whose own mansion has been removed. All that remains there is its working gas station, until the new mansion takes up residence. The resulting combined lot will be set for life—not a fire in sight.

In real terms, Nash may have pulled off creating a hybrid egg, which could then be fertilized with sperm. Such an embryo would have two genetic mothers and one father. If this is real, it's totally radical, paving the way for offspring from *three* individuals for the first time in history. And totally illegal, violating the strict federal ban on editing human embryos intended for reproduction.

It would be so much easier if three people didn't need to be involved—if, say, my husband could loan out some healthy mitochondria instead of a random donor woman, but unfortunately biology doesn't work that way. Only eggs—and thus, only women—can pass down this special kind of genetic material.

The odds of such a transplant actually working are long, and the danger is high, but the post from JohnsMom111 ended with a statement I can't stop thinking about:

> Reading between the lines, ladies, it seems like Dr. Nash might be looking for a woman like one of us to volunteer for a clinical

trial to try to have a healthy baby through his procedure, in TOTAL SECRECY OF COURSE . . . or else his work will never be tested in the real world b/c of the laws. Jillian couldn't say so explicitly, but I can take a hint!

The implications tapped a vein of hope I thought had cauterized long ago: the birth of my own child (mostly), conceived with a little help from the latest technology; and the rebirth of my marriage, defined for too long by helplessness and disease.

But Nash is now twenty-seven minutes late.

I lean into my palm and close my eyes. A throbbing sensation in my skull threatens to gather steam, explode into a migraine. The lounge's posh atmosphere of chatter and jazz isn't helping. I gather my non-designer purse to leave.

"Mrs. Glasser?"

Nash stands at the edge of my booth, a briefcase slung over his shoulder and a black trench coat buttoned up over his towering frame. His face is flushed, as though he's jogged several blocks, and his mane is downright untamed. He gives me a rueful half smile, as though I had a right to expect anything of him.

"Sorry I'm late. Wasn't sure you'd still be here."

I swirl the purple liquid in my glass with a smile, forcing myself not to leap up and hug him. "I'm too cheap not to finish my wine."

"Fair enough." He scoots into the booth across from me and sets his briefcase aside. In the low light, with the panorama of skyscrapers silhouetted in the window, his features stand out in sharp relief: the heavy ridge of his brow, the nose that's a little too pointed, the prominent chin and stern jaw. His handsomeness is aggressively masculine. I can't help thinking of my husband's soft, kind face and even softer middle.

"Thank you for coming. I realize my note wasn't all that . . ." I trail off, unsure where I stand.

He tilts his head. "Conventional?"

"I was going to go with *subtle*, but yeah." I'm suddenly aware of my racing heart. "Do you want to order something?"

"I don't drink." He says it matter-of-factly, without shame. The journalist in me fights the urge to ask why. The prying nature of my job has almost ruined me for normal social interaction.

"Got it." I take a sip of my wine to buy time, but apparently, he isn't one for small talk.

"So how do you know Jillian?" His direct gaze unnerves me.

"Your postdoc?" I wave my hand. "Oh, I don't *know* know her."

He narrows his eyes, and I shift in my seat.

"You've heard of the Mighty Mito Moms? Well, one of our members crossed paths with her and heard about some of the . . . stuff you guys are working on."

"What *stuff*?" A stormy look darkens his face.

I spit out the words. "With the . . . eggs." I lower my voice. "The mitochondrial transplant . . ."

"Jesus Christ." He glances away, muttering something under his breath.

"I thought you wanted . . . ?"

He stares at me blankly.

Okay, maybe he doesn't want volunteers after all.

"Never mind." Mortified, I reach into my purse for a twenty-dollar bill to throw on the table. "I should go."

"No." His hand shoots out. "I need to know what she said."

I repeat the bare bones I learned. "I'm very sympathetic, obviously. All the Mito Moms are. We're the last people you have to worry about."

He sits very still. Too still. Gazes out the window at the shadowy treetops of Central Park. I wait uncomfortably in the silence. Finally, he looks back at me, and his expression is grim.

"She had to blab at the worst possible time."

"She was just excited," I reply, jumping to the defense of this Jillian I've never met. "She knows we're on your side so there wasn't a risk."

"I don't think you understand how sensitive a time this is."

I hold up a hand. "Trust me, I get it."

All anyone in bioethics circles like Ethan can talk about is the FDA's recent draconian punishment of a Yale group who figured out how to engineer a synthetic egg and sperm cell, then create an embryo from scratch—with no parents at all. The scientists argued that they weren't technically breaking the law because they weren't tampering with the genes of a natural embryo, but the FDA disagreed and not only shut down their lab, but announced criminal charges.

Human life is sacred, not fodder for irresponsible experimentation with unknown consequences, the FDA's headline-making statement declared. Ethan read it aloud to me triumphantly over breakfast, practically cheering along with his cereal spoon. *To be human means to have two biological parents—no more and no less. Anything else would be a repudiation of our collective heritage, needlessly redefining and endangering our future generations, and the essential stability of our species.*

Of course, the impact for Nash is just as significant as for the Yale group. Zero parents are as verboten as three parents, and now there can be no doubt about whether the FDA will throw its might behind enforcing the law.

"I just can't believe her," he's telling me. "She's the brightest post-doc I've ever worked with—I'm talking superstar potential. And then to do something so careless? If the press gets wind of this . . ."

"It won't," I tell him firmly. Maybe it's not the best time to mention I'm also a journalist, though my editors at *Mindset* would kill for this scoop. But I don't care. I'm after a much bigger payoff. Either I can leave now and wonder forever, or confront him outright. A memory of Colton assaults me then: the day he was rushed to the ICU in an ambulance as sepsis spread through his veins. *Mommy!* he cried, clutching me as his fever spiked. *I don't want this body anymore!*

I ground myself with a shaky breath.

"I know you don't know me, but the truth is, I think we can help each other."

"You mentioned that." Nash's tone is wary, but I forge ahead.

"There's nothing I want more than to have my own healthy child, and your transplant is the only shot I have. Let me be the first human trial."

He laughs. He actually *laughs*, but the sound is far from mirthful. It's a dry snort.

My breath quickens. "I'm not kidding. I've been to hell and back, and I just want another chance to be a mom. Losing my son . . ." I chomp on my lip. "Please. I would do anything."

He watches me, but his face is inscrutable. I can't tell if he is pitying or judging me. Then he stands and picks up his briefcase.

"You're leaving?"

"I'm sorry about your son," he says, and his voice is gentle enough that I believe him. But then it takes on a harsher edge. "Unfortunately, this meeting was a mistake. I think you should find another doctor."

His eyes betray a sadness that clashes with the hard line of his mouth. Then he turns on his heel and heads for the door.

* * *

JILLIAN

On Friday night, while other people my age are out partying, i.e., getting hammered in some random bar, I'm at home reviewing a lab report.

It's the latest data from Double X—the mitochondrial transplant experiments. An egg's sex chromosome is always an X, while a sperm could be an X or a Y. So combining the DNA of two eggs—two X's—to create a single perfect egg led me to coin the project's shorthand name. Just between me and Nash, since he and I are the only ones working on it.

It's a dream job in more ways than one. Because his fertility clinic is adjacent to his own private lab, he has access to a virtually unlimited supply of human eggs to work with; he gives a price break to IVF patients who donate some of their leftover ones to research. Plus, he's the closest I've come to knowing a genius.

As I underline various stats in the data, I can't help thinking back to our electrifying moment earlier today. Something passed between us. Something that can't be measured or observed. It doesn't matter that he's my boss, or that I'm twenty-four and he's forty-two. The charge between us is undeniable.

I rub my eyes, coaxing the memory back. My cramped studio is dark except for the yellow pool spilling from my desk lamp. No moonlight illuminates The Cave, as I fondly call the place. My only window faces a brick wall, my kitchen is hardly more than a mini-fridge, and the bathroom could be mistaken for a closet. It's a joke, and still, I can barely afford the Upper West Side rent on my postdoc stipend. But in five short blocks, I can walk right into the lab.

Nash rarely doles out compliments. One approving look is enough for me to float for a week. So today's interaction floored me. First, he watched as I demonstrated my innovative method for snipping the nucleus out of a donor egg to preserve more of the integrity of the cell.

Then he shook his head with an I'll-be-damned grin. "You're on your way to greatness, you know that?"

"Come on," I said, though I knew he was right. I've known it ever since my seventh-grade biology teacher, Mr. Sear, pulled me aside and asked whether I would consider skipping straight to a local university. *Undergraduate work would be more appropriate for your level of comprehension and skill*, he told me. In the months that followed, as I aced the bio and stat classes that perplexed college freshmen, I would dwell on Mr. Sear's remark, unpacking its promise and the future it implied.

And now, fresh out of Harvard with my PhD in molecular biology, I'm one of the youngest experts this field has ever seen. And I'm only just getting started.

"I'm lucky to have you." Nash caught my eye. "I mean it."

"Does that mean I get a raise?" My paper mask and magnifying goggles covered half my face, but I'm sure he could tell I was smiling. We were standing side by side at my microscope. To my surprise, he draped one arm around my shoulders.

"How about when you win the Nobel, you'll kick me a percent?"

"Deal," I said. All too soon, he removed his arm. But its weight lingered at the base of my neck, and my shoulders tingled. We'd never touched before. Did it mean something? The gesture was too brief to signify anything other than encouragement, but maybe . . .

An abrupt knock rattles my door. I startle out of my chair—it's after ten PM. No one visits me this late.

"Who is it?"

"It's me," says a distinctive voice. He's *here*? I rush to my mirror and smooth down my hair before opening the door. A late-night visit can mean only one thing.

But as quickly as my hope rises, it vanishes. Nash is more livid than I've ever seen him. His jaw is clenched, his cheeks are pink, and his forehead is beaded with sweat.

"What happened?" I ask in a panic. "Are you okay?"

Without a word, he stomps into my apartment and flicks on the light. It's his first time seeing the place, and I'm embarrassed to show him how modest it is. But he obviously doesn't care; he's staring at me with cold, hard rage.

My mind flies to our farewell hours earlier: I cleaned up my station, recorded the day's progress on the master doc, and said goodnight, still high from our brief contact. He smiled at me and tipped an imaginary hat: *Nice job today.*

"You're fired, Hendricks."

I grip the edge of my console table. "What?"

From his intimidating height, his red face seems volcanic.

"As talented as you are, I just can't trust you. There's too much at stake."

"Excuse me? I'm the best fucking postdoc you've ever had."

"I know." He begins to pace. "But what you did—telling those Mito Moms about our research, which you know very well is now *illegal*—" We lock eyes as he stops short. "What the hell were you thinking?"

"Oh." I smirk. "Yeah, trying to win us more funding is definitely inexcusable. Good point."

"The woman you told spread the news to their whole group!"

"It's fine, they're on our side."

"Yeah, *too* much. One of them just cornered me to volunteer for a trial." He rolls his eyes. "You should have known better. These poor women are desperate."

"So what?" I lift my chin. "They have a right to be. And they've helped us raise money before, so don't they have a right to know where it's going?"

"Not if they're going to blab! I'm surprised the press hasn't already called, and then the feds—and next we're both out of a job, or worse."

Already my mind is racing ahead to how I'll land my next postdoc position with an abrupt dismissal and no recommendation, how I'll make my rent next month without my shitty stipend, and how I would rather eat dirt than ask my parents for money. They run an elite prep school in upstate New York that funnels privileged kids to the Ivy League. As their only child, I grew up in a thicket of expectation and ambition, which intensified when my precocity became apparent. My father used to frame my A+ biology exams around his office, telling visitors, *Jilly's going to make her mark one day.* He even landed a profile of me in the local paper after I was accepted to Bard at age thirteen. And now, after my spark of greatness, this is it? A dishonorable discharge, good-bye and good luck?

Nash is silently watching me, allowing me time to digest the next steps—my inevitable apology, a logistical conversation about collecting my items from the lab, some formal horrible good-bye.

But none of that is going to happen.

Calm settles over me. I will not go gentle into this good night.

"You can't fire me," I say. "At least, you shouldn't."

"Oh really?" I'm emboldened by the tinge of amusement in his voice.

"It would be the biggest mistake you could make."

"Look, I understand—"

"No, you don't." I brush past him to my bookshelf and pull out a biography of the British legends Robert Edwards and Patrick Steptoe.

The cover shows two aging men wearing black-rimmed spectacles and dark suits.

I hold it up. "Remember them?"

"Of course." He crosses his arms. "The fathers of in vitro."

"That's right. They created the first test tube baby in 1978."

"What does that have to do with you?"

"A lot, actually. I'm guessing you haven't read their bio." I clutch the book tightly. "They knew the world would be so scandalized by a baby created in a dish that the experiment would never be permitted, so they were daring enough to carry it out *in secret*, then hid it for the entire nine months of the mother's pregnancy. It was only after Louise Brown was born healthy that they announced it, when no one could question the outcome. And today IVF is as routine as going to the movies."

Nash squints at me. "Jillian—"

"If you remember, Edwards won the Nobel in 2010. Not a bad gamble, huh?"

"You're crazy." He shakes his head. "No way."

"Am I?" I decide to double down. "Or are you a coward?"

My heart is skipping. I know he prides himself on his boldness in going against the establishment. But have I gone too far?

He glares at me. "You know better than that."

"I thought I did. That's why I came to work for you. But what's the point now? We've gotten this far, we know it works—"

"In mice!"

"Which is why the next step *has* to be a clinical trial or it's all for nothing."

"But it's illegal."

"So why are we still testing it?"

He purses his lips, saying nothing.

I hope my use of the word *we* isn't lost on him; I've innovated the methods just as much as he has; to hell with our titles. Our collaboration deserves as equal a billing as Edwards and Steptoe, or Watson and Crick, or any of the famous scientific duos. The cynical side of me wonders if he's figuring out how to take credit for my contributions.

It's practically standard operating procedure for an older male scientist not to acknowledge a subordinate woman's accomplishments, going back to how Watson and Crick failed to credit Rosalind Franklin for her help in discovering the double helix, and now her name is nothing but a footnote in history.

Sure, Nash has heaped on the praise, but he probably still thinks of himself as the pioneer deserving all the glory. Or else how could he come so close to getting rid of me?

Steaming, I grab my cell off my desk. Then, with my back to him, I tap the VOICE MEMOS icon and touch the big red RECORD button. If he ever threatens to fire me again, I won't make it so easy.

I turn around to face him, holding my cell to my chest. "Well? Why even bother?"

"Because," he says quietly, "it's too good to give up."

"So don't." I step closer. "We can do this. That woman gave us the perfect opening. We take her eggs, carry out the DNA transplant in the lab with no one watching, and implant one back in her. Just like a normal IVF patient."

"No." But the force of his denial is undermined by the excitement in his eyes. "It's still crazy. And we would need a healthy egg donor, so that's another person, another liability."

"Not if I do it," I hear myself say. "Then it will just be the three of us." I smile up at him with the satisfaction of a losing player cinching the win. "No one else will have to know a thing."

ABBY: NOW

I get home from school to find Mom and two men from the alarm company going around inspecting all the windows downstairs. She tells me they're upgrading the security system, putting in new sensors and cameras. All I care about is that she doesn't follow me upstairs.

In my room, I eagerly unzip my backpack, where Riley stuffed the testing kit. My pink permission slip for the end-of-year field trip falls out with it. The whole fifth grade is going to Storm King, an awesome outdoor sculpture park, if Mom lets me go. She can be weird about big group outings, as if I might get lost or kidnapped or something. But *she's* not about to come, that's for sure.

She knocks on my door. "You okay? You ran up so fast I thought you were going to trip."

I shove the kit under my bed and open the door.

She's standing there in her usual sweat pants, her hair in a ponytail, no makeup under her eyes. A worry line cuts across her forehead. I don't get why she's so stressed. It's not like we live in Afghanistan.

"I just have to study. I have a big math test tomorrow."

"Since when are you so eager to start your homework?"

I shrug. To distract her, I hand her the permission slip, addressed to MR. AND MRS. BURKE. "I need you to sign this."

"*Please*," she says.

"Please. We're going to Storm King. It's gonna be really fun."

She frowns. "How many chaperones will be going?"

"I don't know; why don't you volunteer?"

My annoyed tone must send a message, because she backs off.

"That's okay." She grabs a pen from my desk and is about to scribble her signature when something makes her pause. She flips over the pink square. Then she lets out a horrified gasp.

"Really, Abigail?"

"What?"

She crumples it up and throws it at my feet. "I don't know what to say to you right now."

I unfold it to find a handwritten note:

My mom's a crazy bitch.

CLAIRE: BEFORE

As I climb the stairs of the 116th Street subway station on my way to meet Ethan for dinner, my cell lights up with a voice mail from a 212 number.

"Mrs. Glasser, this is Rob Nash. Please call my office as soon as you can."

I stare at the phone in shock. The memory of him walking out on me at the bar still makes me cringe. I have never felt like more of a fool.

Ethan and I have hardly spoken since that night, because when I came home, I announced that I'd changed my mind about trying IVF.

What? He was dumfounded. *Right after we met your favorite doctor?*

Of course, I couldn't tell him Nash had been a total letdown. Instead, I said I wasn't emotionally ready to gestate a random donor egg.

The shameful truth is that I don't think I could love someone else's baby as much as my own. I realize how embarrassingly regressive this makes me, like a liberal person who harbors racist prejudices. But I can't help it; blood matters. The last thing I want is to be a surrogate womb for Ethan's child with another woman. And if the child wanted to find his or her "real" mother one day, I know it would kill me.

Staring dumbly at Nash's voice mail on my cell, I realize I've stopped on the subway stairs. Commuters are grumbling in my wake, elbowing past me in an endless irritable chain. But I don't move. Instead I call him back right then and there, pressing my volume all the way up.

"That was fast," he says. "I just called you five minutes ago."

"I didn't think I'd hear from you again." I rush away from the station to a secluded spot under the eaves of a campus building.

"When's the soonest we can meet? Face to face."

Against my better judgment, excitement creeps into my heart. "About . . . ?"

"Let's talk when you get here. I'll be in my office for another hour tonight, or tomorrow until—"

"Stay there. I'm on my way."

I leap into the air like a teenager invited to the prom.

On my way back to the subway, I send Ethan a careful text: So sorry honey, but just found out Eva's dad passed suddenly. Need to go be w/ her tonight.

Eva is my work friend at *Mindset* whom Ethan barely knows. There's no way he can verify the details.

His text pings back: Sorry to hear. Typing dots show up, break off, come back again. Then: Are you avoiding me?

Don't be silly, I tap quickly. See you at home later. As an afterthought, I add a red heart emoji and a kiss face. It's the closest we've come to actually kissing for a week.

Is this what our marriage amounts to now?

I fear that we are drifting further and further apart. It isn't just our shared trauma. It's our profound philosophical divide. Ethan sees the world like a bystander, ready to accept nature's whims, while I see the world like an editor, ready to correct nature's mistakes. I can't stand the way he thinks, and vice versa, but the love we shared for Colton overwhelmed our differences. Now, a second child might be our only hope.

OK, he finally writes back. No kiss face. I wait for a full minute on the subway stairs, hating that our intimacy is reduced to a cartoon icon. But nothing comes.

* * *

Twenty-two minutes later, I arrive panting at Nash's office. It's after six PM and his staff is gone for the day, but he closes the door anyway. The secretive move sends a thrill through me.

He gestures to one of the leather club chairs as he sits at his desk. "Thanks for coming on such short notice."

"Of course. What's going on?"

He presses his palms against the wood and regards me earnestly. "There are serious unknowns. You have to understand that."

"Oh my God." I feel a euphoric grin tug at my lips.

But he doesn't crack a smile. "I can't guarantee the child will turn out normal. We've never seen a human baby born from the DNA of three people."

"But haven't your animal trials proved safe? No deformities?"

He nods. "That's why I'm willing to risk it—if you are. But you could still spend the rest of your life dealing with the consequences."

"I understand."

"I need you to be physically *and* mentally up for this. Are you sure you can handle it?"

A stinging sensation unexpectedly flares up along my wrists—a visceral memory burned into my flesh. I grip the chair, willing it to go away.

"Absolutely," I tell him. "No question."

The sting recedes. I focus on feeling a new baby kick inside me, those first butterfly flutters of life that compare to no other thrill in the world. *My* own baby, and Ethan's. And—

"Who will the other mother be?" I ask, but as soon as the word *mother* leaves my mouth, I want to take it back. "The donor, I mean?"

The woman with the perfect mitochondria will supply merely thirty-seven genes. The other 20,000 or so will be passed down from me and Ethan. She doesn't deserve recognition on my level. I vow never to think of her that way again.

"My postdoc." Nash isn't fazed by my correction. "Jillian's young and healthy, and most importantly, discreet. We need to keep this within the smallest possible circle."

I raise my eyebrows. "Wait, so you trust her now?"

"I trust her not to sabotage her career. If it works, it could wind up being the biggest fertility breakthrough since IVF."

"And you trust me?" I hold his gaze without flinching.

"I could be wrong, but I don't think you're undercover FDA."

"Actually . . ." I joke.

He pretends to wipe sweat off his forehead. "I wish I could laugh."

"So how does it work?"

"The records will show you're a normal IVF patient for insurance purposes. There will be zero evidence. The mitochondrial transplant is a one-hour procedure in the lab. And there's no way to prove it once you get pregnant, unless you submit to specific prenatal tests."

I barely hear the last part because I'm stuck back on the word *pregnant*. The whole thing sounds like either a Disney fantasy or a dystopian nightmare. But I'm willing to chance it.

"I won't discuss it with a single soul," I promise.

"Other than your husband, obviously?"

"Even him." *Especially him.* "The smallest possible circle, right?"

"Okay." Nash seems surprised. "If you're comfortable with that."

I lean in. "I'm not a religious woman, but I do hold one thing sacred above all else: the memory of my son." A familiar closing sensation thickens my throat. "I swear on Colton's life that this stays between us."

Nash extends his palm across the desk. I'm thinking he wants to shake on the deal, but instead he clasps my hand gently in his own. "Then let's make him proud."

ABBY: NOW

I cringe as Mom's eyes fill with tears. The note makes me look like a horrible person:

My mom's a crazy bitch.

I'm going to kill Sydney tomorrow. I bet she wants to get me in trouble so I won't be allowed on the field trip. That way, she can hang out with Tyler alone. If she gets her way, I'll make him swear to ignore her.

"I didn't write that," I tell my mom. "Why would I do that?"

A disgusted noise rumbles in her throat. "You're allowed to hate me, but you're not allowed to lie."

"I don't hate you!" I kick my backpack in frustration. "And I'm telling the truth, okay? God."

She crosses her arms. "So, you want me to believe that someone went into your backpack when you weren't looking and wrote an extremely cruel note in bubbly handwriting? Just like yours?"

I plop down on my bed. "Pretty much."

"Well, that makes *much* more sense." She stomps over and sits near my feet. "I'm not leaving until you admit you're lying."

"I'm not! This is so unfair! When have I ever lied to you?"

"Let's see." She touches her chin in pretend thoughtfulness. "You don't secretly check the Instagram you're not supposed to have? Or fake a stomachache sometimes even though you haven't been sick for years?"

I lick my lips to hide my guilty smile. "How did you know?"

"That's not the point."

"Fine." I slide under my comforter and roll away from her.

"Abigail." She uses her warning voice. "I'm ready for your apology."

"I told you," I say to the wall. "I didn't write it."

"Then who did?"

I throw off the blanket and sit up. "The girl who hates me, okay?"

"Someone hates you?" She frowns. "You never told me that."

"Because she said mean stuff about you. I didn't want you to know."

"About *me*? Why?"

I chew my fingernail. "Since you don't, like, show up to stuff. I mean, no one ever sees you get out of the car."

She's speechless and a little embarrassed. I wait for an explanation. Something more than her usual "I'm not a social person" or "I have anxiety issues." *What are you so afraid of?* I want to ask. But I don't have the balls.

"Kids at your age can be such bullies," she finally says.

I shrug. "Yeah." I pick up the stupid pink slip and study the writing. "It's definitely not mine. I don't do a lowercase *a* like that."

She gives me a weird look that makes me shiver. It's like she's trying to recognize me but sees someone else.

"Hey." I wave a hand. "I didn't do it. Okay?"

She sighs. "If you want to punish me, I get it. I know I've been preoccupied."

"Mom, for the last time, it wasn't me!" I'm almost screaming at her, but I don't care. "Do you think I'm, like, evil or something?"

"Okay, okay. Calm down."

"You know what? You're right," I say loudly. "You have been checked out and it sucks. Sometimes I feel like you're not even here."

"I'm sorry. I really am. I haven't been feeling well."

Normally this would annoy me, but I find myself bracing. "Are you okay?"

She waves a hand. "Nothing you need to worry about."

A tense silence follows. I don't believe her, and she knows it. But she says nothing. After a few moments, I lift my backpack onto my lap.

"Well, I should start studying."

"Okay. Dinner's at six." She jumps off the bed and walks to the door without giving me a hug or even a second glance. I can't help feeling like she wants to get away from me.

Then it hits me: that troubled look on her face?

It seemed a little like fear.

CLAIRE: BEFORE

NINE MONTHS TO GO

For three uncomfortable weeks, I have been pumping myself full of hormones to stimulate my ovaries to release a bunch of eggs, and so has Jillian. Today, at last, is the big day. Nash will take our eggs out in separate parallel surgeries. Then, while I'm back home sleeping off the drugs, he will perform the secret mitochondrial transplant and mix our hybrid eggs with Ethan's sperm.

As if I don't have enough to stress about, a screening test on Ethan's sperm came back low. Apparently, it was from a mild prostate infection, so Nash prescribed him antibiotics, which should have worked their magic by now. Ethan's not too worried—he feels good.

We're aiming to get around a dozen healthy embryos. In five days, Nash will pick the single most viable one to implant inside me. Then we'll hope it sticks. Though *hope* is an understatement. People hope for good weather. I'm aching like a lost sailor aches for land.

I wish I could put faith in God, or destiny, or whatever spiritual force comforts others. Yet I'm far too rational—this is going to be an odds game. At my ripe old age of almost forty, they aren't great. The live birth rate is only fifteen percent, and that's with stone-cold normal embryos.

Ethan is also clinging to our small island of hope. After I told him I had decided to try IVF after all, using my own eggs and "praying for a miracle," his attitude toward me transformed. His distant moodiness and halfhearted pecks disappeared. He started spooning me again in bed. But, I asked, wasn't he terrified of having another child like Colton? *God wouldn't give us what we couldn't handle*, he told me serenely. *We will love him or her no matter what.*

I could only nod in response, too afraid that opening my mouth would start a fight I could never win. His attitude is an outrage, an excuse to do something totally reckless. To risk burdening a child with a lifetime of suffering, only to blame it on "a master plan we don't yet understand," is a sickening evasion of responsibility. But to argue with him is to acknowledge our moral divide, which would impugn his whole career.

It's easier to shut up and do things my way: protect our baby from both of us—my defective genes and his defective thinking. I came perilously close to walking away before. But this second shot at parenthood has inclined me to give him another chance. It helps to remember the night he stayed up with Colton reading the final Harry Potter book in a marathon six-hour stretch, because another day with our son was not guaranteed. Ethan was no doubt an incredible dad, if not my perfect soul mate, and that has to count for something.

* * *

In the waiting room at Nash's clinic the morning of my egg extraction, Ethan draws me close. "You nervous?"

The procedure requires me to undergo sedation while Nash inserts a hollow needle through my vagina, up to my ovaries, to get the goods.

"Nah." I shrug. "It'll be done in 20 minutes."

"Brave girl."

I smile coyly and lower my voice. "Your part will be way more fun."

"I'm not going to touch a thing in there. You think they ever clean that DVD player?"

"I hear *Amateur Babysitters* is not to be missed."

He laughs as a nurse calls him back. "Mr. Glasser? We're ready for you."

"Go stallion, go," I whisper as he gets up.

"I'm bringing strength in numbers," he jokes. Under my sweater, I cross my fingers.

Waiting to be called next, I glance at the other patients on the white leather couches. There are three other women in their twenties or thirties tapping on their cells. Are any of them the mysterious Jillian? I know she is also going to have her eggs retrieved today so that Nash can carry out the illicit mitochondrial transplant this afternoon.

I find myself fixated on one woman with striking red hair—it tumbles over her shoulders in waves worthy of a shampoo commercial. Her face, which is absorbed in her phone, radiates youthfulness—creamy skin, rounded cheeks, a smattering of freckles. She must be barely twenty-five.

That's about how old I was when I met Ethan. Such an innocent time, back in the B.C. era—before Colton. I smile to myself, thinking of the days when he would leave me little love notes around my apartment—*If you're reading this, I miss you right now*, or *Can't wait to* see *(all of) you later.* I saved each scrap in a shoebox that still lives in our closet.

The woman looks up and catches my eye, and any doubt I had about her identity vanishes. Only a shrewd scientist, however young, could possess a stare so penetrating. I tighten my arms across my chest as a thought both wondrous and disturbing crosses my mind: *soon, a piece of her will be in me.*

Jillian's lips stretch almost imperceptibly, but I can't tell whether she means to smile or sneer. Either way, a surprising coldness emanates from her eyes.

I don't like it one bit.

* * *

JILLIAN

I sidle up to Nash as soon as the door to the lab closes behind us. It's been a grueling day so far: he extracted twenty-three of my healthy eggs in a short procedure under intravenous sedation. Claire produced only eleven eggs, so we will have that many chances to form the perfect embryo.

After my procedure, I recovered for an hour in a private room while the anesthesia wore off, and Nash sweetly brought me some apple juice and Tylenol. I was touched that he attended to me himself, rather than a nurse. Then I went home to freshen up and mentally prepare for the transplant. Now it's after four pm, and I'm sore but excited to get to work. Nash dismissed his entire staff early, encouraging his nurses, lab technicians, embryologist, and receptionist to "get a head start on the weekend."

Which means we are finally alone.

"You ready?" I whisper into his ear. He pulls away from his microscope. As our eyes lock, I feel a stab of anxiety. His impassive expression reminds me of when he's about to deliver bad news to a patient. He probably means to seem unthreatening, but he triggers the opposite effect instead.

He looks away. "Soon."

"You better not be getting cold feet." I point angrily at the incubator, where all of our eggs are waiting inside at a toasty thirty-seven degrees centigrade in ninety-five percent humidity. "If I went through all this for nothing—"

"Relax," he interrupts. "It'll happen." But his face is inscrutable.

I wait for him to notice the effort I've made to look good for this moment—which wasn't easy only hours after being knocked out by powerful drugs. At home, after they wore off, I showered, shaved my legs, and curled my hair, then applied eyeliner, mascara, and blush.

But this is not how I envisioned my fantasy . . . the two of us high on our mutual admiration, tearing off each other's lab coats in celebration of our forbidden success.

"Everything ready to go?" His voice is painfully neutral.

"As ready as ever."

Under an inverted microscope powered to 30,000-times magnification, we will extract the nucleus of one of my eggs so all that remains is the shell—including its healthy mitochondria. Then, using my pioneering technique, we'll extract the nucleus of one of Claire's eggs and transplant it into my egg's empty shell to form one perfect hybrid egg, with my mitochondria intact. We'll repeat the procedure for each pair of eggs we have, then mix the hybrids with Claire's husband's sperm.

After five days of growing in petri dishes, each embryo will have grown to around 100 cells. We'll pluck five to ten trophectoderm cells from each one with a laser and analyze them under a microscope in a technique called PGD—preimplantation genetic diagnosis—to make sure none of Claire's harmful mutations were inherited. Then we'll evaluate which embryo is the best candidate for implantation. In the Darwinian world of assisted reproduction, only the strongest one has a shot at actual personhood.

"I'll go prepare the sperm." Nash stands abruptly, his stool screeching out from under him. "Why don't you start without me?" His smile seems oddly strained. "You invented the cell polarization maneuver, so it's only fair."

My mouth opens in surprise. *Are you sure?* I almost ask. But this is my opportunity for greatness, as he himself predicted. There's no way in hell I'm going to argue. The only sad part is that we deserve cameras and reporters documenting this turning point in the history of mankind—the first time anyone has genetically intervened to prevent the transmission of a fatal disease. But one day, hopefully within our lifetimes, I'm confident the world will come to its senses and honor us.

I smile gratefully at him. "I thought you'd never ask."

"You deserve it."

I suppress a twinge of regret, remembering the secret recording I made in case I needed to blackmail him one day. But now I see he's not selfish enough to steal my spotlight. We're equal partners.

* * *

Twenty-five minutes later—longer than usual to prepare sperm—he returns from the adjacent room where semen samples are tested, washed, and stored. I look up from my microscope to catch him wincing. At first, I worry he's in physical pain, but then his lips purse and I realize something is wrong.

"Spit it out," I tell him.

"I didn't want to say anything." He lets out a heavy sigh. "But I just double- and triple-checked. Ethan's sperm count is only four million with two percent morphology."

"What? You've got to be fucking kidding."

Fifteen million is low for sperm, and most of his are abnormal. How are we supposed to create the perfect embryo now?

"There's still a chance," Nash says, reading my mind.

"The odds are terrible. I can't believe this."

"I know."

I set down my pipette and pull off my mask. "What the hell am I doing, then?"

"Finish the job. It's still possible."

"Bullshit."

After all our months of prep, all the strings I've pulled, including things he doesn't even know about, this was one outcome I had not anticipated: doomed to failure by pure dumb bad luck.

"Don't give up." He touches my shoulder. "It ain't over till it's over."

His strained optimism is crushing.

"Okay, okay," I say slowly, thinking. "Give me another half an hour."

"Good. I'll go prep the sperm." He retreats to the other room. "At least we've come this far, right?"

I nod. "Who knows what could happen?"

"That's the spirit."

* * *

When the time is up, he comes back to check on me. "How did it go?"

I switch off the microscope; my eyes are burning from the intense focus. "Mostly fine. Couple casualties."

"What happened?"

"Punctured the cytoplasm on one, tore the nucleus on another."

He frowns. In all our trial runs, I've shown the precision of a marksman.

"Sorry," I tell him, making a point to seem ashamed. "I guess I was nervous."

"So how many hybrids did we get?"

"Nine."

"That could still be enough."

"Hope so." I manage the smile of a good sport. "You're doing the ICSI now?"

Intracytoplasmic sperm injection—shooting the sperm directly into the egg—will give us our best shot at forming embryos. This way, Ethan's shitty sperm won't have to swim to find their target. But with such bad specimens, all nine tries could still fail.

"Yeah," he replies. "Shouldn't take too long."

I keep my expression neutral. "I'll wait. Maybe we can do dinner after? Toast to possibilities?"

"Sure. Sounds like a plan."

* * *

An hour later, after changing out of my scrubs and into the sundress I stashed in my locker, I find myself sitting across from him at a fancy Italian restaurant across the street. It's packed with couples out for date night, and the atmosphere is appropriately romantic: white globe lights decorate the perimeter, and each table has a pink rose floating in a glass bowl.

Nash is dressed in dark slim-fitting jeans and a gray V neck that reveals his pecs and upper arms. I must admit, I never knew his body under his lab coat was so jacked. For a forty-something guy, he is in killer shape.

When a waiter arrives to show us the wine list, I push it away.

"Two vodka martinis, please."

"Coming right up."

The waiter marches off, and Nash winces. "I actually don't drink."

"Oh. Like at all?"

He pauses. "I'm ten years sober."

I wait for details, but he offers none. The revelation makes me strangely happy. As he watches me for a reaction—judgment or disgust—I realize why: he's opening up to me.

"Good for you," I tell him. Then, with an ironic smile, "I'll drink to that."

The waiter returns and sets down two pungent martinis filled to the brim. I delicately raise one, and he touches his plain old ice water to it.

"To us," I say, deliberately pausing before I add, "Succeeding."

He smiles. "Cheers."

My nostrils flare from the burn of the vodka sliding down my throat. Almost instantly, I feel myself relaxing.

"You know," he says, "no matter what happens, I couldn't have gotten this far without you. So, thank you."

Emboldened, I plant my elbows on the table and lean in, squeezing my breasts together. His eyes zero in on my cleavage. Despite the loud voices and clinking silverware around us, we might as well be alone. A pleasant warmth pulses between my legs. Maybe my fantasy isn't so far off after all.

"You really think we have a chance?" I ask.

He shrugs. "Not great, but I'm cautiously optimistic."

I tilt my head. "Funny, that's what I've been thinking about you." As soon as the words escape, my heart stampedes into my throat.

His eyes widen. "Oh?"

"You're a patient man, Rob . . ." I risk a smile, acknowledging my use of his first name. "Don't think I haven't noticed how often you ask me to work late. But . . ."

He clears his throat. "But what?"

"Nothing ever happens."

How many hours I've spent trying to decipher his mixed signals, his appreciative glances one day and minimal attention the next.

"Well, you're a beautiful young woman and I'm your boss. I can't just take advantage . . ." He trails off as if waiting to be contradicted. That lustful look I've witnessed on certain late nights bares itself again. The difference is that this time, we both know it.

Coyly, I slip a finger into my bra. "I'm not that hungry anymore. Are you?"

"I think," he says, "we should get the check."

* * *

As I unlock my apartment twenty minutes later, his body presses up behind mine. He strokes my stomach an inch above my pelvis. Every nerve ending in his path fires up as if for the first time. I'm no virgin, but my body has never responded to touch like this before.

I turn around and lift my face up to his. "I've wanted you this whole time."

He bends down to kiss me. His lips are soft and expressive, edged by sexy stubble. I press my mouth harder against his, and he wraps his arms around me. Making out, we blindly push open the door, traverse my apartment, and fall onto my bed. He rips off my dress and kisses my neck as I drag down his jeans. Naked, he is perfection. Toned, trimmed, and hard.

"Are you sure?" he asks, hovering over me. "You must be sore."

"I'm fine." My vagina *is* tender from the egg retrieval, but I don't care.

I grab a condom from my nightstand and tease him with my tongue as I put it on.

A moan escapes him. "I'm not going to last."

I roll onto my back. "Get on top of me."

We rock together in a blissful rhythm that starts off slow—the cautious union of two bodies meeting for the first time—and then picks up speed until I can feel him in my deepest reaches. Everything else falls away in the throes of mind-numbing pleasure.

But before I lose control altogether, I thrust harder until it hurts, and the pain brings me back. I know my intensity will make him come faster. Soon he does, with a groan of pure ecstasy.

I'm already thinking of the next step. We lie there, panting, until our eyes meet.

"Did you come?" he asks.

"Of course, how could I not?"

"Oh, good. I wasn't sure."

I pull his stubbly chin down to kiss it. "That was hot."

He slides off the condom, and I point to my small garbage can beside the bed. He tosses it in. I lie back against the pillows and close my eyes.

"Be right back," he says, and disappears into the bathroom.

When he returns, he's smiling. "You're something else, you know that."

Oh, I think, *I know.*

ABBY: NOW

As soon as Mom leaves my room, I head under my bed and retrieve the testing kit. I was feeling bad about my plan to sneak into her room while she's sleeping and swab her cheek, but now I don't. She's already convinced I'm a brat, so what's the difference?

It's time to figure out who the real liar is.

At six PM, I go down for dinner—leftovers, nothing special. Dad's exhausted from all his furniture customers, and Mom doesn't mention our fight or the note. She talks more to Dad than me; they discuss boring things like whether he paid his parking ticket from last week. She warns him that a judge could issue a bench warrant if he forgets, and then he could be *arrested*. I swear, she's so dramatic sometimes.

When I tell them I need to study, they excuse me. I spend the next hour in bed on my laptop, researching. She can't eat or drink for thirty minutes before giving the spit sample, which should be fine, since I'm waiting until she's asleep.

Google says that the special Q-tip brush in the kit needs to graze the inside of her cheek to pick up "squamous epithelial cells from the outer epithelial layer of the mouth." Then I have to quickly put the swab stick into this thin plastic tube, where it will mix with something called "DNA stabilization buffer liquid." That way, the sample will stay safe in the mail until it reaches the company's lab in Burlington, North Carolina, where they will separate the DNA from the bacteria and whatever other junk is in saliva. A few weeks after that, Riley should get an email that her report is ready to view, since Riley is the one who registered the new kit.

Mom and Dad's nighttime routine is super predictable. They get into bed around ten, watch one episode of a show, and turn out the lights by eleven. Mom also takes a sleeping pill sometimes because of her anxiety. I'm sort of hoping that our fight today stressed her out enough to take it.

At my bedtime, nine PM, she and Dad come in to give me a kiss and wish me good-night. She asks if I want to read a chapter in Harry Potter, but I tell her I'm too tired.

"Sleep well," she calls from the doorway. "Night night."

Dad blows a kiss. "We love you, Abby Caddaby."

"Love you too," I mumble.

Their footsteps grow quiet as they go to their room.

I throw off the covers and sit up. I can't fall asleep by accident. My alarm clock reads 9:06 PM. I play games on my laptop and kill time on YouTube, getting more antsy by the minute. The usual stuff—cat memes, prank videos—barely distract me. Even secretly checking Instagram is not too exciting tonight.

Finally, at twelve fifteen AM, I can't take it anymore. I slide out of bed with the swab stick and tiptoe down the hallway to their room. It's silent behind the door except for the sound of Dad's snoring.

I close my eyes and force myself to breathe in. I can do this. I *need to* if I want the truth.

I give the door a quick, firm push to get past the squeaky hinges. Once my eyes adjust to the darkness, I drop to my hands and knees and crawl on their soft rug to my mom's side of the bed. The moonlight shines through the slats in the blinds, helping me find her in the otherwise dark room. She's on her side facing away from Dad, with one hand under her pillow and the covers pulled up to her chest. Her mouth is slightly open, and her eyes are twitching back and forth under her eyelids.

I crawl up to the bed and carefully bring the swab tip near her lips, above a spot of drool on her pillow. My heart is beating fast and my hand is trembling. At the last second, I yank it back.

I let a whole minute pass just sitting there on the floor. Her chest rises and falls evenly under the blanket. I decide to do a simple test. If she wakes up, I'll tell her I couldn't sleep. If not, I'll know it's the right time.

I gently touch the blanket near her shoulder. Nothing. I rest the full weight of my hand on it. She doesn't move. It must be the sleeping pill. I'm going for it.

It happens so fast: I insert the swab into the corner of her open mouth so it soaks up the drool. When I twirl it to coat the whole tip, she stirs—her eyes flutter, and she scratches at her cheek. I drop to the carpet. The swab is wet.

I hear the blanket moving around. She must be changing position. Then she goes quiet again. I count to twenty before I peek. She's on her stomach facing the other way, breathing steadily again. She looks so pretty and peaceful with her hair tumbling across the pillow. Part of me wants to climb in bed next to her and forget the whole experiment.

Instead, I army-crawl to the door, close it quietly, and tiptoe back to my room, where I shove the swab into the plastic tube and screw on the cap, which releases the buffering liquid. Then I'm done.

Riley will mail it for me tomorrow after school.

I fall into bed feeling a weird mix of excitement and guilt. I've probably broken a bunch of laws, not to mention Mom's trust. If she ever finds out, I'll be grounded for life.

Soon I'll know whether the stranger is really her cousin. I think back to the message where JH0502 asked if I had a brother. But literally a billion people have brothers. It doesn't prove she's part of the family, right? She could be some random stalker after all.

My eyelids close. Maybe Mom's been telling the truth the whole time.

I've been upset with her. She's been so distracted. But that doesn't make her a liar. As sleep muddies my mind, I land on one last thought:

I hope the experiment fails.

CLAIRE: BEFORE

"Your turn in the hot seat," Nash says to me with a wink.

I squeeze Ethan's hand and climb onto the wax-paper-covered chair in the center of the exam room, then slide my feet into the metal stirrups. In the days since my egg retrieval, nine embryos have grown in Nash's lab in the privacy of their petri dishes, concealing their secret deep down in their DNA, and two have emerged as the strongest candidates for implantation. Nash has advised me to transfer only one embryo for safety reasons. If it doesn't work out, we'll have a shot with the other one. So today he's putting in a single female embryo, a double X. To think I could be the mother of a daughter!

Today is embryo transfer day, and Ethan and I have not been this excited since—well, since I found out I was pregnant with Colton a decade ago and the future still sparkled with possibilities. Ethan rubs my hand with adorable eagerness now, reminding me of that distant, golden era.

On my right side, Nash squirts cold gel over my abdomen to prepare for the ultrasound-guided transfer. My bladder is painfully full, which is required for his visualization. As he strokes my stomach with a probe, a grainy black-and-white image of my empty uterus appears on the flat screen. My womb is disappointingly compressed and narrow, like a flat tire. I picture it filling up with a big round baby.

"I can't believe our child is about to be in there," Ethan says, gazing at the screen.

"In about one minute." Nash holds a thin catheter tube that contains the microscopic embryo in its tip. "Claire, I'll just insert this into your cervix and guide it into the middle of your endometrial cavity, then depress the plunger, and *voila*."

I smile weakly, too overcome to speak. My heart beats erratically. Now there's no going back. In nine months, I could be holding the world's first genetically modified human being. *Please let her be healthy. Please let her be normal.*

"Will it hurt?" Ethan asks. His concern sends a tremor of guilt through me.

"Nope," Nash says. "It'll feel like a tampon but smaller. Ready?"

When he stares at me, an electric dart shoots between us, a charged particle of hope and nerves massive enough to collapse the room if it weren't for Ethan, who misses the moment entirely. He's transfixed by the screen.

I clear my throat. "Let's do it."

After inserting a speculum to view my cervix, Nash slides the catheter painlessly into my vagina. The three of us watch it bypass my cervix and snake up into my uterus.

"Okay, moment of truth," he announces. He's acting relaxed, but his hand is slightly shaking; I feel the catheter wiggle inside me. His nerves are our secret, a strange kind of intimacy we can't help but share. To counteract this closeness, I squeeze Ethan's hand. Nash deploys the plunger.

A white speck shoots out the head of the tube and disappears somewhere inside my womb. In three seconds, it's gone.

"Okay." Nash lets a breath escape as he withdraws the catheter and the speculum. "Now we wait."

Ethan turns to me with an ecstatic grin. He kisses my lips, then reaches over to pump Nash's hand as though their professional beef never existed. Not that Nash has any idea who he is. To Nash, he's Mr. Ethan Glasser, sedate science teacher, not Dr. Ethan Abrams, relentless ideological opponent.

"Thank you so much, man," Ethan says. "You have no idea how big a deal this is."

I silently will Nash to avoid looking at me so that my burning tongue doesn't explode with the truth. Nash gives Ethan a hearty slap on the shoulder, not missing a beat, and the temptation passes.

"In fact," Nash tells him with a smile, "I think I do."

Eleven days later, on a Monday morning, I wake up with sore, heavy breasts and an urgent need to pee. Ethan is already in his office preparing to give a nine AM ethics lecture.

I run to the bathroom to unwrap one of the pregnancy tests from the three different brands I hoarded during the terrible wait for this day. I wasn't supposed to test until *at least* eleven days after the transfer, but I've secretly been peeing on a stick morning and night since day six. Each time, the damn stick has remained a stubborn white next to the pink control line, and I've choked back my panic.

But this morning, as I examine my naked body in the bathroom mirror, something is different. My nipples have darkened to a purplish brown, which has only happened once before.

I hover over the toilet, stick in hand, and pee like the expert I am. It's pathetic, but I could do this in my sleep. I must have blown two hundred bucks on pregnancy tests this week out of sheer impatience. No desire compares to the primal need to know of a new life inside you; to want to bear witness to every moment of its existence. The love I ache to give another baby floods my heart with bittersweet pain. I could wait a thousand years if I knew I'd have one someday. The hardest part is not knowing if I ever will.

I pull up my underwear and sit back against the wall. The blank stick taunts me.

Look away. Three minutes will take an eternity otherwise. But who am I kidding? I hold it up to the window so the sun will illuminate even the faintest line. Particles of dust dance in the light, but the stick remains appallingly white.

Come on.

I squeeze my eyes shut and count the seconds under my breath. When I get to twenty-seven, I can't take the suspense anymore and open my eyes.

There it is. A second line.

Faint is an understatement; it's a wisp of the softest pink, too pale for a visible edge. But pink nonetheless.

I wondered all week whether I would burst into tears if this moment arrived. Instead I just stare, unblinking. The greatest art in the world couldn't be more beautiful than this little line.

I get to be a mother again.

Colton would have been the best big brother. How is it possible for good news to sting so much?

After another sixty seconds, the gossamer pink darkens to a rosier hue, something I can take a picture of and send to—

Nash, I think first. And then, guiltily, *Ethan*.

Another name enters my mind. I notice that my hands have become clenched. Really, the donated few bits of DNA mean nothing in the grand scheme of an entire person. They're like a quick fix for some diseased cells. Over and done. Case closed.

It's my baby now. My little girl.

I sprint to the bedroom to grab my phone and photograph my priceless fortune. Then I text the picture to Ethan: We did it!!!

I write the identical text to Nash, who gave me his cell number in case of emergency. On second thought, I add: You're a miracle worker. ☺☺☺

Then, out of nowhere, an aftershock of dread slams into me. It hits me so hard that I sink onto the bed.

What if she's not normal? What then?

* * *

JILLIAN

At the lab bright and early, I hear Nash's cell phone buzz in the storage locker. He's in the clinic seeing a patient and won't be back for another hour.

I head over to the floor-to-ceiling locker and pause in front of his unit on the bottom left. All the laboratory staff deposit our personal items in private lockers so as not to contaminate our work environment. Nash has never bothered to be secretive about his code—for months, he's pressed 0912 into the keypad, his birthday. For a brilliant physician-researcher, he isn't exactly a whiz at security.

I hesitate with my finger on the zero.

No one else will be here for another fifteen minutes—it's only 8:43 AM.

I can't stand the thought that's been driving me crazy for a week. Is he sleeping with anyone else? But I can't ask him outright. What am I supposed to say: "Do you fuck a lot of women in your spare time? Or just me?"

I glance over my shoulder. Coast is clear.

I punch in his locker code and retrieve his phone.

As soon as I see the name CLAIRE GLASSER on the text, I sigh with relief. Claire is certainly not dating him. And then I notice the picture attached—a pregnancy test—and the words: We did it!!! You're a miracle worker. ☺ ☺ ☺

We? *She* didn't do a damn thing but spread her legs.

We did it—me and Nash. I can't believe we pulled it off.

Claire's misunderstanding doesn't matter. She doesn't even matter, beyond her status as the first subject who volunteered for our research. The child, if it's born healthy, will be the crowning achievement of our career. And one day, the whole world will know it. I marvel at the consequences for science and humanity—if the pregnancy survives, it will be the first-ever child born of three people's DNA.

. . . Including *my* DNA. I freeze, staring again at the photo of that pink line. Somehow, despite all the planning and effort leading up to this very test, I haven't thought much about the personal implications for me. But in a very real sense, I, too, am reproducing.

That means Claire is pregnant with *our* child. An actual human being—not just an egg cell—is going to inherit my mitochondrial DNA, which I inherited from *my* mother. I always imagined I'd be a mother someday, once my career was established and the right man came along—and maybe he already has.

But in about eight months, a baby will enter the universe who shares thirty-seven of my genes. I lean against the locker in astonishment.

My baby, too.

ABBY: NOW

The morning after my successful saliva mission, I'm on my way to homeroom when I spot Sydney heading past me with an ugly smile. I still can't believe she slipped that horrible note into my bag. Calling my mom crazy—it's *seriously* messed up.

I plant myself in her path. "What the fuck?" I say quietly, so any teachers around can't hear. The curse slips out without warning, surprising us both. I cross my arms, feeling very grown-up and powerful, even though she's at least three inches taller.

Her pimply face displays shock, then confusion. "Excuse me?"

"I could get you suspended."

"What are you talking about?"

I hate that I have no way to connect her to the note. "You know what you did. Why are you such a brat?"

She suddenly pushes me—hard.

"Hey!" I cry, stumbling back. My sandals fly out from under me, and I crash down onto my butt and elbows in the middle of the hallway.

She stands over me with sick enjoyment. "Watch who you call a brat."

Tears sting my eyes as she stomps off. A group of younger kids rush past, whispering. I'm sure our "cat fight" will be all over school by second period. *Ugh.*

The bell rings. Five-minute warning.

I'm rubbing my elbows when Mr. Harrison and Mrs. Miller come into view, chatting. I guess they can tell something's wrong, because they both start running.

"Abigail!" Mr. Harrison helps me up. "What happened?"

I wipe my eyes. "Nothing."

"You okay?" Mrs. Miller asks. She rests a hand on my shoulder.

After Sydney's cruelty, her kindness makes me choke up, so I nod and rush to the bathroom before I embarrass myself any more. This is the worst day and it's not even nine AM.

Once I'm locked in a stall, I text Riley: Meet me in bathroom NOW. She's probably already in first period, but we still have a few minutes to spare.

Soon, there's a knock on my stall. "Abigail?" I recognize Mrs. Miller's gentle voice. "Are you hurt?"

I open the door a crack. "I'm fine."

"Do you want to talk?"

I shake my head. The last thing I need is for her to report what happened to the principal, who would call our parents and give us both detention—even though it's all Sydney's fault.

"If you change your mind—"

Riley bursts loudly through the bathroom door. "Oh my God, I just heard Sydney punched you!"

Mrs. Miller's expression turns to horror.

"No, no, nothing like that." I head to the sink to freshen up. "It's not that big a deal."

Mrs. Miller checks her watch. "Okay, well, two more minutes, girls."

"We'll be right there," I promise, as she pushes open the door.

"Don't be late." But she smiles to let us know we're off the hook. "We're finishing the mandalas today."

When she leaves, Riley and I start talking at the same time.

"That *bitch*," I say, as she goes, "So?"

I tell her all the details. When I finish, she looks more confused than pissed. "I wonder why she hates you so much."

"It's so annoying. As if I don't have enough to deal with." I unzip my backpack and hand over the kit containing my mom's DNA sample.

My best friend eyes me with a new respect. "You actually pulled it off?"

"Yup." I'm not sure whether to be proud or ashamed; maybe both. "Can you mail it today?"

"I will after school. How long till they get back to you?"

I shrug. "Couple weeks. They'll email you the report."

She groans. "*Weeks*? That's, like, forever."

"I know."

The bell rings again. As we leave the bathroom, she lowers her voice even though no one else is around.

"What if you reopened your account and contacted the stranger again? See what else she'll tell you?"

I give her a one-eyebrow *please*. "I'd have to sneak onto my mom's email."

"Why? Can't we do it from my computer?"

"Because my mom told their customer service I was being 'harassed.'" I make air quotes to show how extreme she can be. "Anyway, I'm sure it's too late. They already shut it down."

"Nope." She gives me a wicked grin—the same one that got me on an upside-down roller coaster last year. "I checked. They don't delete your data until sixty days after your account is canceled. It's only been, like, a month."

We pause outside Mrs. Miller's classroom. Her voice floats out, discussing mandalas. In ancient cultures, she's saying, they symbolized the connection between our inner worlds and our lived reality: "Think of them as a reflection of your state of mind . . ."

No wonder I chose all black and brown colors.

Riley's whisper snaps me back. "You still have time."

"If my mom found out, she would freak."

"Abs, you're *way* past following the rules. I mean, you stole her DNA. You could probably go to jail."

My stomach sinks like a bowling ball. "Exactly. I've already done enough."

As we walk into class, my forehead breaks out in a cold sweat.

What have I done?

PART TWO

CLAIRE: BEFORE

TWO MONTHS TO GO

I feel the baby moving first thing every morning before I get out of bed: insistent jabs near my pelvis, or dramatic rolls above my belly button. I've never felt so connected to a fetus—honestly, not even to Colton. He was much quieter in the womb. Sometimes, days would pass before he provided evidence of his existence with a mild flutter. If he was a hummingbird, this baby is a bull. And I'm loving the show.

The strength imparted in her kicks tells me everything: she is going to be healthy. Strong. A child with a future.

I've been so enthralled by the world of my womb and counting down the weeks until my due date—February 28th—that I'm totally caught off guard when Ethan asks me over breakfast one morning, "Who's Jillian Hendricks?"

I don't do anything stupid like spit out my decaf coffee. But my stomach flips over like one of the baby's somersaults.

"Hmm?" I keep my eyes on my iPad, where I pretend to be engrossed in the *New York Times* Sunday crossword.

"Jillian Hendricks." He slides the iPad away from me. "The person you've been Googling the hell out of."

I dare to glance up at him and am not surprised to see his exasperated frown. I hate that look; it makes me feel like one of his slacker students.

"Come on, Claire." He sets down his coffee beside his plate of half-eaten eggs. "Your laptop was open on your desk when I went to print something, and her name was all over it."

Okay, it's true that I have become preoccupied with the elusive Jillian—trying to discover her health history, her ethnic background, her political views, her social media activity—but there's frustratingly little online. I wish I could have shrugged off our connection with a thank-you and a good-bye as soon as the pregnancy test dried. But the truth is that the baby's debt to Jillian has been tormenting me. What if my daughter somehow looks like her? What if she's inheriting some tendency to cancer or Alzheimer's or something? So like any good journalist, I've sought facts to set the story straight. It's just so damn hard to learn anything through Google.

I widen my eyes as if in belated recognition. "Oh, Hendricks, yeah, she's this up-and-coming scientist I want to interview for the magazine. But I haven't been able to contact her, so my editor might kill it."

Ethan forks a bite of egg into his mouth, watching me. He chews slowly, suspiciously. I try not to squirm.

"Why?" I demand. "Who did you think she was?"

"I don't know. That's why I asked you."

"Okay." I pull my iPad close again. "Whatever."

* * *

An anxious feeling settles into my chest for the rest of the day. At first, I can't figure out why it's so hard to shake. Ethan doesn't know anything; he couldn't. There's nothing to suspect. But then, while I'm in the middle of folding lavender onesies for the new nursery, it hits me.

What if Jillian decides to enter our lives and threaten everything? What if she feels she has some right to the child—either as a parental figure or as a researcher? We have no contract, nothing in writing setting out the terms of our illegal collaboration.

My mind, already prone to worst-case scenarios, conjures up a wicked scene of her knocking on our door and demanding access to the baby. Maybe she'll want to study the DNA, or worse—far worse—establish her *own* maternal relationship with the child. Every-other-weekend sleepovers, Mommy and Me yoga, alternating preschool pickups . . .

Stop!

That will never happen. She has zero rights. The child will never know her. Ethan will never know her. She's nothing but a ghost from the past.

But still I'm not reassured.

There's only one thing to be done. I need to see her face-to-face, to make sure we're on the same page before the birth.

It also isn't a bad excuse to contact Nash, whom I haven't seen for several months. Since he's a reproductive endocrinologist, he followed my pregnancy closely for the first ten weeks, then referred me to a regular OB-GYN for checkups. He's kept tabs on my health via text—and everything has been perfect—but I do miss our regular visits. I've heard of fertility patients who go back to their IVF doctors to show off their baby bumps. Now that I've popped, Nash deserves to see my big belly; he made it possible.

I text him my concerns about the nebulous arrangement with Jillian, and he replies right away: Don't worry, we'll talk.

A few hours later, he lets me know the three of us can meet next Tuesday. But he doesn't want to risk his staff asking questions, so instead of meeting at the clinic, we're going to get together for lunch in the West 80s.

It's a date, I write back, with a guilty little flutter in my chest.

* * *

When the day arrives, I put on my prettiest new maternity purchase—a turquoise empire-waist dress that flatters my bump. I'm not sure if I want to look good for Nash or for Jillian. Either way, my jaw is tense with anticipation.

"Hot date?" Ethan teases as I straighten my hair, which I rarely bother to do. Icy sleet is hammering the city in advance of a nor'easter, so he decided to come home from work early today—something I hadn't counted on.

"Yeah, right. I have an interview."

"With who?" He stands in the doorway of the bathroom, watching me drag the steaming iron through my wet hair.

"Just a source for a story."

"I figured. Which one?"

Annoyance pricks me, though I'm usually delighted to share the details of my reporting conquests.

"It's about . . . an important drug trial," I lie. "For liver disease."

"Oh yeah? What about it?"

I think back to a developing story the editors discussed in a meeting last week. "We heard the data might be fudged to cover up safety issues," I tell him. "An insider is coming to the office with a tip."

"Cool. Sounds big."

"We'll see. You never know."

"Take my umbrella. It's brutal out there."

I look at myself in the mirror again, then kiss him on the cheek. "Will do."

He rubs my belly as he helps me into my winter coat and boots. "Chinese later?"

"Sure. I'll be home in a couple hours."

He kisses me again before I head out the door.

As I walk down the steps of our brownstone, the freezing wind smacks my face. I shove the umbrella head-on into the gust, but it turns inside out.

"Damn it." Rain slides down the back of my neck, inside my dress.

Struggling to fix the umbrella, I happen to catch sight of Ethan's dark silhouette in our living room window. He must be watching to make sure I'm okay. I wave to reassure him, then plod heavily down the street toward the restaurant. I don't want to be late.

* * *

JILLIAN

Sitting across from Claire and Nash at the Tangled Vine, I can't help wondering if he's secretly attracted to our very pregnant, very married research subject. Especially when he steals a glance at her cleavage in that dress.

Bitch, I think.

Nash and I have been sleeping together for months now, and it's starting to feel serious, at least on my end. But he is still resisting a formal label for some reason, and it pisses the hell out of me. Is it really that difficult to call me his girlfriend?

In a swift, almost violent motion, I throw back a gulp of my merlot and set the glass down hard on the counter.

Nash drags his eyes away from Claire to raise an eyebrow at me.

I pointedly ignore him and focus on her. "So did you just want to thank us in person, or what?"

She pulls her club soda closer and attempts what is clearly a fake smile. "Well, that's one part of it," she says, in a pandering tone that makes me want to slap her. "I want you to know how grateful I am— "

"We know," I interrupt.

She shifts on her chair and glances sideways at Nash.

He wastes no time rescuing her. "I think Claire was very wise to call this meeting. We all need to figure out our roles now, before the birth. In fact, we really should have done this from the get-go, but better late than never."

"The point is, there's nothing to figure out," she declares. "I want you both to know how much I appreciate what you've done, but going forward, that's it. I'm the *only* mother." Her defiant stare is like an invitation to duel.

I laugh. "Oh God, trust me, I have no interest in raising a kid anytime soon."

Her brow relaxes. "Good."

"But you do realize," I go on, "that we've risked our entire careers to do this experiment with you?" It feels good to group myself together with him, on the same side.

She bites down on the tip of her straw. "Yeah . . ."

"Then are you seriously saying that's it? We have no right to follow up on our results? To ever see the child?"

She looks me square in the eye. "Pretty much."

"That's insane." I scowl at Nash. "You can't possibly be okay with this."

He seems to be struggling to say the right thing. This is like winning the lottery only to find the cash stolen.

"We will know that child," I tell her. "That I promise you."

"Excuse me?" she snaps. "*My* child's life is up to *me*."

"Obviously." Nash clears his throat. "I think Jillian was just saying she wants you to consider things a little more carefully."

Claire crosses her arms over her sizable bump. "My daughter is going to grow up to be normal, without her mother sneaking her off to some lab and lying to her dad. Sorry, that's just not part of the deal. Since I'm carrying this Frankenbaby, I get to set the terms."

"Frankenbaby, huh?" Nash gives an amused smile.

"We have no idea how she's going to come out, right?" Claire demands.

"Which is exactly the point," I cut in. "We have a right to know."

Her disdain is withering. "I'll call you."

"Real scientific." I bite the inside of my cheek. "We should have screened her better," I tell him. "This is unbelievable."

"You'd be nowhere if it wasn't for me," she retorts. "You're welcome."

He sighs. "This has been a team effort. We can agree on that much, yes?" I wonder if he senses the strange rivalry simmering between the two of us. *It's my baby, too*, I want to remind them. So what if my genetic contribution isn't as large as hers?

But in the interest of appearing cooperative, I say nothing.

He fixes his gaze on Claire—gentle but firm. "Look, I understand you want us to go away so you can be normal. But this is history in the making. This could help thousands of women like yourself have healthy children. If you shut us out, you wreck that chance." He pauses. "Do you think that's what Colton would want?"

At the mention of her son's name, Claire's resistance appears to crumble. A faraway look comes into her eyes and she stares off into the middle distance, likely absorbed in some memory. Watching her, I can't help feeling pity. She may be unreasonable and infuriating, but losing a child is utterly incomprehensible. A tragedy I can't begin to grasp.

She presses a button on her phone, and the home screen lights up with a picture of a grinning blond boy with an adorable dimple and striking blue eyes.

"He was beautiful," Nash says, after a respectful silence.

Her voice softens. "Thank you."

Another silence ensues.

"We would never hurt the child," I promise. "Her safety and anonymity would always be our paramount concern."

Nash nods at me gratefully. "Absolutely. It goes without saying."

Claire opens her mouth to reply when her eyes lock on someone outside; involuntarily, she cries out. I twist around on the stool to peer through the rain-streaked glass, but all I can see is a blur of pedestrians clutching umbrellas.

"Sorry, I have to go." She slides quickly off her stool and hurries to the door.

"Wait," Nash calls. "We haven't finished—"

But she's already halfway outside, thrusting her arms into her coat and popping her umbrella. We watch her march down the street out of sight.

"Well." I swirl my wine in the glass. "That went well."

He sighs. "I don't know what happened. But I think she'll come around. And you should really go easier on her next time. We don't want to scare her off for good."

"Sure, whatever." I flash him a sidelong glance. "In the meantime, why don't we go wait out the storm at my place? We can head back to work after."

"It's supposed to get worse this afternoon. I wasn't planning on seeing any more patients today."

I pretend to be shocked. "Are you giving me the day off?"

"Only half a day." He pulls out his wallet and throws two twenties on the table. Then he takes my hand. "Let's get out of here."

* * *

CLAIRE

"Ethan!" I shout. "Wait!"

Hunched under a black umbrella, he stomps down the wet sidewalk away from me. I immediately realize he tracked me on the Find Friends app, that his suspicion must have kicked in when I got all dressed up, which I rarely do.

I stagger in his wake as fast as I can, arching my back at the mercy of twenty-five pounds of belly weight. Whenever we get into a serious fight, he flees. That's how I know it's bad. He might escape into his office for hours to get away from me.

But now he has nowhere to hide.

A light at the next block turns red, sidelining him to the curb. I manage to close the gap between us, panting. He acknowledges me with a glare.

"I'm not supposed—to be—out of breath," I stammer.

"Or lie to your husband." The bite in his voice could snap bones.

"It was a last-minute thing. I'm sorry."

The light turns green, and he steps off the curb with a snarl of disgust. I rush after him, grabbing his coat sleeve.

"Honey, I can explain."

He stops dead in the middle of the intersection. "Are you having an affair with that doctor?"

I utter a high-pitched laugh. "God, no."

But can I completely deny that zippy little thrill from seeing Nash again? *Lots of women fantasize about their attractive male doctors*, I tell myself. The power differential is a turn-on, but nothing more.

A yellow cab honks at us and we scurry across the street.

"So why were you with him? And that woman? And couldn't tell me?"

"Well, it's kind of complicated."

"I've got time."

It's obvious I'm not going to get off easy. A half-assed lie will only magnify my betrayal; he'll see right through it.

One possible future flashes before me—if I cooperate with Nash and Jillian, it means hiding my ongoing relationship with them, sneaking the baby off to run tests, covering my tracks with Ethan, letting my child be poked and prodded and studied, potentially upsetting her as she grows up. Not exactly what I had in mind. All I want is for her childhood to be happy, healthy, and normal.

But if I refuse them access to her, what will they do? Just let me ride off into the sunset? I don't think so. Nash seems like a good guy, though I barely know him—or how far he might be willing to go to salvage proof of his breakthrough. As for Jillian, there's something bitter about her brilliance. She already hates me for some reason, that much is clear. I shudder to imagine what she might be capable of, with my child caught in the middle. How ugly might things get before Ethan finds out the truth anyway?

"Claire?" he prompts. "Don't even think about bullshitting me."

The rain is pelting us, making it difficult to see more than a few feet ahead, let alone engage in the most serious talk of our marriage. As I hesitate, he steers me under the red awning of Swagat, our favorite Indian restaurant on 78th Street. It's where we went out to celebrate the night I learned I was pregnant again.

"I'm not moving until you tell me what's going on."

"Okay." I tug at the collar of my coat. "I wanted us to have our own healthy baby. That's all we both want, right?"

He narrows his eyes, unsure where this is going. "Obviously."

"But I couldn't risk reliving . . . everything." I push away a strand of wet hair clinging to my cheek. "So, I went outside the box."

The tiny muscles around his mouth tighten. "What's that supposed to mean?"

"I went to Dr. Nash for a reason . . ." I proceed to explain about the mitochondrial transplant he pioneered to circumvent diseases like Colton's, as Ethan's face contorts into disbelief. When I finish, his stunned pause and horrified stare send a chill down my spine.

"Bottom line," I say with forced cheer, "we're finally going to get what we always wanted!" I grab his limp hand and place it on my belly. "Feel her kick right now."

He snatches his hand away like I've burned him. "Are you telling me this fetus has the DNA of me, you, and *someone else*?"

"Jillian, his researcher. She was generous enough to—"

"You have got to be kidding. This is for real?"

My voice is sour. "I knew you'd disagree."

"Disagree? I don't even know who you are right now."

"I'm a *mother* protecting her *child*." I clench my teeth. "If you can't understand that, then I don't know you either."

"I can't even look at you." He pivots away. "You and that shyster have violated our marriage, my rights, the law, ethics . . . I mean, holy fuck, Claire—"

"*We're having our own healthy baby!*" I scream, nearly in tears.

He backs up like I'm a lunatic. "Maybe you shouldn't have gone off your meds."

A band of shame squeezes my heart. "That's not fair."

"You really don't get it, do you?"

I can't keep the sadness out of my voice. "I think it's pretty clear."

"Yeah? Let me get it straight." He ticks his points off one finger at a time. "You agree to a criminal experiment using my sperm, without my consent, to mess with the human germ line, with potentially permanent consequences for our species, and you expect me to just nod and smile?"

I am gutted with fury and disappointment. Sure, we have our

differences, but in the back of my mind, I've long suspected his moral preachiness is basically an act to ensure upward career mobility. Disdain toward biotechnology is in vogue these days. But in real life, I hoped his rigid ideas would have room to bend when it came to avoiding our second child's *suffering and death*. Turns out my husband is both more sincere and more corrupt than I realized.

"Not only that," I tell him, "I would do it all over again. But maybe not with your sperm."

His lips part like I've sucker-punched him. He angrily pulls his phone out of his pocket and jabs at the touchscreen.

"What are you doing?"

"Looking up the number for OCI."

"OCI? Is that a Columbia thing?"

"No, FDA." He enunciates slowly. "The Office of Criminal Investigations."

I gape at him. "You wouldn't."

His finger hovers over the screen.

"Please." I try to keep my voice steady. "Let's just go home and talk." I bring his fingers to my lips. "Please."

He squints. His face scrunches up and he rushes around me.

As he stumbles headfirst into the wind, I can see his shoulders quivering. And then I understand his haste: he doesn't want me to see him cry.

* * *

JILLIAN

We both know the drill. As soon I unlock my apartment, Nash and I head for my bed, wriggling out of our coats and kicking off our soaking-wet boots. As we make out, an irritating visual pops into my mind from half an hour earlier: him and Claire at the restaurant, smiling at each other like I wasn't even there.

The memory makes me kiss him harder. I shove my hand into his pants and grab his erection, enjoying his moan. There is no way he's thinking of anyone else now.

That's when his pocket starts to vibrate. His phone shimmies out, flashing CLAIRE GLASSER across the screen. He fumbles for it as I knock it off the bed with my elbow.

"It can wait. Unless"—I let him go—"you want me to stop . . ."

He kicks off his pants and flings them to the floor.

ABBY: NOW

When I hear a strange car pull up outside late at night, I immediately sit up and reach for my phone. It's 12:49 AM. The house is quiet. My parents are sleeping down the hall on the other side of the house, so they probably don't hear it.

Underneath my window, the engine hums and a door opens.

A tingle runs over my arms. It must be the cops. Someone must have figured out that I stole my mom's DNA, and now they've come to get me . . .

Holding my breath, I leap to the windowsill and peek behind the shade, expecting to see a swirl of red and blue lights down below.

Instead, I see a normal car. Black or navy; I can't tell in the dark. Then a shadow-person gets out and walks quickly onto our driveway, where my parents' two cars are parked. My relief turns to fresh panic. Does the person want to break in?

I cup my hands around my eyes, but I can barely make out anything. The stranger is sort of short, I think, and bundled up in a puffy jacket with the hood up. I can't see any hair. I think of the extra alarm system my parents just installed. God, I hope they turned it on tonight.

I'm about to rush to their room when I notice the person drop underneath my mom's car. He or she must have spotted me in the window and is trying to hide.

"Mom!" I yell, without leaving my post. "Dad!"

I hear them jump out of bed and run down the hallway. At the same time, the shadow-person pops up, sprints back to the dark car, and drives away. As my parents run into my room, the car disappears into the night.

"What happened?" my mom cries, rushing in with my dad. They're both frantic and wide awake. "Are you okay?"

"I think someone was about to break in." I point outside. "But they just drove off."

Mom lowers herself onto my bed. She and Dad exchange a look that seems like some kind of message—like they know something I don't.

"Was it a man or woman?" Dad asks me.

"I couldn't tell. Should we call the police?"

He gazes outside. "You didn't see a license plate or anything?"

I shake my head. "Sorry." I hop off the windowsill and go sit beside my mom.

"Okay." He bites his lip, still scanning the street. "If you see anything else, let us know right away."

"Can I sleep in your bed tonight?" I put my head on Mom's shoulder. "I'm scared."

"Of course," she says, putting her arm around me.

That's when I notice her body is quietly shivering.

I have no idea who that person was. But I'm pretty sure she does.

CLAIRE: BEFORE

"Pick up your fucking phone!" I hiss at my cell. I'm in tears, locked in our bedroom, while Ethan's predictably cloistered himself in his study. I have no clue whether he's wreaking havoc on our entire life or just stewing in anger. The possibilities are terrifying. Nash deserves to know, to prepare, but he refuses to answer my calls. I fire off a series of increasingly desperate texts:

4:57 pm: CALL ME
5:02 pm: Need to talk ASAP!
5:05 pm: He knows . . .
5:07 pm: WTF where r u?!

Another ten minutes go by. Still no response. If I stare at my Goddamn phone for another second, I will explode, so I toss it onto the bed and tiptoe to Ethan's office down the hall.

I press my ear against the door. It's as silent as a cemetery.

I knock softly. "Can I come in?"

He grunts. I take it as a welcome and push open the door. He's slumped in his leather chair, back to me. When he spins around, there's no mistaking his red-rimmed eyelids and runny nose.

But instead of eliciting my sympathy, the pathetic sight sets me off.

"You should be happy," I snap. "Don't you want our baby to be normal?"

"Normal?" He snorts. "Will it call you Nuke Mommy and her Mito Mommy?"

I roll my eyes. "I am the only mother. She's meaningless." But even as I utter the words, I hear the shrillness in my voice.

"That kid is forever going to be a freak."

My hands fly to my belly. "How dare you! This is your *child*!"

For a moment, his eyes soften with longing—a look I recognize from whenever my period was late. But soon his face darkens again.

"It wasn't supposed to be like this. You, going behind my back, with *him* . . ."

"Nash is a genius."

"Fuck that guy." He grabs his phone. "Tell me why I shouldn't sic the feds on him right now."

"Because," I say quickly, "because the person you're really pissed at is me. So punish me, hate me, but keep this between us. A *family* issue."

I hope my emphasis will snap him out of his impulsiveness. Whenever we feel defeated by grief, we keep hope alive by talking of the family we might one day still share. Family traditions, family dinners, family trips. *Family* anything is our special shorthand for our happily ever after.

My gamble appears to have worked. He puts the phone down.

"For now," he allows. "I haven't made up my mind about anything yet." Then he looks me straight in the eye. "Including you."

* * *

JILLIAN

Forty-five minutes after Nash leaves my apartment, both of us disheveled and satisfied, my cell rings.

I'm in the shower, deliciously sore, when I hear it buzzing on the sink.

I almost let it go to voice mail, except that it might be him. I peek past the curtain and see his name lighting up the screen, so I hop out.

"Miss me already?"

"Listen." His voice sounds weirdly stiff. "We're in deep shit. No time to explain. Pack a bag and get over to my place."

"What happened?"

"Claire blew our cover."

I sink to the toilet. "Oh my God. Where are you?"

"Heading back to the clinic. I'm going to move the leftover embryo to a storage bank off-site, and I've already contacted a lawyer, just in case."

"In case . . . ?"

"I hope we don't need to find out. But I think you should come stay with me tonight."

Naked and dripping wet, I race out of the bathroom to get dressed. "I'm on my way."

ABBY: NOW

When school lets out, it's pouring outside. Mom's car is usually one of the first in the pickup area, but by two forty-five PM, she's still not there. At three PM, I know something is wrong. She's never been this late. Her phone rings and rings and goes to voice mail. I text her a few times: Where are you?! Still waiting. Helloooo? MOM???

Eventually, I give up and call my dad.

He tells me he's in the middle of a big deadline for a customer, but when I explain, he drops everything and comes to get me. When he shows up around three thirty, the last parent to arrive, his worried face fills me with fear. I figured he would know what's going on, but he doesn't.

"Where could she be?" I ask as I climb in the car.

"No idea. I just stopped by home."

"Nothing?"

He shakes his head, checking his flip phone's tiny gray screen.

"And I texted her like ten times."

His brow creases. "How did she seem when she dropped you off earlier?"

"Fine, I guess."

"Nothing out of the ordinary?"

"I mean, she's been weird for a while now."

He skips the left turn toward our house and keeps on going. "Weird how?"

"I don't know, like, distracted. Stressed. Do you know why?"

He looks uncomfortable. "Abs, your mother has . . . ups and downs. More than most people."

I get the feeling he's not telling me something. "Is she okay?"

He presses his lips together. "I hope so. But I'm not going to sugar-coat it. I'm concerned."

My heart clenches like a fist. "About what?"

"Her mental health. She's been sick before."

"What is *that* supposed to mean?"

"It's really not my place to go into detail with you." He avoids my eyes and makes a right turn. We pass a farm with cows grazing in the summer rain.

"Who was that person the other night? Who showed up at our house."

Dad frowns. "How would I know?"

"I don't know. I felt like maybe you did."

He stares out the windshield, gripping the steering wheel.

"So," I ask, my heart pounding, "who do you think it was?"

A firmness edges into his voice. "I already told you, I don't know. And right now, it's more important that we find Mom."

I sigh. "Fine. Where are we going?"

"To town. Maybe she went to Trader Joe's and forgot her phone."

"You just did the shopping."

"I forgot coffee. You know how she is about her coffee."

"You know, if we had iPhones like normal people, GPS could find her in two seconds."

"Well," he snaps, "we don't."

I roll my eyes. "Jeez, okay." It's so lame that none of us have smart-phones; both my parents are freaked out by the idea of "Big Brother," so we're stuck with ancient flip phones that don't even have the Internet. It's seriously embarrassing. No Facebook, no Instagram, nothing. All we can do is text and call. They also taped over the cameras on all our laptops in case the government is spying on us. And they act like *my* generation is nuts because we "don't value privacy."

Anyway, after we check Trader Joe's, we walk to the post office, the pharmacy, and the nail salon, even though Mom does her own manicures and rarely goes to the other places. Dad tries to keep his cool, but I can tell he's getting pretty upset.

When we get back in the car, I suggest calling the police.

"No," he says quickly, "that's not necessary."

"But what if she's not okay?"

He steps on the gas. "Let's go home. I'm sure this is all just a big misunderstanding." But his jumpy energy doesn't match his words. He can't stop checking his phone.

I decide to take matters into my own hands. As he drives home, I punch 911 into my cell. He doesn't notice what I'm doing until the operator's voice comes through the speaker: "Nine one one, what is your emergency?"

"No!" Dad suddenly cries, grabbing my phone away from my ear.

"Hey! What are you doing?"

"We don't need to bother nine one one yet." He snaps my cell closed. "She's probably fine, okay? Let's check at home again."

I don't agree, but we're almost there, so I say nothing. The road up to our house is all dirt and gravel, so the ride is uncomfortable, like the silence between us. When our house comes into view, we both gasp.

Mom's car is in the driveway—and we can see the back of her head in the driver's seat. Why is she just sitting there? Why hasn't she called us back?

We both jump out and sprint to her. She's hunched over the steering wheel, crying, and her face is covered in what looks like brown, wet mud.

A wave of dizziness knocks me sideways.

Mom is definitely *not* okay.

CLAIRE: BEFORE

The apartment feels like the front lines of a cold war. I no longer recognize the place as home. Ethan and I have camped out in different rooms, staking out our territory. The bathroom is a means of escape; the living room, a minefield of dirty looks.

Our standoff is heading past forty-eight hours with no resolution in sight. Ethan refuses to discuss it, almost refuses to acknowledge me at all, as he goes to work, comes home late, eats takeout in his office, and sleeps on the couch.

But he still hasn't called the authorities. As the hours tick by, I pray that his threat of retribution is waning, but it's impossible to know for sure.

Meanwhile, my own drama with Nash has become another source of distress besides being almost eight months pregnant and generally miserable.

Nash hasn't spoken to me since I managed to get through to him and explain what happened. He stayed deadly silent on the call, then demanded that I tell him right away if Ethan calls any officials. Before I could beg for forgiveness, he hung up.

Now he's ignoring all my calls, so I've resorted to texting him from the privacy of the bedroom, where I'm hiding from Ethan this morning under the comforter.

> I'm SO sorry. It would kill me if anything happened to you b/c of me.

I stare at the screen, willing it to light up.

Four minutes later, his response arrives at last:

No news?

His reticence is another jab.

I text back: Nope! Pretty sure he is backing off.

Of course, I have no idea, but I'm desperate to restore Nash's confidence in me. I think of how he put his hand on mine at the Tangled Vine a few days ago, and how gratified I felt to have been trusted with such a great honor. I'm not sure anymore if I deserve it.

My phone has gone silent again.

To prompt more back-and-forth, I fire off another series of texts:

I hate that we have to be so paranoid. You deserve better and so does baby . . . her own father called her a freak!

Made me realize I do need you in her life . . . hope u still agree?

That's when I hear Ethan's footsteps shuffle toward the bedroom, so I shove the phone in my nightstand drawer and dive under the covers, feigning sleep.

He approaches his side of the bed, blocking the window's soft light. I open my eyes. He's already dressed and shaved, and his face is blankly grim—the sum of all his conflicting emotions.

"Hey," I say quietly, in a tone I hope is nonthreatening. "How'd you sleep?"

He rummages through his drawers. "I'm late and I can't find my watch."

"I think I saw it under the bills in the kitchen." I throw off the covers and heavily drag myself out of bed. I feel like I weigh two hundred pounds, though I've only gained an extra twenty-eight so far. "I'll go check, I need my charger anyway."

"Oh. Thanks."

Progress. Our least-hostile exchange in two days.

I locate his prized Tudor where I expected and plod back to the bedroom.

"Found it!" I call in a singsong, walking in to find him bending over my nightstand. My vibrating cell lies in his palm like a grenade.

He gives me a wounded stare. "Why is *Dr. Nash* calling you?"

I freeze, at once delighted and horrified. "No idea."

As my cell continues to buzz, I lunge for it, but he spins away from me.

"Hey!" I cry. "What are you doing?"

"What *else* are you hiding, Claire?"

"Nothing; give me my phone!"

I watch in growing panic as he opens my texts.

He starts to read select ones aloud. "*It would kill me if anything happened to you . . . I hate that we have to be so paranoid . . . I still need you in her life.*"

When he looks up at me, there is something I have never seen in his eyes: hatred. "What the actual fuck?"

"It's not how it sounds!"

He rears his arm back like a pitcher and hurls my phone across the room at full force. It smashes into my mirror, shattering the glass, raining metallic shards over my dresser.

"You've been having an affair, haven't you?"

"No!" I drop to my knees at his feet. "I swear to God!"

"But he had his hand on yours; I saw it myself. When are you going to stop lying to me?"

"I'm not lying!" The lump in my throat gives way to hot, frantic tears. "There's nothing between us and there never has been."

"You think I'm an idiot? You make me sick."

Before I can stop him, he whips out his own phone and taps angrily on the screen.

"What are you doing?"

"Giving that motherfucker what he deserves."

"No, Ethan!" I leap at him, but he steps out of the way easily and I lose my balance. The shock of falling on my hands and knees takes my breath away, but he doesn't come over to help. Instead he holds the phone to his ear and speaks in a low, shaking voice.

"Yes, hi, this is Dr. Ethan Abrams from Columbia. I'm calling for Director Lee." There's a pause, and my entire body goes rigid. I feel the punishment before he utters it.

"Tell him I have a criminal violation to report."

* * *

JILLIAN

Sitting at Nash's granite counter sipping coffee feels like the most natural thing in the world. I could get used to living in his apartment. Waking up beside him, coming home to him. Thanks to Claire's unbelievable screw-up, our intimacy is no longer just about sex. In two days, the danger has elevated our relationship to a whole new level. We're on the same lifeboat now.

Truth be told, the threat is a tad thrilling. I relish his protectiveness, his insistence that we both skip work for the week to prepare for the worst. After hours of discussion over the last few days, he has convinced me that if shit hits the fan, we're not going to run. We will man up and fight. No point in abandoning our whole lives because some asinine law has made us out to be felons.

"Round two?" he asks me now, standing on the other side of the breakfast bar with the coffee pot aloft.

"Sure."

He pours more of the Kona dark roast that smells like heaven. "I just got a text from Claire. Seems like it was all a big false alarm."

"Oh yeah?" My heart sinks, and I realize why: it means our normal, separate lives can resume. "How can she be sure?"

"I don't know. I tried calling; no answer." He sips from his own mug. "But I think we should go back to work today. No point in hunkering down here forever."

"Right." I bury my face in my cup and wait for his invitation that is surely imminent. *Stay one more night?*

But when I glance up, he's staring at his phone, no doubt trying to get back in touch with *her*.

"I don't get why she's not picking up."

"Whatever. I'm going to go take a shower . . . care to join?"

"You go ahead." He taps at his screen. "I'll catch up."

I slide off my stool, but can't quite bring myself to leave. "Are we going to tell everyone at work?"

He frowns. "About Claire?"

"No, silly." I shoot him a meaningful look. "About us."

"Oh. I don't see why. None of their business."

"So we're going to keep pretending, then?"

"Not pretending, just being discreet."

I purse my lips, all too aware of what his reluctance implies. The question is why. Why won't he call me his girlfriend? Why won't he say *I love you*? Why won't he show me off to the world? We're obviously the best part of each other's lives.

But he is not a man who bows to pressure. It's one of his traits I most admire—and loathe. Patience is my only strategy.

"Okay, boss. Whatever you say." The intercom buzzes. "You expecting someone?"

He shakes his head and crosses the room to answer the call. "Yes?"

"A woman's here to see you," the doorman's voice announces. "Claire Glasser?"

Nash meets my gaze in surprise. "Thanks, John; send her up."

I slide off my stool. "What's *she* doing here?"

"Who knows?"

We rush to the door. A minute later, the elevator deposits a very pregnant Claire in the hallway. Her eyes are puffy, her hair a frizzy mess, her face wet with tears. A large duffel bag is slung over one shoulder and she's straining to carry it along with all her extra weight. He reaches out to take her bag.

"What happened? Are you okay?"

"I couldn't stop him." She wipes her eyes. "He called the FDA director himself."

I gasp. She notices me for the first time, and her face darkens. I don't bother to hide what I'm sure is my own hostile expression. Instead I slip my arm through Nash's, in case there's any doubt about his loyalties.

"What do we do now?" I ask him, pointedly shutting her out of the *we*.

"I was thinking we could leave together," she announces, also to Nash. "Get out of town, lie low somewhere the police can't find us." After a reluctant pause, she includes me in her gaze. "All of us."

"No," he says firmly. "We are not running."

"But the police are already on their way!" she cries.

"Right now?"

"Literally any minute. I had to come warn you in person because my phone broke." She glances between us with increasing panic. "Seriously, we should go . . ."

"How could they be so fast?"

"Trust me, when my husband calls, they don't mess around." She looks nervously at the elevator bank. "We could already be too late."

"We're fucked," I mutter. "Way to go."

Nash is indignant. "I don't understand. You said it was a false alarm!"

"I thought so, but . . ." Her cheeks flush. "He thinks we're having an affair."

I snort in disgust. "Why the hell would he think that?"

"We had a bad misunderstanding," she admits. "He actually kicked me out."

"Where are you going to go?" Nash asks. "What about the baby?"

"I don't know. I guess Grand Central. And then . . ." She trails off. "I'll get on a train."

"Isn't that kind of drastic?" I say. "Where will you end up?"

"I'll figure something out. The last thing I need is to get caught up in some media freak show."

I notice Nash eyeing her enormous belly with a weird combination of compassion and anger. "You should go," he instructs her. "Go to some quiet town where you can rest until the birth. It's dangerous for the baby if your blood pressure gets too high . . ."

The intercom buzzes again. He pounces on it.

"Yes?"

"Couple of cops here to see you," the doorman announces. "Sorry, I gotta send them up."

Shit. Nash's finger hovers over the button. "Thank you."

He turns to us with the steely gaze of a boxer before a match.

"Looks like our visitors have arrived."

I'm awed by his composure, which contrasts with my own hammering pulse. Now that the moment is upon us, our trouble no longer seems romantic, just terrifying. But what can I do? Leave him? Leave everything? It's already too late anyway.

"I have to go," Claire says, squatting to pick up her duffel bag.

Nash lifts it onto her shoulder. "How will we know where you are? You said your phone was broken?"

She retreats down the hall. "I still have your number."

"So that's it?" I yell. "What if we can't find you?" *And our baby?*

She steps into the elevator. "I guess you have to trust me." She ignores me, watching Nash with a sadness that borders on longing.

"Wait!" I shout.

But the doors close and she's gone. I open my palms in frustration. "We can't just let her disappear!"

Nash shuttles me back inside the apartment. "She won't. She'll be back."

Shortly, we hear the ding of the elevator and heavy steps out in the hall. My knees buckle. I slide down the wall, but Nash yanks me up, his voice harder than concrete.

"Stand up. We've done nothing wrong."

The knock comes hard and fast.

We stare at each other.

"Taller," he commands. I square my shoulders.

Then he grabs my hand and opens the door.

ABBY: NOW

"Mom!" I shout, opening her car door.

Dad frantically reaches inside for her. "Honey, are you okay?"

She winces, sticking out her left foot. Her ankle is hugely puffy and turning purple. "I-I think it's broken."

"Oh my God! What happened?"

"I was at the park, and—" She sniffles, wiping her face, which only smears the dirt around. "I slipped down the hill and lost my phone. I managed to drive home, but it's killing me."

"Jesus Christ!" Dad scoops her into his arms and carries her inside. I follow behind them. "How'd you slip?" I ask.

"It was an accident."

"An accident?" Dad sets her on the living room couch and props some pillows underneath her left leg. "How do you just fall down a hill?"

"I told you, I *slipped*."

His voice goes from worried to irritated. "Why were you even there when you were supposed to be picking Abby up? I had to piss off a customer to go get her."

"Just to get some fresh air, okay?" She puffs out an annoyed sigh. "Do you really have to interrogate me right now?"

"Fine. I'm going to find some ice." As he stomps off, I put a blanket over her legs. She lies back without meeting my eyes. I can tell she's holding back tears, maybe more. Something doesn't feel right; she's frowning at the blank wall behind my head.

"Hi." I give a little wave. "You okay?"

Unexpectedly, her lips tighten into a self-conscious smile, as though I've caught her. Doing what? But I don't ask, and she doesn't explain. Instead she lifts her arm, and I crawl into the warm nook against her chest, not caring about her dirty face and rain-soaked clothes. "I'll be fine," she whispers. "Don't worry."

I want to believe her, but I can't ignore the way she keeps glancing around, blinking, like she's looking for something that's not there.

When Dad returns with a cold pack, a towel, and a bottle of Advil, he asks me to go to my room to start my homework.

"Your mom and I need a few minutes."

"Why?" she demands, as I hop off the couch. "We were cozy."

"Honey," he says, in a warning tone.

"I have a science test anyway," I tell them. Upstairs, I loudly shut my door, then press my ear against it. When I pick up the faint noise of their voices, I crack it open.

"I don't want to talk about it," she's saying.

"Well, I do. What were you doing there?"

"Can I not just visit a park?"

"In a fucking thunderstorm?"

"I didn't check the weather!"

"Is this about *her*?"

"No!" Mom yells.

"Okay, but this isn't like you."

"It was a stupid accident. I'm fine."

"I just want you to be open with me . . ."

"I told you, I'm *fine*."

"You're not . . ." His voice drops, and I can't hear a thing. After a few more seconds, she says, "*No*," very clearly. "I'm done with this conversation."

"All right," he says at normal volume, sounding disappointed. "I'll take care of dinner."

I hear him walk into the kitchen and start pulling out pots and pans. I tiptoe out of my room and peek over the railing to spy on the living room. Mom's stretched out on the couch with her left leg elevated. The squishy blue gel pack is wrapped around her ankle, and her eyes are closed.

Could the mysterious "her" be my cousin? Was *she* who came to the house?

And why won't they discuss it in front of me?

CLAIRE: BEFORE

At rush hour, no one in Grand Central Station stands still. The place is a madhouse of harried commuters and tourists, all darting in every direction to the various tunnels that stretch underneath the cavernous dome.

I plant my feet in the center of the crowd with my elbows out to protect my belly, studying the train schedule up on the giant board. Every few minutes, another train gets called over the loudspeaker for towns upstate and down south, far-flung and close by. *Boston*, *Peekskill*, *Dobbs Ferry . . .*

It doesn't matter where I go, as long as it's somewhere Ethan and the media and the cops won't think to search. Once Nash and Jillian's arrests hit the newswire, the tabloids won't be far behind. I've worked in journalism long enough to recognize a scandalous story when I see one—a Frankenbaby created amid a purported love triangle. All it needs to blow up is the perfect twisted headline.

It's only a matter of time now until my most shameful secret gets dug up and printed in black and white for the world to see.

"All aboard the five fifty-seven Metro North train to Poughkeepsie on track fifteen," booms a voice overhead, "making stops at Tarrytown, Ossining, Croton-Harmon . . ."

A mass of people swells together like a single organism and moves in lockstep toward track fifteen. I tuck my chin and shuffle forward in the sea of bodies, holding my duffel tight under my arm. The cash I withdrew on my way to the station—four thousand dollars, the bank max—lines the bag in stuffed envelopes. I descend a long staircase, walk along the concrete platform, and climb through the first open door onto the waiting train.

Even if cameras in the terminal later spot my face, there's no telling where I got off later. I'm as good as lost.

A few minutes later, the engine groans and the train jumps ahead. The movement startles me even though I'm expecting it. We pick up speed, barreling through the pitch-black tunnel.

So, this is it. This is good-bye.

No more going home to Riverside Park and our apartment, the bittersweet place where Colton lived and died. No more hovering near his elementary school, pretending he's about to run out with the other kids, or sitting on the bench next to the flower garden where he loved to watch dogs walk by.

Soon the train bursts out of the tunnel into the dreary twilight. The lights of midtown recede in the distance, already miles away, and my heart ices over. Letting go of New York means letting go of the last tangible connection to my son.

I silently vow that no matter what, I will visit his favorite place on his birthday every year—the Natural History Museum. I'll visit with my daughter as a new tradition to honor his memory. Inside my womb, the baby signals her approval with an emphatic punch.

Everything is going to be fine, even if I'm alone and poor, a stranger in a strange town. I don't need Ethan or Nash or a fancy brownstone or a fancy writing career to keep the only thing I still care about on this earth, something no one can steal from me.

In six weeks, I'm going to be a mother again.

* * *

There's no reason I get off at Garrison except that nothing distinguishes it from any other stop along the Hudson line. It's heavily wooded, with single-lane roads winding deep into the hills. The contrast with the city could not be starker. New York's quietest streets still radiate light and life—bright apartment windows, trolling cabs, people riding bikes.

Here on the windy train platform, as commuters hurry to their cars, I feel utterly alone. For once in my life, I'm without a plan.

Am I crazy? Should I turn around and get right back on the next train to New York, back to Ethan?

No. Even before he turned our baby into a crime scene, it was too late. I can't shake his fundamental beliefs.

Nash and Jillian must be in handcuffs by now, being questioned at the station.

Before long, everyone will want to know where I am.

I shiver in the darkness and tighten my coat over my belly.

Headlights flash in my direction. A blue sedan is idling a few yards away. The driver rolls down his window.

"Need help?" calls an older man with a neat white beard. "You look lost."

In the city, I would decline on the spot and call a taxi. But my cell is in pieces on a floor seventy miles south.

"Sure," I say, hesitantly. "Thanks; I lost my phone."

He pulls up, and I climb into the passenger seat. The car smells faintly like cigarettes, but his gentle smile eases my discomfort.

"I was about to head home when I noticed you freezing there. Where do you need to go?"

"I—I'm looking for a hotel. The closest one will do."

He laughs, not unkindly. "Not from around here, are you?"

"No."

"Town's too small for a hotel. I think there's a motel about fifteen miles away, though, near Cold Spring."

"Oh. That's pretty far."

"I'll call you a cab," he offers. "You can wait here in the meantime."

"Are you sure?" I look at the glowing clock on his dashboard, wondering if some sweet lady is cooking dinner for him at home. The thought makes me teary. "I don't want to hold you up."

"No prob," he says, glancing at my stomach. "Who would leave a pregnant lady out in the cold?"

I shake my head. *You'd be surprised.*

* * *

The next afternoon, after a restless night in the nondescript Countryside Motel, I'm ninety-five dollars poorer and in need of more permanent digs. It takes an hour of scouring the Internet on my laptop over the free WiFi to locate a cheap short-term rental within twenty miles. GREAT DEAL AVAILABLE NOW! reads the ad next to a low-res picture of an outdated kitchen with floral wallpaper and a hideous tiled floor. INTERNET, LANDLINE, HEAT & HOT WATER INCL. Apparently, demand isn't too strong in the winter for an old house in a remote stretch of the woods. In the cab on the way there, I wrap my scarf several times around my face to cover my nose and mouth.

The house is one story on a dirt lane, with navy siding and peeling white shutters. Thickets of pines rise all around it, blotting out the weak January sun. Beyond the cliff in the distance, the Hudson River winds between the hills like a glistening snake. There are no other houses in sight.

The gray-haired woman who opens the door makes no attempt to hide her skepticism.

"You're the lady who called?"

"Yes." I smile. "I'm Anne." My middle name. "Thanks for showing it last minute."

The woman clutches her satin housecoat. "No one's called for weeks."

Her unasked question hovers in the air like a test.

I rack my brain. "I'm a writer on deadline and had to get away from the city to finish my novel." I motion to my belly. "Before the baby comes."

"Oh." A smidge of friendliness creeps onto her lips. "You ever read Agatha Christie?"

"I adore her," I say truthfully. "And I still can't figure out how she pulled off *Ten Little Indians*. Total genius."

"I know!" The woman grins. "Well, Anne, come on in. It's very old, but the heat works, and the views aren't half bad."

I follow my hostess on a quick tour, not that there is much to see. A living room with a wood-burning fireplace and a sagging olive couch, an ancient kitchen and modest bathroom, and two bedrooms that smell like an old folks' home but feature giant windows looking west over the vast river. The place shows its age, but it's clean—and private.

"It's perfect. I can pay all cash up front. When can I move in?"

"Saturday? I'm leaving for Florida this weekend and was thinking I'd have to lock it up for the winter. I'll be back in May."

That gives me four months and about two thousand dollars to figure out the rest of my life.

"Great," I tell her. "I'll take it."

* * *

Moving in is the least difficult part of the weekend. Unpacking takes about fifteen minutes of folding and putting away the loose maternity tees and lounge pants I stuffed into my bag. I stow my remaining cash in the back of a drawer underneath some of the owner's cashmere sweaters.

Then I plop cross-legged on the bed. The house is strangely silent. No cars rumble by this isolated corner of the woods, and my ears are humming as if to supply the constant white noise I'm accustomed to in the city.

My laptop lies before me like Pandora's box. For five days, I've avoided going online—a record streak in my adult lifetime. In this other universe, my only social contact consists of taking cabs to the supermarket after bundling my face up to my eyes. Nash and Jillian and Ethan might as well have ceased to exist. Without any Internet or phone, my sense of disconnection is profound. I can almost pretend I really *am* on a writing retreat until I return home to my real life, to Ethan.

But dread is a powerful antidote to fantasy.

I open my laptop and log on. Then type my name into Google News. The headlines show up fast and furious:

So-Called "Frankenbaby" Heralds Brave New World of Reproductive Gene Editing

Doctors Behind Frankenbaby Post Bail; Trial Set for February

Frankenmom Still at Large, Charged With Criminal Conspiracy

The Evolution of Frankenmom: 5 Things You Don't Know About Claire Abrams

I click the last link, my heart racing.

1) *Abrams is a 39-year-old star reporter for Mindset magazine who carries a deadly genetic mutation in her mitochondrial DNA.*
2) *Abrams lost her only prior child, a son, to mitochondrial disease three years ago, when he was just eight years old.*
3) *Abrams grew up an only child in the Westchester suburbs, the daughter of a high school physics teacher and an English professor.*
4) *When Abrams was 16, her mother died of an undiagnosed illness that is presumed to be a result of a severe mitochondrial mutation; her father died of a stroke five years later.*
5) *Abrams embraces a style of immersion journalism that defies the norm, colleagues say. "I have never worked with another reporter as fearless as Claire," said Nancy Bennington, Mindset's editor-in-chief. "Most reporters today make some phone calls and call it a day, but Claire is old-school."*

> *Bennington described some of Abrams' more unusual exploits, including posing as a patient to get into a corrupt drug trial; volunteering to try a synthetic form of LSD for cancer research; and trailing the CEO of a pharmaceutical company to expose a scam on prescription drug pricing. "I can't say I'm entirely surprised she would risk everything to try an untested fertility treatment," her editor added. "If there's anyone who would be first in line for something like that, it's her, especially after what she's been through."*

I heave a sigh of relief. They still don't know. All the press has learned so far is the garden-variety version of me. No enterprising reporter has done her homework yet.

I navigate back a page and skim the rest of the stories. Nash and Jillian are out on bail; a picture shows them holding hands together leaving the station: Nash defiant, Jillian stone-faced, both in shock.

I hope they get off easy. But there's no way in hell I would take any of it back. I close my eyes and zero in on the fluttery sensations in my stomach—the near-constant kicking still enthralls me. It never gets old to feel my baby moving, or to dream of us meeting face-to-face for the first time.

When I open my eyes, Ethan's name is staring back at me on the screen:

Ethan Abrams, Husband of So-Called
Frankenmom, Speaks Out

I click on the story. It's an op-ed he's published in a leading journal for intellectuals.

> *Whether we like it or not, there are technologies emerging today that make possible the creation of children who are not the offspring of one man and one woman, as every human has been*

until this point in the history of our species. But such tools have far outpaced our ethical understanding of how—and if—to use them, as Robert Nash's irresponsible fertility experiment demonstrates. That my wife participated, and by extension involved me, is a source of tremendous heartache, both for me and for the child I will soon regrettably share with two other people.

The creation of a child with genetic material from one man and two women violates a fundamental biological principle and our collective moral commitment to protecting the health and well-being of children. The regulatory system prohibits experiments that expose children to novel genetic origins that could hinder their future psychological development and the formation of their identities. That is why our regulations clearly state that no person can knowingly "alter the genome of a cell of a human being or in vitro embryo such that the alteration is capable of being transmitted to descendants."

Claire and I were desperate for another child after losing our son. She was afraid of passing on her mutation, but instead of having the courage to love whatever baby God gave us, she acted selfishly, out of fear, and now it's time for her to face the consequences. If she is found guilty of conspiracy, she faces a fine of up to $500,000, a jail sentence of up to five years, or both. Given her stunning capacity for recklessness, it doesn't surprise me that she's disappeared now, at eight months pregnant, further endangering the welfare of her unborn child in order to evade her own punishment.

Lest anyone question my role in this scandal, allow me to publicly state that I disavow my involuntary connection to it, and condemn every depraved step leading up to the child's birth.

I dig my nails into my palms. Would Ethan truly have preferred another Colton, with his doomed—but *natural*—origins? Then none of the ethics scholars would be scandalized, and one day they could all show up at the next kid's funeral with Hallmark cards expressing their condolences. Assholes.

I slam my computer shut and leap off the bed. If it's *selfish* and *reckless* to sacrifice everything for the sake of my child's health, then maybe I *am* unfit to be a mother. But I wouldn't have it any other way.

An unexpected wetness drips down my thigh. I reach around my stomach to wick it away. If Ethan is denouncing me in public, then our marriage is really over. The meanness of his words hollows out an ache in my chest all the way down to—

My belly. It's gone rigid, like it's filling with cement.

I look down at my hand.

It's bloody.

* * *

JILLIAN

I wait in the doorway with my arms crossed. "What are you doing?"

It's after two AM and Nash still hasn't come to bed. He's in the living room hunched over his phone, his face bathed in its blue light.

"I'll be in soon."

I shiver in my lacy nightgown that he's failed to notice. "Eighteen."

He keeps tapping his screen. "One sec."

"Eighteen," I repeat. "Do you even know what I'm talking about?"

When he finally looks up, his eyes take a second to focus on me. "What?"

"The trial starts in eighteen days."

In his sigh, I detect a note of annoyance. "And?"

I climb beside him on the couch. "And so we have only eighteen days before the shit storm, and you're sitting here on your phone." I snuggle up against him. "I just don't want to waste any of our time together."

And, I think, *I'm done being ignored*. In the surreal, chaotic week since our arrest and release on bail, we've been lying low in his apartment away from the cameras. We didn't cooperate with the cops when they first showed up, but then they quickly came back with a search warrant on the strength of Ethan's tip and went through Nash's apartment, where they discovered a file in his safe called Double X. It contained handwritten notes from our experiment that he'd saved for eventual publication, and unfortunately that was enough evidence to arrest us and charge us with the crime of circumventing federal research prohibitions.

The tabloid media is having a field day with the story, but their angle is all wrong. They're obsessed with Claire, the already legendary—and missing—*Frankenmom*. Never mind the geniuses required to join three people's DNA into one flawless embryo. Nobody gives a damn who achieved that. Yet Claire, merely a means to an end—the press can't run stories about her fast enough.

But the most appalling part is Nash. In my version of this insane twist of fate, the two of us are supposed to be inseparable by now, united against the world. Even as our freedom possibly slips away, his affection should be one hell of a consolation prize.

Instead, the reality is crushing: he is as obsessed with Claire as everyone else. It's obvious in his distracted voice, in the urgency with which he scours the headlines, in his lack of interest in sex and his preoccupation with his phone.

"You're still looking for her, aren't you?" I say.

"She's pregnant and alone," he replies. "Why do you hate her so much?"

"Why don't you? She's screwed up both our lives, and all you can think about is whether she's okay."

"We have a responsibility to that baby. Can you imagine if she forgoes medical care because she's afraid? It would be totally negligent."

The jealous knot inside me loosens. "You're a good doctor, Rob. But Claire made this mess herself, and there's nothing we can do about it."

"Don't you want to know if the baby is okay?"

"Are you kidding? Of course! But it's just another thing she stole, so now we have to worry about ourselves."

His eyes narrow. "Yes, she fucked up, but she's still my patient. I can't just abandon her."

"She stopped being your patient months ago. She's our research subject. There's a difference. And she cut the experiment short. You owe her nothing."

"Why are you so threatened?"

"Oh, I don't know." I shrug, fuming. "Maybe because I'm about to throw away everything for you, and all you can think about is her."

"I told you, we're not going to jail. They have no proof of any conspiracy. It's just Ethan's word against ours."

"What about the file?"

"It's not hard evidence. It's descriptions of embryos at various points in their development. As far as they know, it could be pure speculation, which is not against the law, last I checked."

I hesitate. I've been dreading this conversation.

"Don't look so worried," he says. "Without Claire giving up some DNA, they have no proof."

I decide not to tell him yet. We have so little time left. "Let's not talk about it anymore." I climb onto him and straddle his lap, planting a gentle kiss on his mouth. "Come to bed. It's late."

He barely kisses me back. "Sorry, I'm not in the mood."

I gather enough self-respect to stand. "Fine. If you'd rather be looking for her, I'll get out of your way."

I march out of the room, slowing in anticipation of him calling my name.

Jilly, wait!

But he says nothing. I peek over my shoulder in time to see him grab his phone once more.

ABBY: NOW

As my mom rests on the couch with her broken ankle wrapped in an ice pack, I feel like she's spiraling out of control, along with my entire life.

Why would she slip down a hill in a rainstorm?

Why won't she tell me anything?

Who was the stranger who walked onto our driveway?

I blink back tears. I'm terrified I'm going to lose her and I have no idea why.

I have to do something, and I don't care anymore if I get in trouble.

Riley's suggestion echoes in my mind: *What if you reopened your account on the genetics site and contacted the stranger again? See what else she'll tell you?*

It's now or never. I dash into my parents' bedroom and open Mom's silver MacBook on her nightstand. Her computer has stored her Gmail password, so it loads fast. I search the inbox for MapMyDNA and find the message she sent to the company five weeks ago asking them to close my account. It takes me half a minute to write them back:

> *Hi, sorry for the confusion but it turns out my daughter still needs her account for her final class project on DNA. Is it possible to reopen it ASAP? If so, can you please make her old username and password work again? Thanks! ☺*

After hitting SEND, I delete the entire chain and block the company's email address so she won't see if they reply. Then I replace her laptop exactly as I found it—slightly off the edge of the nightstand.

It's past five PM now, on a Friday, so they probably won't get the request until after the weekend. I hope it won't be too late, because I have a feeling there's only one person in the world who will lead me to the truth.

CLAIRE: BEFORE

The blood is dark red, like the first day of a period. Sweat prickles down my neck. It's five weeks too early.

I press my stomach. The baby is still moving. She's alive.

But my big belly is stiff as plaster to the touch.

Is it a contraction? With Colton, I had a planned C-section due to him being breech, so I never experienced labor.

Oh God, of all the times to be alone, far from any hospital, far from anyone who can help . . .

Nash. Nash can help. He has to, even if he hates me, because that's what doctors do in emergencies; they set aside judgment and fury and betrayal, and they come to the rescue.

I check his number in my laptop's address book, then drag myself to the dusty phone on the old woman's nightstand and grab it off its cradle. Hearing an ancient dial tone only adds to my sense of unreality. My blood-stained fingers push the buttons of their own accord, and one ring collides with the next as the sticky warmth trickles down my thigh, until, finally, the acute relief of his voice echoes in my ear: "Hello?"

"I'm bleeding," I blurt out. "But if I go to the hospital, they'll find me!"

"Claire? Oh my God, where are you?"

"Upstate. I'm so lost here. I don't know what to do."

"Go to the hospital right now. The baby could be in distress."

"But if they recognize me, they'll take her away!"

"It won't matter if she's dead."

My breath catches. *Dead.* The word shocks something awake inside me, and my decision clicks. I would sooner kill myself than watch my own child die—again.

"Meet me there," I whisper. "Hudson Valley Hospital. I'm going now."

* * *

Half an hour later, I waddle into an empty emergency room holding a towel between my legs. The blood is still trickling out, but slower than before—and the baby is still moving. I haven't taken my hand off my stomach for a second.

I approach the check-in desk with trepidation. My face is all over the city tabloid press, but here in rural Cold Spring, does anyone know or care?

The young lady at reception is absorbed in her computer; her long purple nails clack on the keys. She glances at me with minimal interest.

"How can I help you?"

"I'm thirty-five weeks pregnant and bleeding." I indicate the towel between my legs. "I need to be seen right away."

She seems unfazed as she pushes a clipboard across the desk. "Fill out your insurance information."

"I . . . don't have any." I think of Ethan's amazing Columbia University health insurance that was supposed to have seen me through pregnancy and labor. Then I picture the meager two thousand dollars in the dresser. Who knows if it would even cover this visit? "I'll—pay cash," I stammer. "Is there a payment plan?"

'Yes." The receptionist doesn't bother to hide her pity. How pathetic I must appear: pregnant, alone, and broke.

"The accounting department will send you a bill after the visit. First, we need you to fill out your name, birth date, address, and medical history. You have ID?"

I wince. "Sorry, I rushed out so fast . . ."

In fact, I'm counting on the law that guarantees emergency treatment to anyone who walks into an ER, regardless of their legal status.

"It's okay; just fill out the form."

Name. My gaze sweeps over the desk cluttered with stacks of forms and hospital-branded pens. I scribble ANNE PAGE, and a fake birth date approximating my age. Next, I write the address of the skyscraper that houses the *Mindset* headquarters on Seventh Avenue. It's the only one I know by heart aside from my own home. Former home, I guess. For the rest of the medical history, I check NO next to every major ailment, until I arrive at MENTAL HEALTH HISTORY.

After a pause, I check NO. Then I slide the clipboard back to her.

"Someone will be with you shortly, Ms. Page."

Five minutes later, a chatty blonde nurse leads me into a private room and helps me onto the bed, then takes my blood pressure and pulse and makes small talk about the snow. I appreciate her effort at distraction, but the longer we talk, the more I worry about a spark of recognition.

"Dr. Morris will be in to examine you soon," she says on her way out, after recording my vitals. "You can change into the gown, opening at the back." At the doorway, she stops and stares at me, and I brace.

"Is it your first?" she asks.

"Yes." It's easier than explaining, and safer.

"Ah." Her lips curve into a reassuring smile. "First-time moms are always extra nervous. But by thirty-five weeks, it's very likely your baby will be just fine even if she's born today. Good luck."

I'm still catching my breath as I change into the gown. Soon, there's a knock on the door. A relaxed, fifty-something man wearing glasses and blue scrubs strides in, skimming my intake form.

"Hello, I'm Dr. Morris, and I'll be examining you today. I hear you have some third-trimester bleeding?"

Is he studying my face a little too closely, or awaiting my answer?

"Yeah," I tell him, "I just noticed it. I don't have any pain, but I think I might be having contractions . . ."

"Have you ever been diagnosed with placenta previa?"

I shake my head. He instructs me to slide my bare feet into the stirrups at the end of the bed. "I'll need to take a quick look at your cervix." He holds up a clear plastic speculum. "It shouldn't hurt, but it may be unpleasant, okay?"

I nod, thinking how strange it is that I feel more comfortable with him looking down there than up at my face. I feel a cold squirt of jelly, then the thrust of the device, and his fingers poking around inside me.

"Ouch." The pressure is intense on my sensitive cervix.

"Good news," he says, "everything's nice and closed. Next I want to do an ultrasound to check on the baby."

He wheels over a machine with a small screen that's connected to a plastic wand about the size of a cucumber.

Another cold squirt, this time on my stomach, and he presses the wand firmly into my belly. The screen comes to life with a grainy image of a fetus. Head, torso, arms, legs. I stare hungrily at the screen, at the limbs flickering in the black oblivion of amniotic fluid. A rapid whooshing heartbeat echoes through the speakers.

"Is she okay?" I barely choke out the words.

"She looks perfect! But . . . I do see one thing."

My heart surges into my throat. "What?"

He squints at the screen, moving the wand back and forth over my abdomen. Every fiber in my lungs goes still; I can't breathe.

"It's your placenta. It appears to have partially detached from your uterine wall."

My head feels woozy, like I'm swaying over an abyss. I struggle to focus.

"What does that mean?"

The doctor grimaces. "This can happen sometimes spontaneously, especially with advanced maternal age. You're lucky; the abruption is minor—for now. Aside from delivering the baby, which I don't think is necessary, there's not much we can do except put you on strict bed rest." He frowns, imparting the solemnity of his order. "And I mean, *strict*. The slightest exertion could cause a hemorrhage."

"Oh God."

"Do you have someone at home who can help you?" He glances at my left hand, where my diamond ring still glitters. I haven't had the heart to take it off. "Your husband?"

I clear my throat. "I'll be fine."

His brows knit tighter. "Are you sure? You look white."

"Yes," I say, thinking of Nash. "He's on his way here now."

"Oh, good." He seems relieved. "It's very important that you not overdo it. If you can make it through two or three more weeks, you'll be full-term."

Right at the start of the trial. How can Nash possibly stay?

The doctor pats my hand with fatherly calm. "Everything will be okay, Mrs. Page. Before you know it, you'll have a newborn, and then life will really get crazy."

I force myself to smile. "I can only imagine."

* * *

The doctor makes me undergo a non-stress test and wear an external fetal monitor until he is satisfied that the baby's health is okay. Then I'm finally allowed to return to the waiting room in a wheelchair. I instantly spot Nash hunched in a chair wearing a puffy black coat; a small carry-on suitcase lies at his feet.

"You're here!" I exclaim, grinning despite everything. I've never been so happy to see him, even though he looks pale and tired. His chin has a week's worth of stubble, and his cheeks are thinner than I remember.

He rushes to my side. "I took the first train out. Are you okay?"

"Sort of." I explain my diagnosis, aware of the eavesdropping nurse who is wheeling me. "I'm going to need a lot of help at home."

"Let's get you into bed then. I'll go call a cab."

As he disappears outside, the nurse pats my shoulder. "Your husband seems like he'll take good care of you."

"Yes." I feel myself relax. "I think he will."

She pauses. "I feel like I've seen him somewhere before."

"Oh really?" I stare at the hospital's revolving glass doors, willing him to hurry back and whisk us away. "Probably because he looks like that one actor. What's his name . . . ?"

"What's he in?"

I scramble to divert her. "That one movie . . . with the spaceship."

The nurse shifts her weight from one foot to the other. "I'm not sure which one you mean."

"Oh well." I make a show of clutching my stomach. "I just got another weird cramp."

She kneels beside me. "Do you want me to call Dr. Morris?"

I wince and shake my head. How long does it take a cab to arrive in this small town? Of all the things I miss about the city, transportation at the wave of a hand is high on the list. "I don't think so. I just need—a second." I cover my face and draw a few steady breaths. "Okay. It's going away."

"Sounds like Braxton Hicks. I got them nonstop from twenty-eight weeks on with my first."

"Oh, you have kids?"

It's the magic question. Her face lights up, and I know we're back on solid ground. Talk of her three children keeps us busy until a car pulls up outside and Nash's towering figure appears in the revolving door.

"Oh, there he is!" I announce giddily. As he strides in, I wrap my scarf several times around my face.

"It's bitter out there," the nurse notes, handing the wheelchair over to him.

"Sure is," he says. "Now let's get you home."

* * *

When we're safely tucked into the back of the cab, I take his hand with profound gratitude. "Thank you so, so much. I don't know what I would do without you."

"Let's get one thing straight." His voice is quietly angry. "You have screwed things up beyond belief."

"I know. You can't imagine how shitty I feel."

"I'm only helping you because I can't in good conscience not."

"You hate me, don't you?"

He sighs. "No, I made a mistake and now I'm owning it."

His words suck my breath away. I can't speak for a few minutes. Finally, I blurt out, "You mean it was a mistake to trust me?"

He gestures to my stomach. "To do any of this."

"You're wrong. That's not true."

Tears sting my eyes. He stares out the window. We sit in painful silence as the car winds along the narrow country roads. Eventually, we hit a red light, and he faces me sadly. "I had a life, Claire. A good life, before you came along."

I lock onto his gaze. "And thanks to you, someone else will have a life soon, too."

* * *

Once I'm confined to bed at home, he springs into action. A dutiful companion, he prepares our meals, does my laundry, and goes grocery shopping at the rural Walmart nearby under cover of his winter jacket and new facial scruff. Cash, thankfully, is in plentiful supply. In the several days before his arrest, he withdrew five thousand and then four thousand from his account just in case. He deliberately kept it under the ten-thousand limit that might invite federal scrutiny, and now the money is secreted away in the suitcase he brought.

A stiff routine emerges to order our days. We're living in the same house, if not quite *together*. Though he's helpful and efficient, he won't spend voluntary time with me. He eats separately and sleeps in the second bedroom. If I try to make small talk, he grunts or mumbles a one-word response. It's clear he's resigned himself to being my caretaker, but nothing more, so I stop trying after the first few days. I guess I deserve it.

The bed is my prison, and time passes slowly. All the time, I wonder when the looming trial will draw him away. I know he told Jillian he would be back "soon," after he handled my emergency, and that she wouldn't be able to reach him in the meantime. At my request, he took apart his cell phone to disable the GPS tracking feature. Deep in the woods, we're all but cut off from the world. His entire life hangs in the balance of the next few weeks. And still day after day, he chooses to remain here with me.

As the baby's due date nears, I sense his excitement building despite the tension between us. Each night, he listens to her heartbeat with his Doppler. It's the only time his tense face relaxes into a genuine smile. Even if he is furious with me, his affection for the baby is clear. She is his life's work personified. I'm planning to name her Abigail Grace, after my mother and grandmother. I like to think they would have been proud of me for risking everything to bring her into the world.

In the second week of his stay, I am so restless that I get up to do the dishes, but he scolds me when he finds me. "Don't you dare," he says, carrying me gruffly back into bed. "You're not supposed to be on your feet."

I begin to hope that he might stay for the birth, even as the trial nears. We don't mention it, but its ticking clock might as well be audible throughout the house. Sometimes I catch him sighing out of nowhere or pacing the house like a trapped tiger, and I cringe, remembering his words: *I had a good life before you came along.*

After sixteen days of our cohabitation, I'm still showing no signs of labor, and only one snowy evening remains until the zero hour. If he doesn't arrive tomorrow morning at nine AM sharp at the Lower Manhattan federal court in Foley Square, a warrant will go out for his arrest, and any chance of him dodging serious punishment will disappear.

Do I really want that for him?

When he enters my bedroom with a tray for dinner, I force out the words: "Just go. Please. I don't want to be responsible for wrecking your whole life."

He sets down the roast chicken and steamed vegetables on the bed. "Whatever happens, it will be my decision. Period."

"It's fine," I say, more confidently than I feel. "I'm sure I can get myself to the hospital when the time comes."

"I thought you wanted to avoid going back there."

It's true. If someone recognizes me the next time, the hospital could notify the authorities and seize the baby. But I'm not about to attempt labor alone at home. And if he stays to help me, what will happen to him? A citation for contempt of court? A warrant for his arrest?

"I'll do what I have to do," I insist. "Whatever will keep her safe."

"You can't even get up. And you think you're going to cook? Do a wash?"

"I'll manage."

"That's not an answer."

"I'll ask a neighbor for help."

"Good idea." He flashes a sarcastic thumbs-up. "Just walk a mile to the next house in the snow."

"I'll figure something out."

"You need me, Claire. Admit it."

"I can call someone else." I think hard, trying to determine whom I trust enough and who will drop everything to come help me. Not Ethan anymore. Not my work friends at *Mindset.* My parents are long gone. My Mighty Mito friends, like JohnsMom111, only know me online. I don't even know where they live. And my actual friends from childhood and college tiptoed away one by one after Colton's death; the body armor of my grief repelled everyone, eventually. What relationships do I have to show for my thirty-nine years?

The answer leaves me speechless.

Nash is scowling. "If you start to bleed and can't get help in time, you're fucked."

"And if you don't show up tomorrow, so are you. She's going to freak out if you ditch her." My heart speeds up nervously. "She doesn't know where we are, right?"

"No, not that it matters."

"Are you sure?"

"Claire." He touches my hand. "You're being paranoid."

I snatch it away. "I am not!"

He recoils in surprise. “Whoa, calm down.”

“Sorry, I . . .” I trail off to catch my breath.

“You what?” he says, confused. “What’s wrong?”

I almost confide in him but think better of it. “Nothing. I just don’t trust her.”

It’s impossible to overlook the sneer of her lips and the ambition in her eyes; she seems like a woman whose cunning knows no bounds. I remain haunted by her declaration back at the Tangled Vine:

We will know that child. That I promise you.

The baby squirms in my womb then, filling me with dread.

Her baby, too.

ABBY: NOW

As soon as Dad brings me home from school on Monday, I race past Mom on the living room couch, where she's resting with her sprained ankle, and climb the stairs.

"Hello to you, too," she calls after me. "How was school?"

"Fine," I shout down. "I just really have to go to the bathroom."

Upstairs, I grab her laptop from her room, sneak into my bathroom, and lock the door. Then, for the first time since the museum, I log into MapMyDNA with my old username and password. A shiver of excitement flies through me when the orange-and-blue welcome page loads. My email request worked! I'm still sharing DNA maps with all the same people from school . . . plus the stranger who shares my DNA: JH0502.

I open our message history to send her a new note. I type it quickly before I can chicken out: I think my mom is lying about you, but I don't know why.

Then I turn on the shower, in case my parents start to wonder why I'm in here for so long. The hot steam is not very relaxing, though. It keeps fogging up the screen every time I refresh the page for her reply. While I'm waiting, I kill some time scrolling through my Instagram feed, liking some funny memes and my friends' selfies.

I'm checking out Tyler's pictures of his new guitar when my MapMyDNA inbox pings with a new message:

> I will tell you everything, but can you meet in person, alone? I'll come to you.

Whoa. Alone? What's up with that? I imagine my parents locking me in my room forever if they found out.

But if I meet her at school, what could go wrong? It's not like I'm going to get into her car. Come *on*. Who would be that stupid? I notice a green dot next to JH0502's screen name. She's online now.

OK, I write back. Can you come to my school tomorrow? It's the Garrison Union Free School. We have a break from 12:15 to 1 for lunch.

Her reply comes fast: Perfect. Where should we meet?

We can talk on the benches in front of the parking lot. It's against the rules to go off-campus.

For a minute, there's no response. I'm afraid she's unhappy with this plan, but then she pings me again:

OK. But don't tell your mom. Or you won't get to hear my side of the story.

I reply right away: Don't worry. I wasn't going to.

JILLIAN: BEFORE

ONE WEEK TO GO

It's 8:55 AM, the packed courtroom is buzzing, and Nash is about to march in any second—I'm sure of it. It's been seventeen days and two hours since I woke up to find him gone, and now there's only five minutes left on the clock. I've been counting the seconds until this deadline for these last two excruciating weeks, when every attempt to reach him has failed.

Sitting beside my lawyer at the defendants' table, I crane my neck toward the doors and avoid eye contact with the spectators who have come to gawk at the downfall of "Mrs. Frankenstein." Never mind my Harvard doctorate. The idiotic tabloid media doesn't even have the decency to call me Dr. Frankenstein—only Nash gets that dubious distinction. I'm merely an underling, an afterthought. It's bullshit. Anyone who thinks sexism is a myth has never been a woman in science.

But where the hell is he?

Adding insult to injury, his whereabouts have been the source of incessant gossip; he and Claire are said to be secret lovers who conspired all along to create the Frankenbaby and then escape together without me.

But it's not like he chose her over me. He simply couldn't ignore his professional duty to the baby; I get it. Any minute now—it's 8:58 AM—he'll walk in and set the record straight. Even if he hasn't made a formal commitment to me, our future together is real. It's been his implicit promise every time he's pressed his lips to my naked body. We're going to make it through the trial as a team, impervious to public scorn.

But a toxic voice seeps into my thoughts.

Why hasn't he called?

I close my eyes and curse my doubt.

What we share is special. It's scary to admit, but I'm in love for the first time.

Of course he can't call. It doesn't mean he's purposefully avoiding me. His phone is a liability that could be tapped or traced. He's probably *dying* to see me again.

All will be fine as soon as he walks in. It's 8:59.

"Hey," whispers my lawyer, a rail-thin man with greasy hair and a fast mouth. "Don't look so nervous. Juries can smell guilt like dogs."

I peel my eyes away from the door in time to see the somber judge enter the courtroom, her black robes draped around her diminutive frame like a witch's cloak.

"Everyone, please rise for the Honorable Patricia Clark," the bailiff announces.

Any second now. I glance back at the door again, but the lawyer nudges my foot under the table, and I climb to my feet a disrespectful beat late.

Come on!

"This court is now in session." The judge taps a gavel, the strangers in the jury box eye me with suspicion, the prosecutor flashes me a vengeful smile; but I barely notice them. I am transfixed by the empty chair beside me. For the first time, I consider the possibility that he's not going to come.

That bitch must have trapped him. As if she hasn't fucked everything up enough. Something heavier than lead descends into the pit of my stomach: rage.

* * *

CLAIRE

Propped up on three pillows, we live-stream the start of the trial on my laptop. Nash lies beside me with his arms folded behind his head. Surprisingly content, I think, for someone who is officially now a fugitive.

As the beak-nosed prosecutor launches into an opening statement about the sanctity of human life, Nash rolls his eyes. "Can't say I'm sorry to miss it."

"She sure as hell is," I tell him. "You left her high and dry."

On the screen, Jillian's fury is unmistakable; she's sullen and red-faced, her shoulders pinched and her arms tightly folded. Nash's vacant chair beside her is a glaring rebuff.

"I know. But they would be just as vicious if I was there."

"Wasn't there something . . . between you two?" I've long wondered but lacked the opening to ask.

He hesitates. "There was."

"Past tense?" My pulse pounds; I'm not sure why the answer matters, but it does.

"It wasn't really going anywhere," he says. "I wasn't looking for anything serious, even though I'm pretty sure she was."

"Honestly?" I shift my massive belly to face him. "I didn't trust her from day one."

He seems surprised. "Why not?"

"Just a sense. She's only out for herself."

"But she has an exceptional mind. She might be the smartest researcher I've ever worked with."

"So? She would have blackmailed you in a heartbeat."

He winces. "Maybe so."

The prosecutor, who is pacing in front of the jury box while delivering his statement, stops short on the screen.

"Bottom line, the case against Dr. Hendricks and Dr. Nash is as tight as a drum," he says. "Forensic data experts uncovered a deleted recording on her cell phone, which had been backed up to the cloud, that revealed a conversation between them strategizing about exactly how they were going to pull off this conspiracy, combining Mrs. Abrams' egg with Dr. Hendricks'. The whole thing is as clear as day. The recording will play for the jury now."

Nash gasps as his own voice begins to fill the courthouse. But Jillian stares ahead blankly, not revealing any shock.

"You didn't know about this?" I ask him.

"Are you kidding? We were partners. Why would she betray me?"

I can't help thinking, *I told you so.* But his mounting anger as we listen to the recording is validating. Any loyalty he feels for her will dry up fast now.

After the recording finishes, the prosecutor turns to the jury with a flourish, as if gearing up for some big finale.

"What's especially damning," he declares, "is that this willful manipulation of human life, this three-parent experiment, was no reckless impulse carried out at the request of a desperate mother. It was planned well before Claire Abrams volunteered herself—in fact, she was an unsuspecting part of the plan all along."

The prosecutor curls his lips up in distaste.

"What's he talking about?" I ask.

"No idea," Nash says, as the prosecutor opens his mouth again.

"Ladies and gentlemen of the jury, computer records reveal that this woman"—he points at Jillian—"registered as a member of the online support group Mighty Mito Moms a full *year* before the experiment began so that she could gain the trust of women like Mrs. Abrams, mothers whose children suffered greatly from mitochondrial disease. Our defendant here posed as JohnsMom111 and posted in the group thirty-three times about her nonexistent child's illness so that she could eventually use their vulnerable community as a recruiting platform. Poor Mrs. Abrams fell right into the trap."

The courtroom breaks into murmurs as Nash's jaw goes slack.

It takes me several mind-numbing seconds to speak. "Did you know about this?"

"I swear to God, I had no clue."

I inch away from him on the bed. "How am I supposed to believe that?"

"I turned *you* down at the bar, remember? When I told you to find another doctor?"

I recall my mortifying disappointment that night at the Stone Rose Lounge. "True."

"And her recording proves it. She's goading me on, calling me a coward unless I accept your proposition. She must have been waiting for someone like you to come along, counting on your desperation and then mine . . ."

"Wow." I cradle my stomach, trying to reconcile the irony that the healthiest part of my child has come from someone so damaged.

He is visibly shaken. "I would have fired her immediately had I known . . ."

I touch my face. My cheeks are sweaty.

"Are you okay?" he asks. "You look warm."

I flick my wrist. "Oh, my daughter's DNA is part psychopath. No biggie."

"Not the part that influences personality."

"You don't *know* that," I retort, my voice rising. "Gene interaction is way more complex than anyone understands. It's not like we have a precedent!"

His slow exhale makes me shudder. It seems like affirmation of my fear, but his mind must still be on Jillian, because he says, "I never even knew her. After all this time."

Meanwhile, the prosecutor is on a roll now, his step quickening.

"It would have been bad enough to catfish a regular person. But Claire Abrams is in a different category altogether. Medical records subpoenaed during discovery show that she suffered a mental breakdown after the death of her son, complete with paranoid delusions and panic attacks that required a prolonged stay in a psychiatric facility, where she imagined her son was still alive and kept calling out to him.

"Needless to say, we're not talking about someone of sound enough mind to consent to any kind of experiment. But did that matter to Dr. Hendricks and Dr. Nash? No, they preyed on her despair to fashion her into a willing surrogate. And now this poor child is about to be born to a mental patient on the run."

A surreal fog clouds my vision. There it is, my deepest secret exposed with cruel nonchalance. The shame I've worked for so long to hide, scooped right out of my soul and flung before the world to judge. With immense dread, I look at Nash.

He's gaping at me in disbelief.

I manage a shaky smile. "I guess I also have a lot to explain."

ABBY: NOW

On Monday night at dinner, I'm totally distracted. My meeting with JH0502 is *tomorrow.* What will she tell me? What is such a big deal that she is going to drive all the way to Garrison to meet me in person—alone? And why can't my mom know?

If Mom and Dad notice I'm not paying much attention at the table, they don't seem to care. In fact, I think they're having some pretty big problems themselves. They barely spoke to each other all weekend. It must be bad, because Dad turns on the TV to watch *Jeopardy* while Mom silently serves us microwaved chicken nuggets.

Afterward, I skip dessert and tell them I'm going to sleep early. "Big day tomorrow." That part isn't a lie. They kiss me good-night, and I go upstairs. It's kind of ridiculous how they're barely noticing me tonight.

I brush my teeth and get ready for bed, but toss and turn, thinking about what will happen. After a while, I give up trying to sleep. The house is dark when I tiptoe down to the kitchen for a snack, except for a wedge of light from Dad's office. His door is slightly open, and he and Mom are inside talking. I can't help overhearing their tense voices drifting out. I mean, I *could* plug my ears and go back to my room, but what I hear makes me freeze.

"I didn't just slip and fall," she's saying. "There was . . . more to it."

I tiptoe closer and press myself against the wall.

"What do you mean?" he asks. "I thought you said it was an accident."

"It was. But the truth is . . . I was chasing another vision of Colton."

I hold in a gasp. She was *what?*

"I know it sounds crazy," she's saying, "but he just, like, *appeared* on the playground."

"Oh fuck. This is what I was afraid of."

"Why do you think I didn't tell you? But he seemed so close . . ."

"Honey, no one was there. Tell me you realize that."

Silence.

"Oh God," Dad moans. "You need to go back on the Risperdal—"

"No!"

"There's no shame in taking medication."

"I don't want that shit in my body!"

"But what if you hallucinate while you're driving? This isn't something you can control!"

"I'll look for a therapist."

"I really think an inpatient program would be the most effective—"

"No!" she yells. "I'm not going to Bellevue again."

Again?

"Then somewhere else . . ."

I hear them move toward the door, so I leap under the staircase, where I can crouch in the shadows without them noticing. They walk out of the office, still arguing. As they head upstairs, the steps creak above my head.

"I'm sure therapy will help," she's telling him. "Let me just give it a shot."

"All right. But you have to tell me *immediately* if this happens again. Okay?"

I don't hear what she says next, because they lower their voices when they near my bedroom at the top of the stairs.

All I can think of is that terrible note I discovered in my backpack: *My mom's a crazy bitch.*

Maybe Sydney was right. Maybe my mom *is* crazy.

I'm not sure what Bellevue is, but I'm guessing there's a whole big part of her life she's kept hidden from me. Maybe JH0502 will know.

I feel like I'm on the edge of a mountain, waiting for the ground to fall out from under me. Except it's impossible to see the most important thing: how steep is the drop?

JILLIAN: BEFORE

The courtroom smells like fear and stale coffee. When the judge marches in, I rise unsteadily from my seat at the defendant's table along with my lawyer.

The next few minutes mean everything. Today I find out how long I'll be going to prison—alone—since Nash never showed up. Now that we know Claire is unstable, it makes sense. He can't leave a newborn baby with a crazy woman. I'm not sure who I feel worse for—myself or him; we're both trapped.

This past week has been a horror show culminating in a guilty verdict that surprised no one. My recording, which the prosecutor dredged up using data recovery software, was played loud and clear for the jury. It revealed the two of us discussing the strategic details of how to carry out the mitochondrial transplant—when, where, and how the secret experiment would go down. The jury only deliberated for fifteen minutes before reaching their unanimous verdict.

The only question left is how severe my sentence will be. In cases regarding the welfare of a child, Judge Clark happens to be notorious for her harshness.

As she takes her place at the raised bench, all chatter ceases in the airless room. Between two American flags, a round gold eagle seal with the words U.S. District Court shines in the wood paneling above her head.

Seeing those official symbols cuts through my quiet self-control. This is happening. This is real. I'm about to be sentenced for a crime that has no business being a crime. I'm about to be hauled off to *prison*. I grip the table to fight my overwhelming urge to run.

Beside the bench, the poker-faced bailiff announces, "This court is now in session, the Honorable Judge Patricia Clark presiding."

My lawyer nudges my foot with his own. I know what's coming next, and it will take every ounce of my self-control to accept punishment for the greatest triumph of my life.

Judge Clark's solemn gaze bores into me. "We are here today to issue a sentence in the matter of *United States v. Hendricks*. Ms. Hendricks, you have been found guilty by a jury of your peers of conspiring to expose an unborn child to experimental genetic origins that could harm both her physical and psychological well-being, in contravention of the federal ban on editing human embryos. Before your sentencing, do you have any last statement you would like to make for the record?"

I clear my throat. *Damn you all*, I want to scream. My career is crucified. My parents are too ashamed to return my calls. The man of my dreams is gone, stolen by the woman who wrecked my life. What's left?

"Your Honor, I'm—" I force myself to utter the lie. "I'm sorry for any damage I've caused. I accept responsibility for my actions."

A flick of dissatisfaction crosses the judge's face. "Is that all?"

"Yes, Your Honor." I sit down, unable to make eye contact with my lawyer, whose posture radiates annoyance.

"You had one job," he hisses under his breath. "Be at least a *little* contrite."

I'm not an actress, I think. *I'm a fucking scientist.*

The judge opens her contemptuous mouth. "Ms. Hendricks, you are hereby sentenced to thirty-six months in prison and three years' probation, on condition that you agree to stay away from all human embryo research for a period of ten years. You are to voluntarily surrender in thirty days to the Federal Correctional Institute at Danbury."

I feel my lungs deflate as the air flies out.

Time passes, seconds or minutes, I can't be sure; the courtroom erupts in a flurry of activity and my lawyer says something with an apologetic expression; someone takes me by the arm.

But I can only focus on one thing: Judge Clark is right. Justice must be served. An appropriate punishment extracted from the offenders. But the system is broken, the blame misplaced. I will have to take matters into my own hands.

A raw, crackling energy surges through my veins. It's my old friend ambition, galvanizing me with a new purpose.

A purpose that will sustain me over the next three years.

And after that—

I think of Nash and Claire and the baby—*my* baby. I think of them escaping to safety somewhere, of Claire forcing them to become a family together, a family that should have been mine.

After that, I'm coming for you.

* * *

CLAIRE

THE DAY OF

My eyes snap open at four thirty AM, as usual. Insomnia is my nightly companion these days, when rolling over in bed is a feat and my bladder fills every hour. The house is quiet, except for the sound of Nash snoring in the next room.

With the trial over and his (and Jillian's) guilt declared, he has nowhere to go. Returning home would mean certain jail. We're stuck together now. I swallow past my guilt. Have I trapped him?

No. He came on his own to help me. I never forced him.

But maybe—

The rest of the thought makes me cringe. Maybe if I'd been upfront about my mental health issues from the start, he never would have trusted me, and none of this would be happening. Which is exactly why I didn't tell him, of course.

After the prosecutor's brutal revelation, I waited for Nash to retaliate. Waited for his inevitable anger, suspicion, and disgust.

For three years, I had kept my secret from friends and colleagues, cowering alone in my tower of shame. Only Ethan knew, and he cultivated my isolation by pretending our life was normal. He craved normalcy like it was the point of existence. Eventually he decided that another child would fix me. The truth hurts to admit, but I think our marriage failed years before this new baby came into the picture. It crumbled at the altar of my suffering.

You have to get out of bed, he used to beg me. *We can't live like this.*

I felt sorry for him, but more so for myself. I had no desire to move on if it meant leaving my son behind. In hindsight, I realize how alone Ethan made me feel, and how inadequate, for not managing my pain as well as he did.

I've also come to understand that grief can coexist with healing. The former doesn't stop where the latter starts. Instead, they run on parallel tracks; some days one is ahead, some days the other. A return to normalcy after the death of a child is simply not possible. At best, it's facing every day with a clear head and a broken heart.

After the prosecutor's bombshell, I thought Nash would regard me with cautious suspicion, like Ethan did after my brief stay in the psych unit, as though I might revert to seeing Colton's face in the shadows.

Instead, Nash gave me the ultimate gift: his compassion. "That sounds absolutely terrible," he said, without a trace of judgment. "What a nightmare."

"It was. I lost my mind. It was pretty bad."

Then he stunned me further by covering my hand. "You lost a child. Who could blame you?"

"I should have told you at the beginning. I'm sorry."

"Yes." He was matter-of-fact. "But what does it matter now?"

"You don't think I'm . . . ?" I couldn't bring myself to complete the sentence.

He squeezed my hand. "What people do in grief isn't fair to judge. It isn't really you." He closed his eyes as if in painful recollection.

"What's wrong?"

"I lost my wife to brain cancer eleven years ago."

I gasped. "Oh my God. I'm so sorry. I didn't even know you were married."

"I never talk about her."

We were quiet for a bit, and then he said, "It's why I didn't see myself with Jillian long-term. Just couldn't let go."

I wondered about his use of the past tense; had he let go now? A small part of me hoped so.

"I didn't cope well," he went on. "Drank until I had to join AA. I was totally out of control for a few years."

He studied me for signs of disdain. I remained unfazed.

"We do what we can to survive," I said, "and we're stronger for it."

"Exactly. That's why this whole scandal doesn't feel like the end of the world. Because I've been through worse." There was a glimmer in his eye. He blinked it away. "After that, I can get through anything."

* * *

I lie in bed at four forty-five AM, contemplating what has happened between us since that conversation a few days ago. The line between doctor and patient has grown blurrier than ever. He's begun to linger in my room after a meal, instead of rushing out to be alone, and we spend time at night reading side by side, with our shoulders touching. Sometimes he tells me funny quirks about his wife, like that she collected mustache cups and enjoyed terrible puns, and I share an anecdote about Colton. I told him about Colton's love of making up stories, and how we invented an adventure series about a lonely space robot named Melvin. I also told him about Colton's favorite nurse at the hospital, Lucy, whom he called his girlfriend, and who surprised him with fudge one year on Valentine's Day. By then he was getting his nutrition through a feeding tube, because his stomach was in such bad shape, but the doctors allowed him to taste the fudge anyway. It might have been the last great day of his life. Sharing these private memories has brought us immeasurably closer.

Last night, before we went to sleep, he closed his laptop and said to me, "You know what?"

"What?"

"I came for the birth, but that's not why I'm staying."

"It's not?"

"You're brave, Claire. I've never met anyone like you."

I laughed dryly, in spite of my pounding heart. "Or maybe just stupid."

"Nah," he said. "Not to me."

I took his hand and put it on my belly. "She's kicking. Can you feel?"

As we sat there enjoying the baby's surreal jabs, the moment felt explicitly intimate, like a betrayal of Ethan. But fidelity to my husband was no longer a requirement, so I let Nash hold my stomach until enough time had passed that we'd crossed the boundary of our official roles and were becoming something else entirely. Something that triggered a different sort of jolt inside me.

* * *

Now, at five AM, the baby gives another ferocious kick to my bladder. Time to pee again. I feel warm liquid drip between my thighs. Have I wet the bed? Oh God, how embarrassing.

As I struggle to my feet, clear fluid leaks out between my legs in a way I cannot control. Holy shit. When I stand up, the flow gets heavier. It pours out like a faucet, soaking my panties, creating a puddle on the floor.

"Hey!" I waddle as fast as I can into his room. "I think my water broke!"

He bolts upright and flicks on the lamp. "What?"

I point down at my sopping underwear, too shocked to be embarrassed. A painful hardness flares through my lower back and stomach. I double over with a moan.

"Lie down," he commands. I fall onto his bed as the contraction eases.

"I'm going to check to see how dilated you are. I'll be right back."

Sweat is gathering at my temples when he returns with his gloves on and inserts two fingers into me.

"Wow," he says. "You're already at four centimeters and a hundred percent effaced. Good job!"

"I can't," I groan into the sheets. "I want—an epidural . . ."

"You can." His arms wrap around me from behind, and I find myself being spooned against his chest. "You're so much stronger than you think."

The contractions are relentless. It's a good thing nature won't allow women to give up, because otherwise no one would be born. Over the course of hours, I think, or maybe days, they assault me with steadily worsening pain, closer and closer together. I writhe and scream and sway on my hands and knees. I pace the bedroom and roll on the floor. I lose track of time. He holds me through each one, murmuring about how well I'm doing, even as I shriek that I'm going to die.

After some amount of time, he announces that he's going to check my cervix again. "They're every ninety seconds now."

I gasp in response, unable to form a coherent thought. The pain can't be quantified on any human scale. It's like a spear on fire is gouging out my womb, like my baby has sprouted talons dipped in acid. Part of me feels detached, like a bit player in a perfectly choreographed drama. Somehow my body knows exactly what to do without any guidance from me.

"Claire?" he prompts. "I need to check."

I wrench myself onto my back and slide my legs apart while he checks again, his fingers wedging painfully into me.

"Almost show time!" he says brightly. "Nine centimeters. We're about to meet that beautiful baby!"

I moan as another contraction intensifies, culminates in a jaw-grinding peak that lasts and lasts, then starts to back off. Now I have only seconds to catch my breath between each one. The bed sheets are covered in mucus and blood, but I don't have the energy to care or cover myself up.

"How—soon?" I pant.

"Very. Your labor is progressing fast."

His excited tone lends me some reassurance, even though a fetal monitor, an IV, and anesthesia are nowhere in sight.

"Are you sure—I shouldn't just go to the hospital?" My previous worries about being recognized seem distant and unimportant compared to my current distress.

"You won't make it in time."

Abruptly I feel an urgent need to push, so urgent that my body bears down of its own accord, riding a wave I'm powerless to counteract.

"Good," he coaches. "Hold your breath for ten seconds while I count. Ten, nine, eight, seven. Don't give up! Keep pushing!"

His enthusiasm penetrates my fog before another wave slams through me. He inserts his gloved fingers once more to feel my cervix.

"Go, go, go!" he exclaims. "Don't stop! I feel the baby about to—" His fingers abruptly stiffen.

"What?"

"It's a foot. She's breech."

I go blank; the next unstoppable contraction swells. *No!*

The baby's head was engaged in my pelvis as recently as last week.

"She flipped," he mutters. "It must be because of your placenta . . ."

A noise that doesn't sound human escapes my throat—it sounds like an animal dying in the wild. I gather my wits and scream at him.

"Take me to the fucking hospital!"

He shakes his head, grimacing.

"I don't care about the cops; call nine one one!"

"It's not that," he says. "She's coming right now . . ."

A shriek erupts from my rib cage as I feel my most sensitive region split apart, shredding millions of nerve endings I never knew existed. My eyesight briefly flickers to black.

His demeanor is scarily calm. "Claire, you're going to deliver this baby. I saw breech maneuvers done during my training. Just push like you've never pushed in your life!"

A sudden clarity penetrates my haze. I know what I must do. I grit my teeth and channel every ounce of strength into my lower half.

"Good," he encourages, wedging his fingers deep inside me, twisting her body. "Keep going. Legs are out, the cord's pulsing, just the shoulders and head now! Another big one; you can do it!"

My sight dims again with the excruciating effort and I'm so close to fainting I can see spots, but I push through it, harder this time, hard enough to expel whatever is left in my body, organs and all. I feel him jiggering the baby little by little, loosening her shoulders from the rigid confines of the birth canal. Then her big round head squeezes through, and like a dam breaking, the pain floods out. Relief engulfs me; it's like weightlessness after being crushed.

"You did it!" he cries.

I open my eyes to the most beautiful sound I've ever heard—an angry wail. The baby's body is gray and covered in white vernix, but rapidly blossoming to pink. He places her belly-down on my chest, the veiny blue cord still pulsing between us. A sob wracks me as we lie skin to skin. Her tiny heart beats against mine.

We made it. From now on, forever—*we*.

She whimpers as I stroke her. Then her two dark eyes squint up at me. She looks nothing like me or Ethan. Her nose is more delicately sloped, her face heart-shaped, her hair strangely reddish.

Nash hovers behind my shoulder. "She's perfect."

I'm surprised to see that his cheeks, too, are wet.

"Welcome to the world, Abigail Grace," I whisper.

She hungrily puckers her pink lips, and I cradle her face to my breast. When she latches on, immense gratitude washes over me. It was all worth it. Every loss, every hardship. I watch her serene face as she suckles, half closing her eyes in pure contentment.

The sun pokes through the curtains, catching the copper in her hair, and all too soon, I remember the hostile world awaiting us outside. Then I realize this is only the beginning.

I peer up at Nash. "What do we do now?" I ask.

"The only thing we can," he says. "We love her."

PART THREE

ABBY: NOW

In exactly two hours and fifteen minutes, when the bell rings for lunch, I am finally going to meet up with *her*: JH0502. I don't even know her real name. I've thought a lot about those letters and numbers but can't make sense of them. We don't have any *H* last names on either side of my family, going back to my grandparents. And 0502 could be May 2nd—her birthday?—or just random numbers. So many questions with no answers.

Mrs. Miller is up at the board demonstrating 3-D perspective with a sketch of train tracks, but I can't concentrate. All I can think about is what the stranger might tell me, and why it's such a big deal that my mom can't know. Just the thought of my mom stresses me out. I feel like she's on the verge of some epic breakdown. I mean, rolling down a hill after a fantasy of my dead brother? It's, like, insane.

"Dude," the boy behind me hisses. "Wake up."

"Hmm?" I snap to attention to see Mrs. Miller frowning at me, holding out a fat piece of chalk. "Abigail, do you want to demonstrate how to draw a rectangular prism?"

"Sure," I agree.

Thank God for an easy class.

When the bell rings, Riley and I head toward our lockers together and I tell her about the upcoming meeting.

"Today?" Her eyes go wide. "Wow. This is gonna be huge."

"I know. She wanted to come meet me in person."

"How come?"

"To *tell me everything*. Whatever that means."

"And you have literally no idea who she is or what she looks like?"

"Nope."

Riley flicks her locker open and puts her books inside, then squints at me. "I don't know about this, Abs."

"It's not like I'm gonna get kidnapped or something." I snort, but don't mention the tightness in my chest. "Anyway, aren't you the one who kept telling me to contact her again?"

"I didn't think she was going to show up in real life!"

"Even better. We'll finally get the truth."

"Just be careful." She lowers her voice as other kids swarm the locker area. "Didn't your parents tell you she was some random stalker?"

I shrug. "Yeah, but maybe they're lying."

"Either way"—she slams her locker shut—"I'm keeping an eye on you. Okay?"

"How?"

"Simple. You're meeting at the drop-off area, right? I can see it from Mr. Harrison's classroom. I'll just have lunch in there."

I want to hug my kickass bestie, but I also don't want to show her how nervous I am.

"Thanks," is all I say.

"Of course. I've got your back."

* * *

When the bell rings for lunch, the other kids rush to the cafeteria to be first in line for barbecue mac 'n' cheese while I struggle upstream through the crowd toward the front doors. As I slip out, Mr. Harrison shows up behind me, walking next to Mrs. Miller.

"Well hello, Abigail," he greets me. His height, thick beard, and bushy eyebrows make him seem gruffer than he really is.

Mrs. Miller waves, looking pretty beside him in her tight skirt, black pumps, and silky shirt. She smiles at me awkwardly.

OMG, are they going on a lunch date? I can't wait to tell Riley later.

"Is your mom picking you up early?" Mr. Harrison asks me as we all step outside.

"Um, no. I'm just meeting a . . . friend."

My face heats up, but I have no reason to be embarrassed. I haven't done anything wrong. I call out, "Gotta go," and hurry to the circle of benches at the drop-off point.

"Have a nice lunch," he calls, as they walk off together to the parking lot. I watch from a distance as they get into separate cars. So, I guess it wasn't a date. Oh well.

I can feel Riley's eyes on my back, though I can't see her through the dark-tinted glass of the classroom. The parking lot is busy. A bunch of cars are coming and going, but no one seems to notice me. My stomach growls, since I forgot to pack a lunch, but there's no way I'm going to risk missing this for mac 'n' cheese, so I wait it out. Five minutes go by, then ten. We only get forty-five minutes for lunch. Where is this person?

A shiver crawls down my arm. I whirl around, but nothing is there except the pink rose bushes underneath the school windows.

The sound of a car coming makes me perk up.

Never mind. It drives past the school.

I bounce my knees. I stand up and sit down. I jump on and off the bench, twirl my fidget spinner, and eventually shrug at the tinted windows, where I know Riley must be as confused as I am.

When thirty-five minutes have passed, I know this flake isn't going to show up, and if I wait any longer, I might be late for my math test. I can almost hear Riley's voice in my head: *She blew you off? What the hell?*

I rise in frustration, both disappointed and a little relieved.

The questions continue to pile up, unanswered.

Did she change her mind? Or does she have something *else* in mind?

CLAIRE: NOW

I am not crazy. As I limped around the house with my throbbing ankle all weekend, it was the mantra I kept telling myself. I wish I believed it.

The worst part is that Rob believes I'm losing it. Or should I say, *Michael.* Even after this whole decade of living a lie, I still have not fully mastered the habit of thinking of him by his alias, or of responding to mine, *Lisa.*

It was another lifetime ago that we suffered through the uncertain early months of Abby's life in hiding until he phoned in a desperate favor to one of his wealthiest former patients, the wife of a hedge fund manager. She had borne twins thanks to his assistance after years of infertility, so she leapt at the chance to help him. She spotted him ten grand in cybercurrency to purchase social security numbers and fake passports for us on the dark web, complete with new identities as Michael and Lisa Burke. The documents were passable enough for us to open bank accounts and get driver's licenses so we wouldn't have to live off the grid.

But without his old identity, he could no longer work as a doctor. "Michael Burke" lacked proof of medical school attendance as well as board certifications in any specialty. Rob agonized terribly in those early months about how he would earn a living to support us, since my career as a journalist was also a no-go. "Lisa Burke" had no connections at any media outlets and no clips to show potential editors.

We had to start from scratch. When Abby was an infant, I decided early on to focus all my energies on motherhood—in part because I couldn't envision leaving her for the day to take on any kind of job, and in part because adding childcare to our considerable burden of expenses was simply not feasible. So it all fell on him.

In the beginning, he found work as a construction laborer, helping to lay foundations for new houses all over the Hudson River Valley. The job was backbreaking, but it paid in cash each day off the books. He would come home with black dirt caked under his fingernails, covered in sweat, aching for the old days—his lab, his patients, his glamorous clinic facing Central Park West. But if he hated every minute, he rarely complained.

He became quite skilled at building things with his hands. Then one day when Abby was fifteen months old and learning to walk, she bumped her head pretty badly by colliding with the sharp edge of our glass dining room table. I told Rob we had to get rid of it, but we couldn't afford a replacement, as we were still living month to month at that point. Matter-of-factly, he announced, "I'll build one myself." And that was how his woodworking hobby started.

He set up a workspace in our garage designing and making custom furniture on the weekends for fun. Over several years, he honed his craft. I think it gave him an outlet for creativity that he sorely lacked without the ability to pursue research. The pieces were amateur at first, but they were undeniably stylish. He sought exotic woods with attractive amber patterns and swirls, like African bubinga, poplar, walnut, and red cherry. Our house began to fill with his pieces—a new round kitchen table, a toy box for Abby, a jewelry box for me.

By the time Abby turned four, his skill had reached new heights, and I urged him to list a few items on Etsy, the online marketplace for handcrafted goods. It was just a lark—we hoped for a few extra dollars—but what happened was nothing short of remarkable. In the span of just six months, his Etsy store for custom woodworks began bringing in more cash than his construction job. A wait list developed for his kitchen tables, at a thousand dollars a pop. He realized he could make two per week if he quit his day job, which is exactly what he did next. He also found no shortage of customers for coffee tables, end tables, desks, and small gift items like cutting boards, iPad stands, and small nightstand boxes.

We remained in our modest two-bedroom home long after we could afford something nicer, just so we could build up our savings—and eventually pay back the ten thousand to our original rescuers. Finally, when Abby was eight, we felt financially stable enough to upgrade to our current place—one acre of land with a detached in-law suite in the backyard that he converted into his working space. His online store is still going strong; the best part is that he loves the work, and he's able to make a decent living anonymously, from home. The Michael Burke of today is a veteran craftsman with strong, dusty hands, a couple of splinters, and a long list of satisfied customers who are ignorant of his complicated past.

Even though we have technically been Michael and Lisa for a decade now, we are still Claire and Rob to each other—our real names have become private terms of endearment, to be whispered in our bedroom after Abby's gone to sleep.

But he hasn't called me Claire for the last few nights, since I showed up at home crying and covered in mud. I guess I don't blame him. I must truly seem insane.

As soon as I confessed my hallucination to him, the ground beneath us shifted, just as I'd feared it would. His eyes whirred with cold clinical analysis, assessing the severity of my relapse. He used to say he didn't hold my history of mental illness against me, but I never fully believed him. Sure, we grew close quickly in the early years, developing a romance in spite of—or maybe because of—the extreme isolation we had to maintain. Abby brought us together on a deeper level. Raising her as two equal partners, as the only mother and father she's ever known, sealed our commitment for life. Though we never had an official ceremony, we've long considered ourselves married—happily.

And yet.

Under many layers of practiced normalcy, the stigma of my mental breakdown has remained. Perhaps I'm paranoid, and he's denied it, but I sense that he's been on guard all these years, watching me carefully for the return of any troubling symptoms. I've worked hard to defeat that instinct in him, to prove that I'm a steady partner worthy of his trust. For a decade, I've reliably taken care of Abby, managed our home life, and maintained my health to the best of my ability—growing our own organic produce, cooking nutritious meals, swimming, meditating, and doing yoga.

Then in *one* short conversation this weekend, I managed to obliterate all my gains. In a few breathtaking minutes, I reverted from wife back to patient.

But the truth is, my hallucination has also rocked me to the core. Colton at the park seemed impossibly vivid, just like the vision a few months ago at the museum. That first one sparked a private, distracting obsession that left me distant and moody. On any given day, I'm filled with intense longing, cursing myself for indulging a fantasy, and aching for "him" to return. I blame myself for the latest episode. In a moment of weakness on my birthday a few weeks ago—fifty!—I literally wished for this to happen. I wished to set eyes on Colton one last time.

Then, sure enough, he materialized. I was alone at the park last week, meditating. I looked down, and there he was at the far edge of the field. His blond hair was whipping in the wind as he skipped beside a row of tall fir trees. It was an aspirational version of Colton, the healthy kid he should have been and never was.

But "he" was clearly my neurons misfiring, trespassing down old routes they have no business visiting. I think the fact that I'm so disturbed by it is a good sign. It proves I'm not having a total psychotic break, just a few temporary disconnections. I even understand the pathology behind it. The trauma of suddenly seeing J at the museum must have triggered my dormant PTSD. After that first delusion, I was left weakened, fragile, and primed for another episode. The second trip wire was the recent close call at our house. We still don't know who was lurking outside in the middle of the night. My frantic mind, combined with my own irrational longing, conjured the second delusion.

See, I reassure myself, *there's a perfectly rational explanation*. And if I'm able to reason, it must mean I'm not crazy. Despite the note that Abby left for me.

I declare my mantra to the empty kitchen as I take a raw chicken out of the fridge. I'm preparing Abby and Rob's favorite dinner of Thai coconut soup, the tacit context being that I am *just fine*. But despite my efforts to focus on the recipe and move beyond all this nonsense, I find my thoughts circling back to that magical flash of my boy at the park.

* * *

I'd climbed the steep stairs to the vantage point on the hilltop and sat on the cement bench that overlooks the playground. The Hudson River sparkled down below in the valley, and the swaying trees calmed me as I waited to pick Abby up from school. Quiet Bluebird Park is my favorite spot to visit whenever I have a free hour, since I don't have to worry about being recognized. I tried to meditate on being present, though my fears perpetually torture me: J with a gun, J breaking in, J kidnapping Abby. When she first got out of prison, eight years ago, terrifying panic attacks began to strike me out of nowhere—the kind that leave you gasping and choking for air. So I took up meditation and yoga in desperation (and started carrying Xanax everywhere just in case).

At the park, I deterred the familiar horror reel with the only tools at my disposal—nature, beauty, breath.

After a time, I opened my eyes to notice a drizzle spraying down under shifty black clouds. The air crackled and rumbled, and I knew I should leave before the sky let loose. Abby would be waiting for me soon, and she hadn't brought an umbrella to school.

As I stood, a swift motion caught my eye, something dark and fast near the giant trees that line the field at the bottom of the hill. I turned to get a better look—

—and let out a cry of shock.

It was my son.

His hair was as yellow as the summer sun, and he'd gone back in time to six or seven years old, with the knobby knees and noodle-thin arms that concerned me back in those days. He'd always been such a picky eater that I fretted about his weight, and true to the old days, his T-shirt and shorts hung off his skinny body. But unlike the real Colton who was confined to a wheelchair, this fantasy one was running across the grass. I knew it was impossible. But I was too dazzled to care.

I yelled down the hill louder than the storm clouds: "Colton!"

A mistake, but I couldn't stop myself.

He didn't look up. He was too busy picking up a stick.

"Colton!" I screamed again, cupping my hands around my mouth.

But "he" still didn't hear. He was too far away.

I rubbed my eyes then, struck by a belated terror. My head was pounding. I felt woozy and feverish. I should have run straight back to the car. My very real daughter was waiting for me.

But, shamefully, I ignored the voice of reason and doubled down. I ducked under the railing and stepped onto the grassy knoll that led down to a playground. From there, I could catch up to him on the open field.

"Hey you!" I bellowed.

The angle of the hill was so steep that I crouched for stability. The grass was already mucky; the drizzle was turning into a downpour, but I didn't care, because "he" finally noticed me; it was like my warped mind was rewarding me for giving in.

When our eyes met, he flashed me the eeriest grin: *I know you and you know me.* Then he bolted in the opposite direction, toward the parking lot. Was it a game?

He's not real, I reminded myself—at least I had the wherewithal to pause there—but I broke into a sprint down the hill anyway.

"Stop!" I yelled. "Where are you going?"

His small figure was retreating, winding through giant fir trees, almost out of sight. The rain obscured him even more, and I felt that I would dissolve into the wet grass if he vanished again. There would be nothing left of me but muddy grief.

"Wait!" I shrieked. "Please!"

I lost my footing, but there was no room for error. I couldn't catch my balance, and rapidly I lost control, tumbling down the hill like a rag doll, knees banging together, head spinning, arms flailing. I couldn't stop, I was only picking up more and more atrocious speed as some part of my brain fired with total clarity: *this is not going to end well.* Near the bottom, there was no gentle slope to ease my fall, only a metal chain-link fence that encircled the playground. I slammed into it feetfirst, hearing a terrible *pop* in my left ankle a second before the agony set in. My vision blurred with the rain, and I clawed at my eyes to stay conscious.

My last thought was of my son, but he was nowhere to be seen.

* * *

I'm not crazy, I tell myself again, breathless with panic, though I'm safe and warm in my kitchen now. It was just my heartache manifesting, and I let it rule me. I need to be stronger in the future. I can't let my family down, even if it means losing Colton forever. I mean, I've already lost him. Isn't that the point?

My heart's walloping my ribs. I feel myself nearing the edge of sanity: that bright binary line between reality and a darkness no human should ever encounter. Fear of the brink makes me grip the cold counter. I am in control.

"Mommy," says a breathy little voice in my head.

No!

"Go away!" I shout.

Not again!

"Mommy," the voice taunts again, and I realize it's not in my head at all, it's coming from somewhere else, somewhere close by. I whip around to open the refrigerator, but no one's in there.

The house is quiet again, but my adrenaline is spiking. There's raw chicken all over my hands that I've just smeared on the fridge, and I can't remember what I was doing, but I'm gripping a knife.

I set it down and back away from the counter.

"Mo-o-ommy," it calls. "Come play with me!"

Fuck. It's Colton's voice, no matter how much I want to deny it. How could I imagine something so clear?

"Outside!" the voice announces, and I think it *is* coming from near the front door. Is it? I barely trust my senses anymore. I'm straddling that bright line, no matter how much I want to stay grounded. As I rush to the door, I might as well be hurtling myself over the edge. My head feels top-heavy, like it might roll off.

I run outside, barefoot, just in time to catch a glimpse of him—it is him!—jogging around a bend in the street, away from me. Again, he wants me to chase him. He wants to finish the game in the park. I'm mesmerized by the sight of him running—a feat I'd only dreamed of during his life. I hear the smack of his sneakers scraping the pavement as he vanishes out of sight.

This time, I can't let him go. I sprint over the driveway's crunchy gravel, then onto the hot pavement, my sprained ankle protesting with every painful step.

"Colton! Wait!"

I can't seem to reach him no matter how fast I sprint; he's gone. It occurs to me that he isn't restrained by the physical universe. Since he's not real, he can disappear at will. Meanwhile, my lungs are imploding and my ankle's throbbing. There must be a reason he's visiting me again, a message from beyond. So why won't he let me catch him?

"Where did you go?" I yell at the empty road. "Hello?"

I strain to hear his little voice calling out to me. Nothing.

Panting, I bend over in the middle of the street. My soles are on fire, and I can barely suck down enough air to breathe. It dawns on me that I will never catch him; I'm not supposed to. A sob bursts out of me. I'm not sure whether I'm crying or laughing, whether he's real or I am.

A car drives up the road. It's a silver Honda with a slight dent in the bumper—just like mine. I don't bother to get out of the way. *Go ahead and hit me*, I think. *Put me out of my misery.* I almost wish it would. But the driver must see me, because it slows to a stop a short distance away. It *is* my car. I recognize the license plate. Oh, God.

I bury my face in my hands. The sour grease of the raw chicken turns my stomach, and when Rob and Abby step out of the car, I'm a gagging, sweaty, filthy mess. The horror in their eyes seals the deal; I've officially lost my mind.

"Mom?" Abby utters in disbelief. She gives me a wide berth, as though whatever is wrong with me might be contagious.

Rob rushes to my side. "What happened? Are you okay?"

"I saw him again." My tears are falling like a steady rain. "He called for me."

My husband lowers his eyes. "Oh, honey."

"I'm so sorry."

"It's not your fault. But with the right inpatient treatment, you *will* get better. It will only mean a few weeks away, and we can visit—"

"No!" I scoot backward, my first instinct to escape, but there's nowhere to go, nowhere to hide. "No hospital!"

Though his eyes are full of sympathy, his stern voice pins me down like an invisible net. "First thing tomorrow morning, I'm checking you into the neuropsych unit at New York–Presbyterian."

ABBY

In my room, hiding under my covers, I'm trying to process what I just saw: my mother *is* crazy. There's no more *verge* of a breakdown. It's real, and it's happening.

I want to cry, but the tears won't come.

Is this her big secret, the thing she's been hiding from me? Somehow, I can't believe this is it. Or maybe I don't want it to be.

What about the stranger who ditched me? I'm so confused.

I want to confront my dad, but he's too busy dealing with my mom. Her feet are bloody, she's freaking out about going to the mental hospital, and the kitchen reeks of raw chicken. I figure it's best to stay out of their way.

While they're in the living room arguing about something that sounds like "anosognosia," I head into the kitchen and quietly clean up her mess: scrubbing the cutting board, wiping down surfaces, putting away dishes. Then I pop a frozen lasagna into the still-preheated oven and tiptoe back up to my room to wait an hour for the *ding* of our sad dinner . . . maybe our last one together for a long time. This thought finally shakes loose the lump in my throat.

I'm sniffling alone in my room when my phone chimes with a message.

Riley: Can you come over????

I text her back: Not a good time. I don't have the energy to go into detail.

Typing dots show up in the bubble, and then she pastes a screenshot of something. I double-tap to enlarge the text. It's an email: Congratulations, your MapMyDNA sample has been analyzed and is now ready to access!

My mother's report—sent to Riley because of my Internet restrictions.

Me: *OMG!!! Did u open it?*
R: *Nope, waiting for u!*
Me: *Leaving now.*

* * *

The bike ride to Riley's house takes me seven minutes—record time. Mom and Dad barely notice me leave. I often do my homework at her house, so it's not a big deal. Once Riley and I are locked in her room, it takes us a few minutes to log in to the report and locate the stranger (JH0502) on the site's social platform to ask her to share DNA maps with my mother (LB2345).

Once JH (hopefully) agrees, it will be clear at last whether they are related—and which one has been lying to me. We send the invite from my mother's account and wait.

Beside me on the bed, Riley hugs her knees to her chest. "I can't take the suspense!"

The screen gives her face a bluish glow. Outside the window, the sun is setting, and the sky is turning purple, like a bruise. I still haven't told her about my mom.

"I want to log in to my account for a sec," I announce.

I take over and give sharing permission to my mother's profile so that I can compare my traits with hers. I don't tell Riley, but I'm hoping to find some evidence that I didn't inherit her craziness. It's comforting that we're different in lots of ways already. She has brown hair and I have red; she's short and I'm tall. But on a deeper genetic level, am I destined to become like her anyway? I wonder if, along with wet earwax and blue eyes, the trait report includes something like "chance of mental illness."

"Um," Riley mutters, interrupting my thoughts. "Aren't you supposed to be *exactly* fifty percent related to each parent?"

I give her a look that says, *duh*. Everyone knows that.

She points at the screen, frowning. My DNA map overlapped on my mother's map says that we share 49.9 percent of our genes.

I snort. "It's obviously a mistake."

Riley wrinkles her nose. "Isn't MapMyDNA, like, the top testing company?"

"I thought so, but who knows?"

I'm now annoyed that we ever embarked on this stupid experiment. The last thing I need is some lab error to get in the way.

"It's less than a percent off, so I guess it's not *that* wrong," Riley says, trying to make me feel better.

"Whatever." I wave my hand. "I have bigger problems."

"What does that mean?"

I open my mouth to tell her about my mom when her email buzzes with a new message: JH0502 has agreed to connect with LB2345.

We both let out a little shriek of excitement.

It takes ten seconds to log out of my account and back into my mom's.

You have one new connection!

"Click it!" Riley urges.

I can't wait to solve this mystery. I press the word connection, and the screen refreshes with a cheerful new announcement in bright-orange text:

You and JH0502 share 0% of your DNA.

Wait, what? My mom has been telling the truth this whole time?

I slump back against the bed. "I thought for sure they were cousins!"

Riley seems disappointed. "Wouldn't your mom get all weird when you asked her about this?"

"*Super* weird. I could swear she was hiding something."

"And wait, how can you be related to *both* of them, if they aren't related to each other?"

I consider this strange new twist. "JH must be through my dad's side?"

"Then why would she tell you she had history with your *mom*?"

"I have no idea." My head is spinning like the Gravitron ride, going around and around but never getting anywhere. It's hard to think straight.

"Look." Riley points at a link under my mother's profile. "We can download her raw data. All the DNA sequences."

It's a huge file that takes a whole minute to download. When we open it, there's nothing but long strings of random letters and numbers.

I sigh. "Great. Now what?"

"You need someone to, like, read this for you. And your file, too."

"I guess I could email the company . . ."

"No, silly!" Riley punches my arm. "Take it to Mr. Harrison tomorrow!"

I picture our gentle giant of a science teacher, with his scruffy beard and big shoulders and thick glasses. If anyone can help me make sense of this, it's him.

At this point, he's my only hope.

CLAIRE

Lying in bed next to Rob always used to make me feel safe. But tonight, I find no comfort in his embrace. The tightness of his arms around my shoulders reminds me of the restraints in the psych ward.

"Relax," he whispers. "I'm on your side."

I allow myself to go limp against his chest. But I don't want him to think I'm giving in. "Listen," I say evenly, "Today was horrible, but I'm feeling better. I really don't think I need to go anywhere."

He sighs. "This is the toughest part of relapsing."

"What is?"

"Returning to lucidity. But it's a trap—it doesn't mean you don't need help."

A quiver of ice shoots through me. Nothing is scarier than distrusting my own perceptions. My most cherished fantasies have sold me into madness.

I bury my face in his neck, inhaling the musky scent of his skin. It smells like home. "Why is this happening? Everything was fine for so long."

He strokes my hair. "Some genetic tendency, probably, combined with an environmental trigger."

I abruptly sit up. "I know what the Goddamn trigger was."

Neither of us needs to say her name; if J hadn't appeared out of the blue with her wicked smile and her sickening obsession, none of this would be happening.

"It won't help to fixate," he says gently. "Try to let her go."

"But she came to our house!"

"We don't know that for sure. And what else could we do, anyway? We already upgraded the alarm."

"What if I'm gone and something happens to you guys?"

"It won't," he says firmly.

"What if someone at the hospital recognizes me?"

"It's a chance we have to take. But it's been over a decade . . ."

I cringe, imagining some asshole leaking my location to the press, then reporters tracking down Abby at school, shoving mics in her face, splashing her image across the Internet: FRANKENBABY FOUND! The media is a particularly nasty instrument of torture. Hell, it might not even matter if I get recognized. If J knows where we are and wants to out us as revenge, it's all over anyway.

Rob rubs my back. "Don't worry about anything besides getting well. I've got the rest covered."

"Don't you think I'm myself right now, though? Honestly?"

"Honey, if you saw what I saw today, you wouldn't try to negotiate. On meds, you'll be much more stable."

I can't decide which is worse: being fuzzy and numb, with a cotton ball for a brain, or being at the mercy of a delusion that could strike anytime.

"The longer you put this off—" he starts.

"Okay, okay, I get it."

"So you'll go to Presbyterian tomorrow?"

"I guess. How long do you think it will take?"

"Three weeks at most."

A lump rises in my throat. I picture Abby falling asleep without our favorite nightly ritual—me reading her one chapter of a book aloud.

"I've never spent more than one night away from her."

"I know," Rob says, "but it's more important for you to get well."

The hell I will soon enter comes rushing back from a place I've long repressed: the sterile beds, the moaning patients, the brisk nurses, the coarse gowns, the shitty showers and the prickly armpit hair, no razors allowed . . .

"I don't want her to see me there. It's too awful."

"You don't want her to visit?"

"No. It might kill me, but I'd rather be dead than leave her those memories."

"Fair enough." He shakes his head as if contemplating something surprising.

"What?"

"Even with all this, you still want to protect her the most."

I smile sadly. "Isn't that what it means to be a mother?"

* * *

The next morning, I wake up at the crack of dawn to pack a suitcase and say good-bye. I still can't believe this is what my life has come to, but then I think back to spraining my ankle on the muddy hill, and running barefoot into the middle of the street, and I know I'm doing the right thing. It's no way to exist. I got better once; I will fight to get there again.

When I open Abby's door, she scrambles to sit up in bed, as if bracing for an unpleasant encounter. It's all too obvious how much she has come to dread my presence.

I hang back in the doorway, giving her space. "I'm so sorry, sweetheart."

"For what?" she asks.

"Being sick. I have to go somewhere to get better, and it might take a while."

"How long?"

"A few months."

"Oh." She nods slowly, looking far too burdened for her eleven years. I yearn to fold her into my arms. An old memory resurfaces of her as a happy toddler plopping into my lap. God, how I miss the simple joy of her little hand clutching my leg.

Now I venture to the edge of her bed. She flinches but doesn't scoot away. A victory. "I'm going to miss you so much. But I'll be better when I come back."

"How do you know?" Her eyes probe mine with a skepticism I haven't noticed in her before: the doubt that is the hallmark of growing up.

"Because I'm going to work as hard as I can. And whenever I set my mind to something, I get it done."

I think: *It's why you exist.*

"Okay," she says, unconvinced. I realize I haven't been the greatest model of achievement in her lifetime, having burrowed into my supporting roles of wife and mother, leaving no trace of the fearless journalist I used to be.

I silently vow to do something great again when I recover—to make her proud.

But I don't tell her; I can't bear to see that skepticism creep into her face again.

"You seem fine now," she says. "Are you sure you have to leave?"

It takes all my self-discipline to share my shame aloud, even though I know it's not a personal failing; it's the hand I've been dealt.

"I've been struggling," I admit. "The . . . vision I see sometimes, it's a bad sign. It means I'm sick, even if I don't always feel that way."

"Oh, Mommy." She stuns me by flinging her arms around my neck. "I hope you get better really soon."

I hug her back, luxuriating in the weight of her head on my shoulder. I rock her gently, picturing my reserves of strength and love flowing into her, fortifying her for the tough days and weeks to come.

As for the guilt, I'll keep that to myself. It's contrary to nature for a mother to abandon her child, even if it is for her, as everything is, in the end.

ABBY

At school drop-off in the morning, as the other kids are laughing with their friends and rushing to first period, my heart feels heavier than all the textbooks in my bag. No one knows I've just said good-bye to my mom for who knows how long.

My parents' silver car inches out of the lot and disappears. I don't want to be a baby and start crying, so I tuck my chin and walk to class like everyone else. But I feel weirdly alone in the middle of the crowd. My dad is driving her to the hospital in New York City and he's not getting back until tonight, so for the first time, I'm going to come home from school today to an empty house.

The day passes slowly—art with Mrs. Miller and English with Mr. Avery drag on until third-period science, with Mr. Harrison. My only distraction from thinking about my mom in a mental hospital is solving the mystery of my genetics report.

When Mr. Harrison finishes his lecture on gravity and Newton's apple, the whole class rushes out to lunch. I wait for the last kid to leave the room, then sit in a red plastic chair on the other side of his desk.

"Hey there," he says cheerfully. "What's up?"

"Can you help me with something?"

"Sure, as long as you don't mind if I eat my lunch." He sticks his hand inside a brown paper bag and takes out a sandwich sealed in tinfoil.

My stomach growls as he unwraps it, but this is more important than food.

"It's about this." I give him the printout from my backpack of my genetic report: it shows how my DNA map overlaps with my mom's and with JH0502's—even though they don't overlap with each other. On the printout, there are pie charts and percentages and colorful pictures of chromosome pairs spread out from one to twenty-three.

"Oh, is this from our class project?"

"Sort of. After we all did the saliva test, some weird stuff happened." I tell him that a stranger on the site invited me to connect, since we share some common heritage. I tell him about our messages, the long-lost cousin thing, and the failed meet-ups.

Then I fib. "My mom also decided to take the DNA test to research her ancestry," I say quickly. "But her report shows that she and the stranger are *not* cousins—even though I'm, like, related to them both. So, I don't get it."

Mr. Harrison seems troubled. "You said this stranger tried to meet up with you in real life?"

"Yeah."

"But you've never actually met her?"

I think of the lunch date she flaked on with no explanation. "Nope."

"Hmmm." He glances at the printouts. "Well, she obviously lied to you. She is not your mother's cousin. I would be very careful, Abigail."

"What do you mean?"

"It's very suspicious for any adult to try to meet up with a minor over the Internet. I literally can't think of one good reason. Have you told your parents?"

"Yeah, they said they didn't know her. But she's still related to me, right? I mean, DNA doesn't lie."

"We all have hundreds of distant relations, so a slight overlap with someone is not meaningful."

"But why would she lie about being on my *mom's* side? And she asked if I had a brother! It was like she knew."

He makes a disgusted face. "First of all, half the population has a brother. And sadly, there are some sinister people out there who will make up anything to trap you."

Exactly what my parents said. I guess I should have believed them after all.

"For all you know," he says, scanning the printouts, "she could have contacted lots of other minors on the site who happened to share some random segment of DNA and told them the same story, asked them the same questions, and you happened to be one who—"

He breaks off as his eyes widen. "Son of a gun."

"What?"

"There's a mistake in your mother's report." He points at the page. "You and she can't share forty-nine point nine percent of your DNA. That statistic is impossible."

"Oh, yeah." I wave it off. "Someone must have messed up."

"Jesus," he mutters. "I thought this company was legit. Their labs are CLIA approved—I checked into it before our group project."

"Oh well." I take out another, heavier stack of papers from my backpack. "Anyway, here's all the raw data from where my report overlaps with the stranger's. I was hoping you could tell me which genes we share?"

Now that I know she's a creepy stalker, I would love reassurance from Mr. Harrison that our DNA doesn't match in any important places. The last thing I need to worry about is whether I've inherited genes that will make me both crazy *and* evil.

The data's long strings of numbers and letters, like *gs1027* and *rs12885300 (C; C)*, ate up all the ink in Riley's printer. It's gibberish to me, but Mr. Harrison squints at it and types some stuff into his computer.

"I'm researching on the SNPedia," he explains, as if that clears things up. "It's a big encyclopedia of genetic information."

"Oh, cool."

"Wait a sec. You share *mitochondrial* DNA?" A few seconds pass with him just staring at our reports. Then he gives me the strangest look—like he's seeing me for the first time. He presses two fingers between his eyebrows the way I do when my head hurts.

"Is everything okay?"

He clears his throat. "Yeah. Sorry."

"What's wrong?"

After an awkward pause, he says, "Abigail, have you discussed this with your parents?"

"No, should I?"

"I think so."

"Why?"

"I'm sorry; it's really not my place to say."

"Um, okay." As I jump up, blood rushes to my head.

"Wait. Promise me you won't meet up with anyone you don't know in real life?" He extends his pinkie to swear on. I curl mine around it.

"I promise."

* * *

After school, I'm stuck waiting in the parking lot for the bus. It's slow, because there's only one assigned to our district and it stops at the high school first. The five-minute drive home will probably take me an hour. Riley's at dance practice, my dad's still in the city, and none of my other friends take the bus. It sucks watching everyone else get picked up by their moms.

I hope my mom is okay. I hope *I'm* okay. I really don't know what to think anymore. Why won't anyone tell me what's going on? As soon as my dad gets home, I'm going to ask him once and for all. I'll blame it on Mr. Harrison. Because now I *know* my parents have been hiding something from me. Something bad. Mr. Harrison must have discovered some horrible mutation in my DNA. And my parents haven't told me because they don't want me to freak out.

I did have a headache the other night, plus I've been tired, and not very hungry. What if I'm sick and everyone knows but me? What if—oh my *God*. What if I'm *dying*?

I double over on the bench, holding my stomach.

"Abigail? Are you okay?"

Mrs. Miller is walking quickly toward me. Her black blazer is flapping in the wind, and her long skirt swishes around her ankles.

"You look sick," she says. "Do you need help?"

I want to fake being fine, but I can't. "I . . . don't feel so good," I admit.

"Where are your parents?"

"Um, they're away. I'm waiting for the bus."

"Do you want a ride home?" She holds up her car keys. "I'm happy to drive you."

"Really?" I want to hug her. And then climb into bed until my dad gets home.

"Sure, let's go."

I follow her into a blue Jetta in the parking lot that smells like it was just cleaned. I tell her my address, which she puts in her phone's GPS, and off we go. My breath is still coming in short gasps, but I don't want to have a panic attack in front of the coolest teacher in school, so I concentrate on getting it under control. *Breathe in, breathe out.*

She glances over at me, and I know she can tell I'm suffering. "I'm here for you, you know. In case you want to talk."

"Thanks."

I don't say anything else, but she's still watching me out the corner of her eye. I pretend not to notice. There's a small smile on her lips, like she's smiling to herself rather than me.

I realize I still don't know much about her. She started at our school only six weeks ago, after our last art teacher left without warning. One day in March, Mrs. Blake stopped showing up—a family crisis, the principal told us. For about two weeks after that, our first-period class was stuck with different substitutes until Mrs. Miller started, and quickly won over the class's affection with her relaxed rules and cheerful personality.

"So . . . do you live in town?" I ask her. Small talk is a good way to calm yourself down, I've learned. It forces you to act normal.

"Yeah, about five minutes from school. Makes for a nice commute."

"Were you always an art teacher?"

She flashes me a sideways glance. "Not always."

"Oh." I wait for her to say more, but she doesn't. "What else did you do?" I ask.

"Different things. I like art, though. It's fun, and the best part—no tests, right?"

"Yeah, totally. Everyone loves your class."

"Thanks, I appreciate that."

After a few more minutes, my house comes into view along the bumpy road. As usual, the streets are empty.

"Well, thanks for the ride."

"Of course." As we pull into the driveway, she hesitates. "Abigail, are you sure you're okay by yourself?"

The more I think about it, the more I'm dreading being alone. If I *am* dying, how long do I have left? What if I start to breathe so fast I pass out? Who will help me?

"You know," she volunteers, "I can wait with you until your parents get home if you want."

"Only my dad is coming home. My mom . . . went away."

"Oh, okay. Well, it's up to you."

"I don't want to take up your time . . ."

"Don't be silly! It's my pleasure."

I accept her offer with relief.

Inside, I give her a quick tour of our downstairs, pour her a glass of Diet Coke, and turn on the TV in the living room. We settle into the couch and find an entertaining show on Animal Planet about puppies, and soon I find myself relaxing slightly. Between her comforting presence and the cute dogs, I can almost convince myself that everything is normal. But the second my dad gets home . . .

I snuggle under a heavy throw blanket my mom knitted years ago, back when we were all happy and healthy. Maybe the fraying yarn still carries some of those good vibes.

After a while, I notice Mrs. Miller distractedly checking her phone.

"Do you want to watch something else?" I ask.

She puts her phone down with a guilty smile. “No, this is fine.”

When the show finishes a half hour later, we both get restless. I’m obsessing, and she keeps staring out our front window with obvious impatience.

“You can go,” I say. “I’m fine, honestly.”

“Oh no, I can wait.”

We change the channel to a musical theater show with terrible singing and dancing. It’s so bad, it’s perfect. We take turns making fun of the characters. My jokes are silly, but hers are surprisingly mean—and funny. It’s shocking to hear myself giggle.

“Thank you for staying,” I tell her. “Seriously.”

She grins. “Anytime.”

That’s when my dad’s Honda pulls into the driveway. We both jump at the sound, even though we’ve been expecting him. My chest instantly tightens. It’s getting dark outside, and he gets out of the car in the shadows. We can’t see his expression.

“*There* he is!” she says. “Finally.”

We walk to the door. I notice she lags a few steps behind me.

When I open it, he gives me a tired smile. “Hi, sweetheart.” He bends down to hug me, but the second he notices her, he freezes. Then he sags against the doorframe; his mouth opens, but no sound comes out. I stumble backward, confused.

“You . . . ?” my dad chokes out. “How . . . ?”

I’ve never seen him so spooked.

“It’s just Mrs. Miller!” I reassure him. “From school. She drove me home.”

She steps out from behind me. “Please don’t be upset.” She sounds strangely emotional, like she’s trying not to cry. “I’ve been waiting to see you for so long.”

PART FOUR

JILLIAN

"I know you weren't expecting me. But look how things worked out!"

I risk a smile. It isn't a straightforward smile, and I wonder if he can pick up on its complexity, on the suffering that shades my joy. Can he glimpse what I've been through? It wouldn't surprise me; the humiliation and despair are embedded in me like shrapnel. First from the women's prison, now a distant but traumatic memory; and then from my failure to resurrect anything like a career in the aftermath. Not to mention the bitter loneliness that stains the life of a former felon, who is no longer an acceptable friend or colleague or daughter.

All along, one desire kept me going.

"You—?" He points in shock at me, then Abby. "*You* know *her*?"

I feel my smile expand now, breaking through the pain. "I do."

He's speechless—and not in a good way. He rubs his eyes, his gold ring glinting in the doorway's yellow light. I want to rip it off. But I've prepared myself for a less-than-ideal reunion. Claire's toxic influence on him won't disappear overnight, even if she's out of the picture.

"I just . . ." He blinks rapidly. "I can't . . ."

The things I ache to tell him hover on my tongue, stifled for too many years by abandonment and despair. My nerves spasm with relief. All the years of wondering, waiting, and looking have not been for nothing. Up close, he looks more dignified than I remember, now that his hair has gone salt-and-pepper gray, his face has thinned, and the wrinkles around his eyes have deepened. These marks of time upset me: a whole decade that could have been ours—lost. It takes all my discipline not to throw my arms around him, this man I no longer know, but who has fueled me through all these painful years.

He is still aghast. "What are you . . . ?"

"I had to find you guys," I say simply. It's the truth.

He yanks Abigail by the arm, and she's too bewildered to resist. "Dad, what—?"

She doesn't see his face as he pulls her close, the protectiveness writ large in his furrowed brow. He loves her. That much is clear. She is his creation. *Our* creation.

But he's shielding her with his body as if bracing for an attack. After a second, I understand: he thinks I want to punish him for leaving me high and dry. The thought makes me literally laugh out loud. My intentions couldn't be more different.

"Don't worry, I'm not here to cause trouble. I forgave you a long time ago."

I reach out to shake on a truce, but he recoils from my hand.

"Jesus, I'm not going to burn you."

My anger rises, but I remind myself that I'm not the only one who was unjustly punished. He's done hard time in his own way, a prisoner informally sentenced to years of hardship monitoring Claire. He's been stuck in the wrong life, just as Abby's been stuck with the wrong mother. What they don't realize is that I've come to set them free.

He narrows his eyes. "I don't even know you anymore."

"Nothing's changed. I'm still Jilly."

My old nickname doesn't seem to penetrate his shell of suspicion. How thoroughly has Claire brainwashed him? Is he too damaged to tell the good guy from the bad? But he was always brilliant. Surely a spark of the original Robert Nash must still be smoldering, if only I can reach it.

"Dad!" Abby wrenches herself free. "What is going on? How do *you two* know each other?"

I address him. "She doesn't know anything, does she?"

He lowers his eyes.

"Tell her. She deserves to know."

"Know what?" she demands. "Am I dying?"

"No! No, nothing like that." He kneels and takes her hand. "This was not how I planned to do this. But . . ." He licks his lips. "Honey, you're a very special person . . . a very unique person . . ."

I can't stand to watch him dance around our accomplishment.

"I'm not really your cousin," I blurt out.

She shrinks away from me in horror. "Wait, what? *You're JH0502?*"

"Yep. That was the easiest thing to tell you until I could explain everything in person. The truth is, I'm your—"

"My colleague," Nash interrupts. "She's my former colleague. Back before you were born, when I was . . . a doctor."

Abby stares at him. "What? You make furniture."

"Well," he says, "a long time ago, in another life, I helped infertile couples have children. And I did research in my own lab."

Abby smiles in confusion, as if he's telling a joke but forgot the punch line. "I don't get it."

"I'm serious," he tells her. "Long before you were born, I went to medical school at Harvard, graduated at the top of my class, and did a fellowship in reproductive endocrinology at NYU, then opened my own clinic and lab in New York City."

Abby looks back and forth between us, totally speechless. I can tell she's starting to believe him, but none of it makes sense yet.

"In other words," I cut in, "your dad was a pretty big deal. Which is why I went to work for him."

"Huh?" she says. "You guys worked together?"

He nods. "We researched early human development—how to avoid passing on terrible genetic mutations."

"And you were our greatest experiment," I declare proudly. "Your mother carried a fatal defect in her DNA, and we intervened so you would be born healthy—we gave you my mitochondria instead of hers."

She stares at me, motionless. I can almost see her mind turning over the pieces of this puzzle, attempting to make their extraordinary shapes bridge the gap between all she knows and all she doesn't. "You . . . *made* me?"

"Yes."

Her lips quiver. "Dad! Is this for real?"

He nods. "And every single day since you were born, I've thanked my lucky stars that you turned out to be such a healthy, beautiful girl."

"Luck had no part in it," I correct him. "We knew what we were doing. The point is that you and I share my mitochondria—the DNA that is passed from a mother to a child. So that means . . ." I wait for Nash to cut me off again, but this time he lets me seize the opening. "That means I'm also your mother."

She lets out a noise somewhere between a moan and a snort. Nash cringes as we watch her digest this news. I want to shake him, to remind him that *I'm* the one he ought to thank, not his fucking lucky stars.

"You're joking, right?" She presses her forehead. "This is a really mean prank."

"It's true. Our DNA map proves it. We share the thirty-seven genes exclusive to mitochondrial DNA."

She scowls at Nash. "So, like, my whole life has been a lie?"

"Don't say that! You have a great life!"

"Then how come you and Mom never told me?"

"Well, we got in some trouble back then," he says vaguely, "so we kept things quiet. That's why we don't go out much. We wanted to give you a normal childhood."

"When were you planning to tell me?"

"When you were a little older." His smile is apologetic. "But now you know."

"So, I'm healthy? But I have *three parents*?"

Nash winces; he's afraid I'm going to mention Ethan. But that would only provoke more antagonism on his part, as if things aren't bad enough. I shoot him an expression that I hope says, *Don't worry, I'm on your side.*

Then I crouch to Abby's level. "I had to find you. Before you were born, your parents came here, and I never got to meet you, but I couldn't stand not knowing you at all."

"How *did* you find us?" Nash demands, in a tone of outright hostility.

I speak to Abby. "I joined MapMyDNA knowing that pretty much everyone was doing home genetic tests, hoping you were too. I checked the site for three years until you finally popped up."

"What?" Abby cries.

"Yep. When we messaged, I was dying to meet you, but your other mother—she didn't want me in your life. It looks like she fed you lies and pretended I never existed."

"That's not fair!" Nash objects.

"Oh, you want to talk about fair? How about shutting me out of her entire life!"

He falls silent. He knows that he screwed me over, even if it was a passive consequence of his entrapment, not a deliberate choice. And that's the only reason I've forgiven him. After my own three-year sentence, I intimately understand the frustrations of an unjust fate: there is nothing worse than missing out on your own family.

Except if they belong to the woman who stole them.

I cup Abby's pale face in my hands. "Sweetie, you're the daughter I never knew. I didn't even know your birthday, so instead, every May second, I wrote you a card."

"Why May second?" She frowns. "Wait, isn't that . . . 0502 . . . your screen name . . . ?"

"That's right. The day we created you, twelve years ago."

She inhales sharply as I unzip my purse and take out the stack of cards I've tied together with a pink ribbon. "I saved them all. For you."

She slips off the ribbon with shaking hands. The cards scatter at her feet, a colorful bundle of pastel and glitter. I wonder where we'll be on her next birthday. Together, abroad? My mind flashes to the glory that awaits us once we clear the last remaining hurdles. Then it's on to international fame, a comfortable fortune, a place in history.

Because once Nash comes to his senses, we can focus on publishing our results in an international journal. Abby will need full-body scans, whole genome sequencing, tissue biopsies, the works. The data must be as comprehensive as my other, private records.

But if we don't act soon, it will be too late. Foreign scientists are racing to make our breakthrough, now that other countries have woken up to the depravity of letting fatal genetic defects pass between generations. The U.S. is still regressive, but similar research is under way in China, Japan, and the U.K. No one has managed to engineer a three-parent baby yet, but sooner or later, some team will do it and they will reap all the rewards. Unless we show the world the truth.

Then the dam choking off our lives can finally give way. Nash and I can apply for political asylum in whatever country we're offered jobs—I'm thinking professorships, funding, our own lab—and we can all begin the remarkable life we deserve. Better late than never.

I can't wait for my mother to witness my dramatic comeback. *I had it all wrong*, she'll tell me. *You never deserved what you got.*

"Is that why you came to work at my school?" Abby asks, gazing up at me with her indigo-blue eyes—the same color, I notice, as mine.

"I had to find a way to get to know you. Since it's the only middle school in Garrison, I figured we could meet that way. I wanted to tell you the other day at lunch, but . . . I lost my nerve. I wasn't ready yet."

"All this time"—Nash gapes at me—"you've been at her *school*?"

"Only since March."

"And you come forward now, right when her mother's gone to the hospital?"

Without missing a beat, I say, "I'm sorry to hear that."

"Bullshit!" He picks Abby up and muscles past me into the house.

"Dad! Why are you being so mean?"

"She's a dangerous person." Then he hisses at me: "Stay away from us. I'm going to report you to her school first thing in the morning for fraud."

I wedge my boot into the door right as he slams it.

"Will you, *Michael Burke*?" I cock my head. "For fraud?"

His righteous sneer evaporates.

"Great," I say brightly, "so here's what happens next. You and Abby come with me. We're going to have dinner at my house, and then you can go. Is that so bad?"

He stares at me in disbelief.

"What?" I ask.

"Are you threatening me?"

"Don't be silly! I just want more time to catch up."

"Seriously, you can't do this!"

"Do what?" I grin at Abby to show her how unnecessary his stress is.

He mutters a curse I choose to ignore. "One dinner," he says slowly. "And then you'll leave us alone?"

"Whatever you want." I flash him an innocent smile. Later, when he comes to his senses, he'll thank me for getting him out of this nightmare.

Abby clutches his shirt. "I don't want to go."

He glares at me. "Neither do I."

"Oh, come on." I beam with enough enthusiasm for all of us. "It'll be fun!"

ABBY

"Let me just grab my backpack," I say as Dad starts following Mrs. Miller to her car. "I need my history book for the test tomorrow."

"You're such a good student." She smiles over her shoulder. "Just like I was."

I still don't get why Dad agreed to go with her. I just know something isn't right. Dad had this weird look in his eyes the second he saw her, something I've never seen in him before. Like he was trapped.

But why would he be so uncomfortable around Mrs. Miller, everyone's favorite teacher? I guess she's not really a teacher, though. All these weeks of her art class, and she was only there for me. Because she's my . . . part mom? And he's a *doctor*? He's always making tables and covered in dust. I can't imagine him working with her in a science lab, creating me from scratch.

It is completely nuts.

But it does sort of make sense, in a super sci-fi way. I've always wondered why I didn't get Colton's horrible disease. *You were born lucky*, my mom once told me.

But I wasn't lucky . . . I was made. No wonder I can't remember the last time I stayed home sick from school. I am the healthiest kid I know.

If Mrs. Miller is partly to thank, why is Dad so upset with her? Why did he and Mom pretend she never existed? God, I wish she was here right now.

"Abby!" Mrs. Miller calls from the driveway. "Let's go!"

I hear her engine rev up and a door slam. My backpack is on the living room floor where I dropped it earlier. I don't have a test tomorrow. But I do have a cell phone. I've been lied to a lot lately, so when Mrs. Miller told us *one dinner and then you can go*, I'm not sure I believe her. After all, she did fake being an art teacher. And she must have been the one who walked up to our house that night. I'm starting to think she's more creepy than cool . . . maybe even dangerous.

Dad never wants to bother the cops, but if he won't, I will.

* * *

In the car, I sit in the back seat and Dad sits next to her up front, staring silently out the window. She's as upbeat as she is at school. Except now, her cheerful energy makes my stomach feel like a rubber band stretched too tight.

"I'm so happy you guys are coming over!" She pats Dad's knee affectionately. "Good thing I bought lots of food. Do you still like your steak rare?"

Dad keeps his eyes on the window. "I'm not hungry."

"You will be."

The car zooms around a bend, heading deeper into the woods. The road is pitch-black and tall trees close in all around us, crowding out the sky; we might as well be going through a tunnel. Inside my backpack, I feel the comforting edge of my phone.

"How about you?" Her blue eyes meet mine in the rearview mirror. "How do you like your steak?"

"Um, we don't eat red meat. My mom won't touch it since it made her sick when she was pregnant."

Mrs. Miller's face scrunches up. I realize I've said the wrong thing.

"I'll try it, though," I say quickly. "Why not?"

"What about you?" She glances at Dad, keeping one hand on the wheel. "Deprived of your favorite meal all these years? What a shame!"

He shrugs. "I don't miss it."

"Well, everything changes tonight." Her tone is weirdly excited.

The car rumbles along, turning off the paved street and onto a bumpy dirt path. The familiar whistle of the Metro-North train blares in the distance, so we must be near the tracks; they follow next to the Hudson. The thought comforts me, because otherwise the forest is too thick and dark to tell where we are. I don't see any other houses either, just a bunch of trees swaying in the wind.

Soon, we make a sharp left and pass a sign that reads CHERRY MILL LANE. A little cottage comes into view. It reminds me of a house in a fairy tale, with its one-story sloped roof and white siding and bright-red door, tucked into the forest. I think of the witch who lived alone in the woods in "Hansel and Gretel." Didn't she try to, like, eat kids?

We stop on the driveway. Mrs. Miller hops out and opens my door.

"Welcome!" She reaches out to help me, and her hand closes around mine. Dad hurries around his door and breaks us apart.

"I'll take her." He picks me up like I'm a little kid. My backpack dangles off my shoulder.

"I can walk," I say, but he doesn't put me down.

Mrs. Miller walks inside, humming, and Dad follows nervously, as if expecting someone else to jump out. He squints at the bushes and looks over his shoulder, holding me tightly.

"Oh, cut it out." She smiles at us from the doorway, but there's frustration in her voice. "I won't bite."

Dad's face is blank. That means he's past anger and on to something worse. He stops a few feet away, hesitating, and her tone switches from annoyance to sympathy.

"You've been through so much. Let yourself enjoy a night off—you deserve it."

"I don't need a night off. I need to go check on my wife."

Her expression turns cold. "Is that what she makes you call her now?"

"All right." Dad shifts me higher on his hip. "We're going. I'm calling an Uber." As he takes his phone out of his jeans pocket, I am filled with relief. This is getting *so* weird. Mrs. Miller is clearly jealous of my mom. "I wouldn't do that if I were you," Mrs. Miller says lightly.

He glares at her. "Really?"

"All the food will go to waste." She winks at me like we share a secret. "Come on in, let me feed you."

I smack his chest. "No, I want to go home!"

"Listen to me," he whispers, his voice almost vanishing in the wind. "If we don't go in, things could get a whole lot worse."

"Why?" I whine. "*Please.*"

"Trust me." Then he announces, "We're coming."

He slips his phone back into his pocket and marches us into the house, gripping me so I can't jump down and run away. I spot a number twelve above the mailbox.

As we enter the shabby cottage, my panic comes roaring back. I may not be dying, but I sure as hell don't feel safe. I wish my mom, or Riley, or *someone* knew where we were.

Mrs. Miller's friendliness is dizzying. I want to shake her. My confusion mounts as she proudly shows us through her house, pointing out the Oriental rug she got on sale, the rustic wooden dining table, and the vase of fresh pink lilies on it. The ceilings are low and the place is old and tiny—just a living room, kitchen, bedroom, and bathroom—but I must admit, when she lights the wood in the fireplace and the orange flames crackle to life, the cramped space transforms into a cozy room.

"Sit, sit," she tells us, pointing at the fluffy brown couch in front of the fireplace, while she goes to prepare dinner. Even Dad acts calm as we sit and warm our hands.

In the kitchen, she takes off her blazer and drapes it over the back of a barstool. "What can I get you guys to drink? Hot cocoa?"

"Do you have marshmallows?" I ask.

"Sure do!"

If I'm stuck here, I might as well have my favorite drink. "Okay, thanks."

"Just water for me," Dad mumbles.

"Pellegrino, with a lime?"

He perks up in surprise. "You remember that?"

"A decade isn't *that* long," she teases. Her face turns pink, and I notice that her makeup is perfect—not too much, but enough to make her eyes pop and her skin glow. She is beautiful, especially when she's happy. No wonder everyone at school loves her.

Are we hostages or guests? Suddenly I can't tell.

Just to be on the safe side, I sneak my cell phone from my backpack into my sweater pocket when no one is looking. Dad is busy keeping an eye on her, and she's chopping vegetables, boasting about how great a cook she's become.

"I had to teach myself after—oh, never mind. Abby, do you like mushrooms in your salad? I know your father doesn't."

"No, thanks. My mom is the only one who eats mushrooms."

Crap, I did it again. Mrs. Miller frowns as though I've disrespected her in class.

"Let's not talk about her tonight. I'd rather not spoil a wonderful evening."

Dad rubs his hands together, but he doesn't say anything. It's so unlike him.

"Your mother has done nothing wrong," he whispers to me. "Everything she did was out of love for you."

"What was that?" Mrs. Miller comes around the counter holding a wet dishrag. "What did you say?"

He lifts his chin. "I said, her mother was incredibly brave. You can't deny that no matter how much you hate her."

Mrs. Miller's eyes flash in rage. "Was I not clear the first time?" She smacks the rag on the edge of the table. "Enough about her!"

I scoot closer to Dad on the couch, but that pisses her off even more.

"Your hot chocolate is getting cold!" she barks.

I leap up and follow her into the kitchen. Dad stays behind, watching me. Why won't he do anything? I don't understand. He's the one who, when I was fighting with Sydney, told me I should never appease a bully.

At the stove, Mrs. Miller is frying up some steaks in sizzling butter. A bowl of salad is on the counter, and sweet potatoes are heating up in the oven. It all smells amazing, but I'm not hungry. When she hands me a mug of hot chocolate topped with marshmallows, I don't want to drink it, but I know I have no choice.

"Is it good?" she demands.

"Delicious!" I tell her. "So good."

Her wrinkled brow relaxes. "I'm sorry if I got edgy, okay? I just want us to have a good time."

"It's fine." I bury my face in the cup.

"Remember, you're my little girl!"

I choke on a marshmallow. She pats my back.

"It'll take some time to get used to. But you know what?" She brings her face close to mine. "There is nothing I am prouder of than helping you come into this world."

I force myself to smile. *Thanks?* It's impossible to picture myself as a bunch of cells in a dish, and just as strange to imagine her in a lab with my dad instead of in front of a classroom. There must be a reason she is no longer a scientist. I think of my dad's mysterious words: *We got in some trouble back then . . .*

"Did you also get in trouble?" I ask.

Her face darkens. "Quite a bit, thanks to your other mom."

The phrase is clearly meant as an insult: your other, *worse* mom.

I have no idea what to think, but she doesn't explain. Behind her, in the living room, I see my dad bring his silently vibrating phone to his ear and whisper into it, but Mrs. Miller cranes her neck to follow my gaze and he drops it just in time.

She turns back to me with open arms. "Don't worry; it was all worth it for you."

I allow her to hug me. But her touch sets off my panic again because she holds me too tight, for too long. *We are hostages*, I think. She knows we can't run away, because where would we go? Deeper into the woods? When she finally releases me, her eyes are watery, and so are mine.

"I've waited so long to do that," she says. "Thank you."

I wipe my forehead. My cell starts vibrating in my sweater pocket. I quickly reach into the pocket and send it to voicemail. Mom must have been trying to reach Dad, now me. I'll call her back after I take care of business first. "Can I go to the bathroom?"

"Of course; you don't have to ask. It's not class." She points me down the hall.

I walk slowly on purpose and avoid my dad's stare. I don't want her to think we're communicating behind her back. But I wish I could somehow let him know that I'm taking charge. When the cops show up here at 12 Cherry Mill Lane, I'm sure he'll be proud.

Weirdly, there's no lock on the bathroom door, just an empty circle where I guess a lock used to be. Oh well. I turn the faucet on as loud as it gets and take out my phone. *Please have a signal.* Two bars. Good enough. I tap 911.

And then I see an angry blue eye peering at me through the hole.

I let out a scream as the door suddenly swings open. "I knew it!" She grabs the phone out of my hand before I can press CALL.

"No!" I yell. "That's mine!"

Dad appears behind her, furious. "What do you think you're doing? Barging in on her in the bathroom?"

"She stole my phone!" I cry, feeling hot tears build up behind my eyes. "Please, I promise I won't use it; just give it back."

With a snort, she marches away from us and stops in front of a bookcase in the hallway. On top of it is a small box I hadn't noticed. She puts her thumb on it and it pops open. When she turns around to face us, she's dangling a silver handgun.

My dad gasps. I dart behind his legs, my sob finally letting loose. We're trapped.

"It's strictly for safety," she says calmly. "Living alone in the woods, you know."

"You can't just hold us hostage!" Dad shouts.

She rolls her eyes. "Quit being so dramatic. I just want to have a pleasant dinner without interruption." She turns up an empty palm. "I'll need yours as well."

My heart roars in my ears. I wonder if he's figuring out a way to attack her. His shoulders tighten; he looks frantically around the tiny cottage for an escape, a weapon, anything.

"The *phone*," she snaps. "Was I not clear the first time?"

"Fine." He takes his cell out of his pocket and tosses it. She catches it easily and puts both our phones into the small gun box, then slams it closed.

"But if you so much as touch a hair on her head," he warns, "I will kill you with my bare hands."

"Oh, get a grip," she says, walking back to the dining room table and pulling out the head chair. Then she sets the gun down beside her fork. "Now let's eat, shall we? It's getting cold."

CLAIRE

I am living my old nightmare. The most depressing place in the world is an inpatient psych unit: the wary nurses rushing from room to room, answering the beeps of machines and the howls of patients, the blur of white everywhere—sheets, walls, gowns—everything sterile, immaculate, impersonal; the lack of privileges—nothing sharp, we're all safety risks, all packed together in this place of last resort. The schizophrenics are the noisiest; they jabber the most, in different tones. The psychotics are the quietest, but the scariest. When I arrived, I was wheeled past an unblinking man sitting ramrod straight in his bed, scowling at anyone who passed.

I've suffered through the intake process with Rob, passing security checks and signing consent forms agreeing to evaluation and treatment. Now that a semiprivate room has opened up after a four-hour wait, I'm stuck in a bed that's protected from my fellow delusional companion by a thin blue curtain. Every so often, when her meds wear off, she cries out that the television is beaming radiation into her brain. Being here is enough to make anyone crazy if you weren't already.

And that's what I keep coming back to: *I'm not like them.*

Not anymore. A long time ago, I needed this kind of place. They saved me from the shadow of Colton that haunted me at night, from the voice that told me to jump out the window where he was waiting, to punish the staff who was denying me my son.

But now I know he is dead and gone. I *should* never see him again, despite my recent frantic episodes. Maybe my lucid periods mean that my relapse will be easy to control with meds and I'll be able to go home sooner than we estimated. A week, maybe two? The thought of Abby going to sleep without me is devastating. This is the first night in her entire life I won't be there to tuck her in.

My door unlocks from the outside and a nurse marches into my room, her face covered by a blue mask, but I can see her weary eyes; they're underscored by purplish circles and they apprise me with caution. She thinks I'm one of them.

She approaches me with a clipboard and a plastic water cup. "Lisa Burke?"

I sit up. "That's me." I've checked in under my new name so they don't pull my old records and connect me to the identity I've worked so hard to hide. As far as Rob told them, this is my first voluntary hospitalization for hallucinatory PTSD and depression. I have never been to this hospital, but it's still possible someone could recognize me. Even if they do, though, they couldn't prove it.

The nurse checks the number on my wristband and compares it to my chart, then holds out the water and a little white pill. "Here's one milligram of Xanax to help you sleep."

I will be a model patient. I will get out of here soon.

"Thank you." I swallow it. Then I lay back against my stiff pillow. Its harsh detergent stench reminds me of how far I am from home.

"How are you feeling?" She holds a pen over the clipboard, ready to notate my chart. I notice she's backed up two steps, in case I try to grab the pen and stab her. The staff never get too close to a wild animal in a cage. And multiple systems are in place in case backup is required. I know, because I've tested their limits before.

"I'm feeling pretty good right now. I don't think I'll need to stay very long."

She scribbles something, but her expression is unreadable. Is she secretly laughing at me? All crazy patients must say the same thing, just like prisoners who think they were wrongly sentenced. *I don't belong here. There's been a mistake.*

"Okay, Mrs. Burke. I'll be in to check on you around midnight." She shuffles backward to the door with her eyes on me, never letting down her guard.

"Wait! Can I call my husband? I want to say good-night."

It's torturous not to have my cell phone, which I surrendered on admittance.

She considers the sincerity of my plea. So far, I have no marks against me. "Fine. I'll take you to the supervised area. You can dial out from there."

We walk down the hallway to a small room shielded by Plexiglas, in direct view of the bustling nurses' station. There are two black landline phones on a wooden desk in front of plastic chairs.

I eagerly take a seat and dial Rob's cell from memory. It rings and rings. No answer. I call again, aware that my nurse is watching me closely from the other side of the glass. My time is running short. I press the phone to my ear. After three more rings, he picks up, but instead of his usual "Hi, love," he sounds strangely urgent.

"Honey!" he whispers.

"What's wrong?"

"We were—"

Click. The line goes dead.

What the fuck?

I redial, but it goes straight to voice mail. I try again. Voice mail.

The nurse pokes her head in. "All done?"

"Almost." I punch in Abby's cell. It rings once, then voice mail. We don't have a landline at home. There's no other way to get in touch with them.

I rush out of the room and almost collide with a doctor in a white coat. She gives me a dirty look, and two security guards instantly appear on either side of me. Their expressions are menacing.

"Sorry, I didn't mean to . . ." I try to veer around them, but one of the guards blocks my way. "Can someone help me?" I yell. "I need help!"

My nurse appears at my elbow. Her eyes look as tired as ever. I wonder if she's as desperate to get home to her child as I am to get to mine. "What's wrong, Mrs. Burke?"

"I think my family's in trouble."

She trades a grim look with another nurse, who's watching me from the station with one finger on a red intercom button.

"Seriously, I'm not crazy! My husband sounded really upset!"

"Everything's fine. He just left a few hours ago, remember?"

Terror leeches into my bloodstream. I don't think I imagined his distress.

"No, I think something bad happened."

She tries to escort me back to my room. "Paranoia is common with your illness."

"Please." I dig in my heels. "Someone needs to check on them!"

Her voice acquires a no-nonsense edge. "Mrs. Burke, you need to return to your room."

"No, I need to find them!" I shake her off and sprint back to the phone area but am quickly intercepted by the two guards. The next seconds pass in a screaming blur as they pin my arms behind my back and plunge a needle into my thigh, its sting so acute that I fall to my knees.

Then the pain ebbs and blackness rushes in.

JILLIAN

Abby and Rob stare sullenly at their food. "All this . . ." Nash gestures suspiciously at the spread. I wonder how much he remembers of that special night a dozen years ago, during the summer we fell in love. "I don't understand," he says. "Why did you have all this ready in advance if you didn't know we were coming?"

Still sharp as a tack. "Actually . . ." I give Abby a sad smile. "I was going to drop it off for Mrs. Schaeffer tonight."

Her fifth-grade history teacher has just started chemo for breast cancer, and the school organized a drive to deliver meals for the family.

Abby's pout deepens. She can hardly take her eyes off the gun at my elbow. "Won't they be hungry now?"

"They weren't expecting it. I'll take my turn tomorrow instead."

I peek at Nash. It's essential to remind him that I have a good heart, that I'm still the woman he fell in love with, even if I need to apply a firm hand to get us moving in the right direction.

But my charity doesn't seem to have dented his cynicism. He pushes a piece of steak around on his plate without eating it. "I still don't understand," he says. "How in the world did you get a job at her school? Don't you have to be fingerprinted to work in education?"

"Not if you've worked in a New York school before."

"So . . . identify theft?"

"Great minds think alike, Dr. Burke."

Abby's fork freezes above her salad. "What's she talking about?"

He sighs as though I've done him a great injustice by forcing him to be honest with her.

He at least summons the courage to meet her indignant gaze. "Your mother and I had to go undercover for protection. We got fake names—" He shoots me a scornful look. "Not a *real person's* identity! We would never endanger someone else for our own purposes."

Abby's eyes bulge at this aftershock to the main shock, but little does she know the earthquakes aren't over yet. I rest a hand on her arm, relishing the comfort that is my right to offer her. I picture us abroad, holding her hand as we cross a busy street in Prague or London while strangers admire our red-haired resemblance. And it won't matter that I didn't physically give birth to her, because I did intellectually; I'm the mother who made her possible.

She snatches her arm back and tucks it under the table.

I snap at Nash, "Oh, please. The real Mrs. Miller wasn't harmed in the least. She quit teaching last year."

Once I did the legwork to find an art teacher somewhere in New York state who had recently left the field, the rest was no big deal: piecing together her résumé from social media, securing a reference from her former school, reaching out to Principal Hastings at the Garrison Union Free School for an interview. It's the only K–8 school in town, so access to Abby was a shoe-in. The old fool took to me right away. He has a reputation for favoring pretty women. And he was in a bind; he was only too happy to hire me. I didn't know Abby's name when I started the job—only her screen name from MapMyDNA—but because I'd spotted her at the museum, I quickly recognized her in class. The position offered me the perfect perch from which to observe her up close while I executed my long game.

Truth is, of course, I had to create the opening for myself. Art was perfect: easy to teach, and no parent-teacher conferences that would force a premature confrontation. Once I singled out the teacher I wanted to replace, the job opened up in short order. Calling in a few threats to someone's loved ones can work wonders. People will fold like cards if they think their family's safety is at stake—not that I would actually hurt anyone, of course. I'm not a monster, despite Nash's apparent doubts; I'm simply strategic.

"In other words," he tells me warily, "nothing's changed."

"What is that supposed to mean?"

He mutters an insult under his breath.

"Excuse me?"

He sets down his utensils, and his irate eyes drill into mine. "I should have known from the beginning."

My heart flips over. "Known what?"

"You think you're better than the rules. You exploit any vulnerabilities you can find."

"Come on, that's not fair! In an unjust world, you can't always play by the rules. *You* of all people should understand that."

"If *you* hadn't betrayed me with that recording, none of this would be happening," he snaps. "But you just *had* to go behind my back and hand them proof."

"I was protecting myself!" I retort. "You don't know what it's like to be a young woman in science, with hotshot men exploiting their postdocs. Not that it matters anymore."

He scowls. "I never would have done that to you."

"I realized that later. Unfortunately, by then it was too late." A bitter silence ensues; an opportunity. "I'm sorry," I announce. "I regret that more than you know."

He nods—an acceptance? If so, I wonder if forgiveness lies around the corner. He pushes back his chair and stands up. "I need more ice."

I motion to the dispenser on the fridge, then chase my edginess with a gulp of dry Cab. The alcohol tamps down my stress. Too bad he doesn't drink. He could use a glass himself. I remind myself that dwelling on our bad times is unproductive. There will be much to accomplish in the coming days after we cross the border to Canada.

Time to change course. After he returns to the table with a glass full of ice, I fish my wallet out of my purse and remove an old photo, its corners worn down to nubs. In sepia tones, we're arm in arm, laughing, having just stumbled off the Cyclone at Coney Island. Right after the camera clicked, he drew me close and whispered in my ear, *I want to fuck you right now.* And he did, in the back of a cab, on our way back to Manhattan. We were so enthralled with each other that summer, before Claire torched it all.

I slide the photo across the table. "Hey, remember this?"

He blinks in surprise, like I've given him emotional whiplash. In an effort to build goodwill, I remove the gun from the table and place it down by my feet, out of sight.

An audible sigh escapes Abby. No wonder she's barely said a word. She's scared shitless.

"Want to see him before you were born?" I ask her. "Here."

She silently takes the photo from me.

"Handsome, right?" I smile.

She nods. Reaching across the table, he plucks it out of her grasp. I watch his eyes carefully for an inadvertent twinkle—that memory was undeniably one of our happiest together. As he gazes at our faded past, I think I see a shade of nostalgia cross his face.

"The good old days," I reflect. "You haven't forgotten, have you?"

"No," he says. "I haven't." He offers me the briefest smile. "In fact, could we discuss something privately for a minute? There's something I want to ask you."

"Sure." My interest is piqued. I must admit I'm delighted by any chance to score alone time. "Do you want to go in my room?"

"Yeah. We'll be right back," he tells Abby. "Wait here."

As I lead him away from the table, being careful to scoop up the gun just in case, a faint jingling noise catches my attention. So faint, I'm not sure if I imagined it. I look over my shoulder to see that Rob is following behind me, having just passed by Abby.

"What was that?" I ask.

"What was what?" he says.

"That sound."

He and Abby both stare at me blankly, but Abby's stare is not professional enough. Her twitching lips give her away.

I backtrack over to her. Her hands are folded tightly in her lap.

"Open your hands," I command.

She pauses, searching for a sign from Rob.

"Come on," he urges me. "Can't we talk?"

"Open your hands!" I bark at her.

Reluctantly, she pulls her hands apart and *my car keys fall out.*

"What the fuck?"

I raise my gun at Rob, and his hands fly up. "It's my fault, okay? Not hers. I saw you put them in your blazer when we got here." He glances at my blazer, which is still draped over the barstool in the kitchen where I left it. "I got up to get the ice and I took them out of the pocket, then slipped them to her just now so she could try to leave without me. She didn't even know, so please don't do anything to her."

I gasp. I wanted nice, I tried nice, but now it's too late; now it's punishment time. For both of them. I whirl on Abby.

"Don't shoot me!" she begs. "I'll do whatever you want."

I calmly lower the gun to my side, knowing the wound I'm about to inflict will hurt more than a bullet. "You don't know anything about Ethan, do you?"

"Who's Ethan?"

Rob stiffens. Torment manifests on his face like physical pain.

"Tell her," I demand. "Or I will."

A moan escapes him. "No . . . Jillian, please . . ."

Abby shrinks in her chair. "Dad, you're freaking me out. Who's Ethan?"

He lifts his head slowly, clinging to the last moments of an illusion he's been keeping up for a decade.

When he meets her gaze, his strained voice fills the silence: "Your father."

ABBY

"That's impossible." I find myself flattened against my chair, unable to back up any further. "I don't know what you're talking about."

"It's true," Jillian says. A minute ago, she was threatening to shoot us, and now her face is soft with kindness again. I have no freaking clue what is going on—who she is, who my dad is, who I am. Or whether we will ever get out of here alive.

My dad's mouth is moving, but I don't hear his words; my head is a heavy balloon about to float away. I feel myself swaying, and the world blurring, until two firm hands grip my shoulders. I open my eyes and he's right there—my dad, the only dad I've ever known, his face exactly the same as it was a minute ago, yet somehow forever changed.

"I love you, Abigail. You will always be my daughter, no matter what."

I jump up and run to the opposite wall. "Get away from me. You've done nothing but lie my entire life! I want Mom!"

"She lied to you, too," says Jillian, closing in on me, her long pink skirt swishing. Silver bangles clink together on her wrists—bangles I admired at school only a few hours ago. "I came to tell you the truth."

I stare at the man whose real name I don't even know. "When were you going to tell me?"

His eyes fill with tears. I have never seen him cry.

"We didn't want to burden you with this until you were older." I can see that he hates himself right now, but he's also desperate to convince me he's not a total jerk.

"Don't touch me!" I yell, as he reaches for my hand. "I don't even know who you are!"

"I'll tell you everything." He slumps against the wall near me, but not too close. Jillian sits on the floor across from us and hugs her knees. She's watching him with a strange focus, like he's the only person in the room. I can't help staring at her gun, and when she notices my fear, she places it behind her, out of sight.

"Go ahead," she urges him. "Tell her."

He takes a deep breath. "My name was Robert Nash, and I was your mother's doctor. I oversaw the experiment we did to create you, so you would be born healthy."

"Don't let his humility fool you," she interrupts. "He was the greatest fertility researcher of our time."

After watching her lash out, it's shocking to see her flatter him; she seems kind of, like, *obsessed* with him.

But he ignores her. "Your mom came to me with . . . her husband. Ethan."

He pauses to let this sink in. I can't picture my mom with anyone but him. It makes no sense.

"They wanted another baby, but you know about Colton. They didn't want that to happen to you, too."

"So you're not Colton's dad, either?"

"No."

That explains why I've never seen a picture of them all together. There are plenty of Colton and Mom. I always figured he was the one behind the camera. Not some other guy . . .

"In fact," he tells me, "I never even met your brother. He died before they came to me. It's *why* they came to me."

"Why didn't you just tell me before?"

"We didn't want you to feel different from anyone else. Especially at your age, when fitting in seems so important . . ." His voice trails off. "I don't know, maybe we should have. We were afraid that it would ruin your childhood."

"I just can't believe I was a lab rat before I was even born."

"There's no shame it," says Jillian. "You're lucky. You should be grateful."

"Give her a minute," he snaps. "She has three parents. How would you feel?"

"If I was healthy?" she says. "Pretty damn good."

They both fall silent. I rub my eyes. A wave of exhaustion is hitting me, and I can't stop checking every five seconds that Jillian is not about to reach for her gun again.

"Jillian's right, you know." He grits his teeth. "If we'd let nature take its course . . ."

"Too bad your mom got us in trouble." Jillian rakes her nails across the carpet, leaving a gash in the fibers. "Even though she promised us secrecy, she told Ethan, a big shot in the ethics world at Columbia, and he reported our work as a federal crime. No one in this country is allowed to edit eggs or embryos for human reproduction, and he didn't agree with us doing it."

"It does sound kind of creepy," I admit. I picture them hovering over a dish of cells that would one day become me, squeezing drops of different people's DNA into the mixture and swishing it all together.

"Why?" Jillian shoots back. "If it saved your life?"

"I don't know. It just seems wrong." I raise an eyebrow at him.

"I've been thinking about that question for a very long time," he says. "What makes it *seem* wrong, when in fact, by intervening, we helped you avoid a terrible fate."

"And? What's the reason?"

"Ethan would give you a whole philosophical argument about why we shouldn't play God. But honestly, I think he was just scared of disrupting the status quo."

"Even if that means some kids die an early death," Jillian says angrily.

"Right. We decided that the harm of being born to three parents—struggling with your identity, for instance—would be way less than the harm of being born very sick to two parents. That's why we felt the experiment was the right thing to do."

"But then I got sent to prison." Jillian shakes her head as if she's still surprised. "Our country is backwards."

He sighs. "Yeah. And I ran away to help your mother. She had no one when you were born. But we've had to live a very quiet life because we broke the law."

I'm barely breathing. "Wait, you guys aren't even *together*? You just live together?"

I think I might throw up. I picture them swing dancing around the living room, doing crossword puzzles in bed, planting veggies in the garden. How could it all be an act?

"No!" he cries. "Don't think that. Our marriage may not be official, but it's as real as any other."

"Because you got stuck together?"

"Because you brought us together. We loved you at first sight, and then eventually, we fell in love with each other, too."

Neither of us realizes how Jillian is taking this until she stands up with a snort. "That's bullshit. There's no way you could love that mental case." Her furious eyes land on me. "He's telling you a fairy tale."

"I am not! Honey, I'm telling you the truth."

I glance between them, unsure who to believe.

Jillian rolls her eyes. "He put up with her because he's a good man, and he sacrificed everything for you—but it's not too late to get it all back. That's why I came."

He frowns. "What are you talking about?"

"I came to set you free."

She smiles for the first time in an hour, a real smile of hopeful excitement. He scoots closer to me, breathing fast. The contrast between them fills my chest with panic.

"First thing tomorrow," she announces, "we're driving to Canada. Once we're out of the country, you won't have to live in fear anymore. We can finally work on publishing our research, and the rest will follow: Jobs. Money. Fame." She grins at me. "You're our ticket to freedom."

A sound like a retch comes out of his throat. "You've got to be kidding me." He stands up, picks me up, and throws me over his shoulder, the way he used to when I was little and refused to go to bed. "This is batshit crazy."

"You'll sleep in my bed," she tells him, not missing a beat. To me, she lets out an apologetic sigh. "I hate to do this, but I think it's best if you sleep in the basement. I wouldn't want you to do anything stupid like try to run away. It's just for one night, okay?"

What?

"No way!" I cling to his neck. He attempts to comfort me with a squeeze, but his face reflects my horror.

"Don't worry," she says. "It's heated with a cot and blanket. You'll be fine. We'll regroup tomorrow."

She walks to a door in the far corner that I thought was a coat closet. But it opens to a staircase.

What can I do? I don't want to piss her off again, especially with that gun, so I follow her, holding my backpack. She flips on the light to guide my path. A single yellow bulb hangs from the ceiling. The smell of musty wood and dust nearly choke me as I go down the stairs. The air probably hasn't moved for a century.

There's a small metal cot and blanket on a cold concrete floor, plus a half-underground window, an oil tank, and a pile of logs. Past the circle of the light, I can't see a thing. The rest of the basement is totally dark. A shiver crawls over my arms. What else might be living down here?

"Night night," Jillian calls. At the top of the stairs, she gives me a sad little wave, as though she's being forced to do this. "See you bright and early!"

Then she slames the door—and slides a lock into place.

CLAIRE

Light hits my eyelids. Not the soft pink sunrise I wake up to every morning at home. This light streams from the ceiling, harsh and artificial. I squint at the nurse standing over me with a clipboard. She's wearing the same blue scrubs and tight bun as before, but her under-eye circles are covered with concealer. It must be a new day.

"Feeling better?" she asks. "You had quite a night."

"What?"

"The guards . . . don't you remember?"

The memory returns in a flash—being tackled and drugged. Now my empty stomach churns with nausea and hunger.

"How long was I out?"

"About twelve hours."

"Have you heard from my husband?"

She shakes her head. "Not yet. Sorry."

I bolt up, but my head sways, so I lie back down. Out of habit, I reach for my cell on the nightstand, but it's not there.

"Take it easy. The tranquilizer could still be wearing off."

I don't want to take it easy. I don't care about my illness. Only one thing matters. But I can't show any panic, or they'll drug me again.

"Please," I say as evenly as I can. "May I call him?"

She checks her watch, whose pink band is adorned with Minnie Mouse cartoons. It's the only bright spot in her drab uniform. I wonder if she has a little girl, too—if she understands the torture of separation.

"It's almost time for rounds. The doctor will want to evaluate you."

"Please? I just want to make sure my daughter made it to school."

She hesitates, apparently weighing my request.

"There's a big test today," I lie. "It's really important."

"Fine. But make it fast."

"Thank you!"

She leads me to the phone station. In the hallway, we pass several patients who are headed to a group therapy session. One young man has a single shaved-off eyebrow and his eyes are darting around suspiciously. An unkempt woman dodges some imaginary ghost, veering too close to me and reeking of body odor. I jump back in disgust. Then I realize I'm still wearing the same clothes I blacked out in, my face is an oily mess, and my teeth are coated in sludge. Maybe I *am* one of them.

"You have five minutes," my nurse says at the phone bank. "No more."

I punch in Rob's cell. My yearning to hear his voice is stronger than my need to pee or eat or drink. But his instant voice mail shatters my hope. I try Abby's cell, but her ironic voice mail greets me: *Hi! I'm not here right now, but my assistant Alice will take your message. Alice?* Then the robot voice: *Record your message after the beep.*

Abby was so proud of herself when she came up with that prompt. It made us both chuckle. Now it fills me with dread.

I hang up and call her school. It's one of the few numbers I have memorized.

"Garrison Union Free School," the receptionist answers, "how can I help you?"

I picture the cheerful blonde woman whose nails are often painted to match the school's colors, navy and pink. She's like cotton candy—all sweetness, zero edge.

"Carla!" I say brightly. "It's Abby's mom."

"Hi, Mrs. Burke; how's it going?"

"Pretty well, thanks. I'm actually out of town, and I wanted to make sure she got to school okay. I can't get in touch with my husband."

"Oh, let me check." A chirpy musical chorus plays on hold. It couldn't be further from the mood in this suffocating phone booth, where my time is almost up.

When she comes back on the line, her voice is apologetic. "I'm sorry, but she stayed home sick today."

"What? No, that can't be right. She never gets sick!"

"I'm sorry. Is there anything else I can do?"

"No, that's all right. Thank you."

I keep the phone to my ear to buy myself another minute.

Abby is ridiculously healthy, the polar opposite of Colton. I can't remember the last time she took a sick day. A single letter breaks on the shore of my mind.

What if *J* is somehow behind this?

With all those cameras in the house and the new alarm system we installed, it seems impossible. How could a petite woman break in and accost a grown man and a child? Yet I can't shake the fear. Am I just being paranoid? But she *did* seemingly show up at our house that night, and she *did* lure Abby to the museum.

One part of my brain is yelling at me to get a grip—*you're being irrational*—but I shut it down. I listen to the louder voice, the one egging me on.

I march out of the phone booth.

"All done?" the nurse asks.

"Yes. I'm going home today."

"What? You haven't even started the protocol yet."

"I checked myself in voluntarily. I'm not a danger to anyone or myself, so no one can stop me from leaving."

"But you just had that massive panic attack. Why don't you at least wait for the doctor?"

"I don't have time. My family could be in trouble."

"This is your illness talking. At least consult the doctor!"

She might be right, but I'll be damned if I'm going to let it get in the way of taking care of my girl. There's no way I can work through my anxiety and PTSD issues if my family's safety is in question. There's no way I can stay here.

I give her an impatient smile. "Thanks for your concern, but what I really want is my stuff back. And a cab."

"But it's against medical advice."

"Are you going to get my things, or should I ask someone else?"

"After last night, the attending won't give you the green light to leave. You're not ready."

"But you can't legally keep me here. I'm a voluntary patient."

"Yeah, but the hospital could seek a court order to commit you," she warns.

Fear bristles in my chest. I need this woman on my side.

"You have a little girl too, don't you?" I ask, gesturing to her Minnie Mouse watch.

She looks at me in surprise. "Yeah, my daughter is nine."

"Almost the same age as mine. And she needs me right now."

The nurse sighs like she's failed me, but it's also a surrender.

"No one could talk me out of this," I promise. "It's not your fault."

"Okay." When she touches my shoulder, there's no longer an implicit threat—only kindness. "I hope you find what you're looking for."

JILLIAN

Nash and I lie a mile apart in the bed in near silence. When the wind gusts, the trees outside howl and the windows rattle. On such a blustery night, all I want is for us to keep each other warm. It's all I've wanted for a very long time. I wonder how well he remembers my naked body and the things we used to do to each other.

His angry breathing now disrupts the effect. He hasn't spoken a word since I slid the gun into my nightstand drawer and turned off the lights. What is this, a cold war? We're sharing the same blanket, but he's edged himself inch by inch to the opposite side, as though I wouldn't notice. If he's waiting for me to fall asleep first, it's not going to happen. We're both flat on our backs staring up at the ceiling. He's stripped down to his boxers and T-shirt; I'm in my sexiest silk nightgown.

But he's impervious. I bet he's still thinking of *her.*

I fume in silence until I resolve to break the spell. We must keep moving forward; our future together depends on it.

Eventually, I let my pinkie graze his thigh.

"Stop." His voice cuts through the quiet. "Don't."

"Oh, just relax." I turn on my side to face him.

He doesn't follow suit. "I can't believe you're making her sleep down there."

"She'd run away otherwise."

He throws off the blanket. "How much?"

"What?"

"To leave us alone. Ten grand?"

I blink as the insult sinks in. "You think I'm after a *payoff*?"

"What else?"

"I already told you. I'm getting us out of the country so we can pick up where we left off." I scoot closer to him, though there's still an arm's length between us. "You deserve so much better."

He snorts. "Seriously, I'm willing to negotiate. What do you want?"

"That's it."

"Come on, everyone has a price."

"Enough." I almost slap him. "You should be thanking me."

"Yeah, because you've been so accommodating."

I decide to appeal to his rational side.

"I'm giving you a way out. What more could you ask for?"

"What if I don't want to go?"

That's her talking, I think. *Not him.* The genius I knew would never settle for a mediocre life with an unstable woman. The reminder of her influence deflates my rage; it's bound to be transient. Like a virus, it needs to run its course. Only then will he finally be free.

The covers rustle as he sits up. "What if my biggest problem is you?"

"I get it. But once we've started over, you *will* thank me. When was the last time you set foot in a lab?"

It's hard to see in the dark, but I think a shadow of yearning crosses his face. Proof that the real him is still intact under all those layers of deprivation.

"You've paid a terrible price," I say gently. "But it doesn't have to be forever."

His response comes a beat late, as though he's mustering up the conviction to fight me. "That part of my life is over now. I moved on a long time ago. You should, too."

But his pause spoke otherwise.

"Did you?" I slide my fingertips over his bare ankle.

"Jillian." He kicks me away, but not roughly. "I'm married now."

"Does she do this?" I slip a hand into his boxers and fondle the underside of his balls the way he used to love. It was always his shortcut to ecstasy.

I'm half expecting a knee in the gut, but to my delight, my massive gamble pays off: his coiled legs go limp as he emits a quiet moan.

"You like it like this," I whisper, curling up alongside him, caressing his shaft. He pants, his body radiating heat. It's been years since I've slept with anyone, but my hands remember what to do. The right strokes come back like muscle memory.

In no time, he rolls on top of me and grabs my wrists. I want him to pin me against the bed and fuck me. I don't mind that he's smothering me under his weight. The motion of our bodies is oxygen enough. Even with my underwear and his boxers still on, it's already hotter than any encounter I've had in a decade.

"Put it in," I beg him. "I'm not going to last."

"You have a condom?" he asks.

"No, I don't care."

"Let me just check."

Maybe it's the eagerness in his voice, or my belated awareness of his soft dick, but as he reaches for my nightstand, a heinous thought occurs to me. I let out a shriek as he jerks open the drawer and seizes my gun.

In the dim light, he fumbles to release the safety, and I throw myself at him with all the power I've got; the force of fury redoubles my strength.

He's ready, but not ready enough. With no time to position the trigger, he settles for blocking his face with the gun as I collide with him. We both fall off the bed, and I immobilize him with a swift kick in the groin, an easy target. He manages to punch my shoulder, keeping the gun out of my reach, but he doesn't count on my teeth sinking deep into his ear.

A guttural cry escapes him as the metallic taste of blood soaks my tongue. I can't help gagging. But then he writhes on the floor, and his grip on the gun goes slack. I snatch it triumphantly and wield it above him.

He reaches for his left ear. "What the—fuck?" The top of it is missing a chunk; I realize the fleshy piece is still in my mouth. I spit it out onto his leg.

"You forget I was in jail. You learn to fight dirty pretty quick."

"Please." Blood saturates his exposed cartilage, dripping over what remains of his ear. "Don't shoot. Abby needs me."

"Are you going to cooperate from now on?"

"Whatever you say."

"You'll leave town with me?"

His anguish intensifies. "Yes."

"Tomorrow?"

"Yes."

Satisfied, I withdraw the gun. "Get back into bed. I need to tend to that wound."

He scrambles onto the bed without protest. Blood drips onto the white comforter, but who cares; we'll be gone in the morning.

I lock the gun back up in the high-tech box that will only open for my fingerprints. Such a silly mistake, thinking I could reach him with sex. Of course not. After his isolation with Claire, trapped for so long in her skewed universe, it might be weeks until he recovers and embraces our second chance. I knew he needed me to get him out of there. But his psychological deterioration is worse than I expected. It's going to take more time than I thought, but pretty soon, we'll have all the time in the world.

Once he's back under the covers, I retrieve a towel, a glass of water, and a first-aid kit from the bathroom, and get to work tending his wound. He yelps when I dab it with rubbing alcohol, but I hold his head and whisper gently until I'm done. I bandage it up with gauze, then offer him two Tylenol plus an Ativan so he can get some rest.

"That's okay." He pushes the meds away, but winces when his ear rubs the pillow.

"You're in pain." I press the pills into his palm. "There's no reason to suffer."

Reluctantly, he takes the glass of water and swallows them.

I pat his knee. "Good job. Now go to sleep. Tomorrow's a big day."

He lies down again and closes his eyes. In a few minutes, his anxious breathing slows to a quiet rhythm. Watching him slip into slumber feels more intimate than sex, more restorative than sleep. I relish the solitude of this special form of togetherness: just us, yet just me, bearing witness to the peaceful rest of a saved man.

* * *

I wake before he does when the first morning rays filter through the blinds. He's still conked out: mouth half open, snoring lightly, a spot of drool on the pillow. I hate to wake him, but the gauze is soaked with blood and the towel under his ear is bright red. I hope he doesn't need stitches. A stop at the ER is not in the plan.

As I'm considering doing the stitches myself, though I don't have anesthesia, the sound of breaking glass startles me. I leap off the bed and Nash's eyes open. Abruptly he is wide awake.

"Where's Abby?"

Shit. I had almost forgotten about her.

He staggers out of bed cupping his ear, but now there's no time to change the bandage. We run across the cottage to the basement and clamber down the staircase to discover that our worst fear has come true. All that remains of the window is a rim of shattered glass, splattered with white paint.

Abby is gone.

ABBY

I try not to cry as I run. But it's hard not to. I've never felt more alone.

The fresh air helps, even though my shoulders are covered in scratches that sting in the breeze. Branches on the forest floor crunch under my feet. A blur of trees passes by as I sprint toward the road.

"Come back here!" shouts a frantic voice in the distance. It's her.

Don't look back. I'm terrified I'll see her gun. I think of a bullet flying into my head, knocking me down dead.

"Wait!" she shouts. "We can talk about this!"

My heart is pounding so hard I worry it might explode. *Don't cry.* I think of bullets and run faster. My gasps sound like a choking person. A dying person. I run faster still.

I force myself to double my pace, keeping my mind on the prize—the main road. I don't hear my dad yelling after me; God, I hope she hasn't shot him. Oh, God.

I'm far enough ahead that I think I can lose her. There's a rustling sound way behind me near the cottage—her feet crunching over the leaves—but I see the main highway just up ahead, and it gives me another insane burst of energy.

By the time I reach the pavement, my feet are aching and my sneakers are all scuffed up. My backpack feels like it's filled with rocks. When I finally work up the nerve to look over my shoulder, it's a relief to see that she isn't chasing me. The path is empty. I listen for footsteps in the distance, but the forest has gone quiet.

Am I really free? I can't tell if it's another trap. I have no idea what to think about anything anymore.

Last night, I couldn't sleep at all, so I ended up in that nasty cot just *thinking.* If you had told me in class yesterday that my favorite teacher would have kidnapped me and locked me in a basement . . . And yet the more I think about it, the more it makes a horrible kind of sense.

She always was extra nice to me, even if I wasn't paying attention. Sometimes I would look up from a worksheet and catch her just watching me. It never creeped me out before because I figured she was making sure I wasn't secretly passing notes. But now I get it.

I am her experiment.

All night, my mind looped around the same shock until I got too worked up to lie there any longer. My back was aching on the curved pad. So I climbed out and went over to a dusty corner where some old stuff was piled up. Empty cardboard boxes, a broken vacuum, a gross spider web, and . . . a full metal paint can. It was very heavy. I waited.

As soon as the sun came up, I swung the can as hard as I could at the only window, which was half-underground. I couldn't believe my luck when the glass actually broke, and the white paint flew everywhere. If I was any larger, I wouldn't have fit, but I dragged the cot underneath the window, hopped up, and squeezed out of the hole with my backpack. All I have now is my $30 allowance and a couple of school binders; no phone.

At least I'm free. But I feel bad leaving my dad behind—I mean *him* . . . whoever he is.

Dad or not, I can't stand to think of him suffering back there. I heard them fighting last night; there was a crash and a thump, like a person falling on the ground. I don't know if her gun went off, but after that, it was silent. I may be pissed, but I definitely don't want him to die.

I've got to find a way to get him out of there. I wish I had an aunt or uncle, or some other family member who could help me. I wish I could go to my mom, but she's totally lost it. This is way too serious for my friends, and if I ask for help at school, they'll call the cops. And that would be even worse. They would arrest *him*, not her. My skin prickles. No way am I getting the cops involved.

As the sun climbs higher in the sky, I walk along the edge of the road with absolutely no clue where I'm going. On my right side is the forest and beyond it, the river. On the other side of the road is a steep hill with more trees. My stomach growls, reminding me that I haven't eaten since barely touching dinner last night. My tongue is sandpaper; its surface is all rough and bumpy. Thinking of water makes the dryness even worse. I try to swallow, but I have barely any saliva.

A low horn echoes in the distance. The Metro-North train. If I squint through the trees, I can see its silver cars hugging the Hudson.

It goes to New York City. I don't know anyone there, except—

Jillian's sarcastic voice runs through my head: *Ethan, a big shot at Columbia.*

I stop cold. I'm going to find my father.

* * *

About a half hour after I decide to head in the direction of the train station, without a map, food, or water, a beat-up Ford Explorer pulls up beside me on the road. A teenage girl with large hoop earrings rolls down her window.

"Hey, you okay?"

I'm so hungry and thirsty that I shake my head.

"You want me to call someone? Your parents?"

I clear my throat. "No, thanks."

She frowns, her thick mascara weighing down her lashes. "You look younger than my sister, and she's not allowed to walk to school by herself."

"I'm allowed."

She turns back to the wheel. "All right, well . . ."

"Actually, could you drop me off at the train station?"

"If you're running away or something, I can't—"

"No, my dad's picking me up in Manhattan. I just had a little fight with my . . . stepmom . . . so I need a ride."

"Ah, family crap!" She smiles like a big sister might. "I know all about it. Hop on in."

* * *

The drive takes less than ten minutes, and my new friend is nice enough to share a PowerBar and some water with me. I'm so grateful I almost cry. Maybe it's because of all I've been through, not knowing who I can trust, but her kindness hits me hard. When I grow up, I want to be just like her: a person who will help others in need.

On the crowded platform, no one pays attention to me. People in suits are typing on their phones or reading their tablets. After I buy a ticket, I sit close to one woman on a bench so it seems like we might be together, in case anyone's wondering why a fifth grader is alone.

Soon the train shows up, and everyone is sucked into the chaos of climbing on and grabbing a seat. I walk through a few cars until I see an open seat next to a fat man dressed in a business suit whose buttons are bursting. He's bald, with a white mustache and a honker of a nose. He reminds me a bit of Santa Claus, if Santa commuted to work in New York City. His head is resting against the window and his eyes are closed. I hope he doesn't wake up and ask me too many questions.

After I take my seat, the train jumps forward. We're off.

To where? I don't know where Ethan lives. I don't even know his last name, only that he reported the experiment and caused a bunch of trouble.

Wait. If my parents had to change their names and go into hiding and worry about being recognized, that means the world must have known about them. And how would anyone know unless . . . ?

The man next to me is snoring.

"Excuse me." I tug his sleeve.

He startles awake.

"I'm really sorry, but um, can I borrow your phone?"

His eyes land on my dirty hair, my sweaty tank top, and my scraped shoulders.

"I fell off a friend's trampoline," I quickly explain. "But I'm fine. I just forgot my phone . . . and I need to look something up."

"Are you—" He glances around at the nearest passengers. "Are you by yourself?"

"I'm going to meet my dad at Grand Central. It's no big deal; I take the train all the time."

He seems surprised. "You don't see a lot of kids doing that these days."

"My parents are cool," I say, wishing it were true.

"Well, good for them."

He hands me his iPhone. I thank him and wait until he rests his head against the window again. Then the screen is all mine. I bring up Safari and type into the search bar: THREE PARENT BABY NY.

More than three thousand hits pop up. I click on an article that's eleven years old from the *New York Times*:

So-Called "Frankenbaby" Heralds Brave New World of Reproductive Gene Editing

Wasn't Frankenstein a monster?

I don't want to read it, but I can't look away. I skim the words fast, as if that will make them less hurtful. A few phrases jump out: *illegal experiment, criminal charges, crossing an ethical line, the first genetically modified child.*

The last phrase jogs a memory from a few months ago—the day we went to the Natural History Museum, when we passed some protesters who were chanting against GMOs. I had never seen people in Garrison parading around with colored signs and yelling about anything.

If those people were that pissed about genetically modified *food*, how would they feel about a genetically modified *human*? Would they think I'm really that different from them? So different I shouldn't have been born? Would no one want to be friends with me if they knew?

I stare at my fingers. They're long and bony with short round nails. Nothing special. I touch my cheek. It's soft and cool. Same as any other cheek. I don't *feel* genetically modified, whatever that means. I feel like a regular person. But maybe something poisonous is running through my blood.

For the first time, my mom's frustrating behavior clicks.

All this time that I've been mad at her for staying at home like a loner, for not showing up to my soccer games and recitals, it's not just that *she* didn't want to be discovered. She didn't want *me* to be.

A name at the end of the article catches my eye.

> Dr. Ethan Abrams, director of the Bioethics Department at Columbia University's Mailman School of Public Health, disavows his connection to the child in the strongest terms.
>
> "Let me be clear," he said in an exclusive interview with the *Times* marked by outbursts of raw emotion. "I was betrayed by my wife and her cowboy doctor. That baby was created without my knowledge or consent. I had nothing to do with it."
>
> When asked about the criminal investigation, he said, "What they did breaks norms that have existed since the beginning of time. Human beings are not meant to be manufactured like an assembly line, with spare parts chosen from multiple people. The real victim here is the child who will spend a lifetime paying the price—if not with medical problems, then with social and psychological stigma."

This guy's my dad?

Ouch. Deep breath.

My hands are shaking when I close out of the article. What is the point of going to meet him if he wants nothing to do with me?

Outside the window, the river is flecked with diamonds in the sunlight. I'm annoyed at the peaceful blue sky and the white clouds. If the world were normal, I'd be in school, goofing off with Riley in . . . art class. Ugh. Never mind.

I consider my options: go to the city to try to meet Ethan, or get off the train and go back to an empty home? I wish I could talk to my mom, but she's too sick to help me. I could call the school, ask to talk to Riley, and explain the situation. But then she would call her parents, who would call the cops, and I'd be in even worse trouble.

No, I guess I should stay on the train. Maybe Ethan will change his mind when he sees I'm not a monster. Or maybe he'll blow me off. Worst case, I'll go back home anyway and figure out another plan to free my "dad." And best case, Ethan will help me rescue him, and together we'll stop Jillian once and for all.

* * *

It's almost eleven AM when I get off the subway at Broadway and 168th Street, near Columbia University's School of Public Health. The neighborhood is nothing like Garrison. Store windows are shuttered, litter is all over the streets, and some homeless people are wandering around rattling cups for change. A sketchy guy on the corner watches me run to a steel building behind Presbyterian Hospital.

I rush through the revolving glass doors into a domed building with a very high ceiling. But my relief at being inside soon becomes fresh anxiety. I couldn't be more out of place. Some med students are studying in a lounge behind a glass wall. Two doctors walk by deep in conversation, their high heels clicking on the glossy floor. I catch a few words: *interpretation of the biometric data*. This is clearly a place where important grown-up things are happening. I feel like an extra in the wrong movie. My parents would kill me if they knew where I was.

The receptionist, a woman with chunky black glasses, asks where I'm going, and I tell her I'm here for Dr. Abrams.

Her brown eyes widen. He must not have a lot of young visitors. "Is he expecting you?"

"Um, not really. No."

"I'll call and announce you. What's your name?"

"Abigail." After a pause, I add, "His daughter."

"Oh! I haven't seen you around before." She gestures to the elevators. "Third floor, room 301. I think he's teaching, but he should be back in his office soon."

"Thanks."

The elevator surprisingly goes down instead of up. The dropping ground makes me feel off-balance, possibly headed in the wrong direction. I step into a quiet hallway with no windows and pass several glass office doors until I find the right one. I peek inside, then jump back when I see a man at a desk. My father?

I suddenly feel a wave of guilt. I don't even know if my other dad is okay, and now I'm going behind his back to meet a stranger who might hate me.

My hands are clammy and my heart is hammering, but I'm not turning back now. I'm done living a lie.

I drag myself to the door, hold my breath, and knock.

CLAIRE

As soon as my cab home from the hospital pulls up to the house, I know something's not right. It's Tuesday morning, and both of our cars are in the driveway. Rob must have stayed home all day to take care of Abby instead of picking up his regular shipment of wood from his supplier. But why would neither of them answer my calls?

Maybe they both caught the same bug. Or food poisoning. They're doubled over a toilet, so they can't make it to the phone. I want to muster the energy to be pissed. I want to march in and find them both sick as dogs and feel awash with relief and fury, but mostly relief.

Instead, I walk in to a chilling silence. The house smells stale, like the trash needs to be taken out. Abby's pink sneakers, which she always kicks off in the foyer, are gone. I expect to see Rob's keys and wallet on the console table, but the surface is bare. Yet both the cars are outside. They *must* be home.

I cup my hands around my mouth. "Honey? You guys upstairs?"

I listen for the flush of the toilet, the creak of footsteps. Nothing.

"Hello?" I yell. "Anyone home?"

Hearing my panicked voice echo through the empty house confirms that this whole situation isn't just in my head. This isn't some paranoid fantasy I indulged to escape the hospital. This is real. My family is missing.

But the *cars* . . . They must be home.

I spring into action, searching one room after the next. Kitchen, living room, dining room, bathroom. Taking the stairs two at a time.

Guest room, Abby's room, our room, bathrooms. No trace of them. In desperation, I start whipping open closet doors. Twisted scenarios knock on the door of my consciousness, but I refuse to let them in. I'm the bouncer of my own sanity. If I don't keep out the worst thoughts, they'll paralyze me, and what help would I be then?

Once I've gone through every closet, searched the backyard, checked under the couches and beds, behind the shower curtains, and in the garden shed, I finally think to search the cars.

Our Honda Accord is locked, and since I don't have the keys, I peer through the windows. The same old travel coffee mug is in the cup holder and abandoned sweater in the back seat. And to think that just yesterday, Rob and I were inside driving to the hospital and our biggest problem was my mental health.

I peek underneath the car, and that's when I see it: a dirty black box about two inches long and three inches wide, stuck on the undercarriage with a magnetic strip. It takes considerable strength to rip the thing off. A cryptic symbol is printed on the back: a red Wi-Fi signal with a blue arrow. A green light is blinking on the display. I quickly pick off the cover and remove two double A batteries. Then the light goes dark.

What the . . . ?

Someone has been tracking our car.

Jillian. That fucking bitch. It has to be.

Before I lose my nerve, I dial the three digits on my cell that I have spent a decade avoiding: 911. If Rob and I end up arrested on our outstanding warrants, so be it. I'd rather spend the rest of my life in prison than find him and Abby in a ditch somewhere because I was too cautious to seek help.

When the dispatcher answers, I shout at him in frantic, stumbling language.

"Slow down," he interrupts. "Are you in immediate danger?"

"My family is missing," I explain, trying to control my gasps. "I found a tracking device on my car and I know who did it; she's a psychopath; you have to find them!"

"Take a breath. When did you last hear from them?"

"Yesterday. But I was out of town, and today my daughter didn't show up at school, and my husband is unreachable."

"Can you describe them?"

"My husband is tall and thin, with salt-and-pepper hair, and my daughter is eleven, with wavy red hair and freckles. She wears pink sneakers . . ." My voice breaks. "Please hurry. They could be anywhere."

"Can you describe the perp you believe is involved?"

I'm pacing on the driveway, kicking up rocks and dust at every turn, but now I close my eyes and envision Jillian at the museum. "She's about five five, I think, with cropped red hair . . . very fit . . ." I think the word *pretty*, but can't bear to say it.

"Okay," the dispatcher says. "I'll need to take your information for the report, and then I'll send this over to the Cold Spring PD to open a case."

"Thank you," I breathe. "Will they start quickly?"

"Right away, ma'am. There's no waiting period when a child goes missing. We'll give you an update as soon as we can."

After I hang up, a grenade of pure venom explodes inside me. I imagine myself slitting Jillian's throat, scratching out her eyes, strangling her with my bare hands. If we ever meet again, nothing will stop me from killing her.

JILLIAN

Watching Abby disappear into the forest is crushing. There's no way around it. But once she's out of sight, I make a snap decision: we need to cut our losses and get a move on.

When I make it back to the cottage, I venture down to the basement, where I handcuffed Rob to her metal cot under threat of the gun as soon as we found her missing. I find him now yanking his arm uselessly against the cuffs, cursing me out. His wrist is ringed with red marks from his violent attempts to dislodge himself. But when he sees that I'm returning solo, he freezes, and his eyes fill with fresh panic.

"She got away?"

"Yep. Which is why we have to leave. She's a liability now."

"Are you serious? She could die out there! She has no food, no water, nothing!"

"Oh, don't be so dramatic. She'll find her way to a friend's house or something."

Though I'm playing it cool, her abandonment stings. She was an important part of the plan. Without her scans and blood work, our study will suffer. But thanks to my other data, we still have a shot at world fame. It's for this reason, despite my disappointment, that I allow myself a twinge of admiration for her escape. I recognize a little of myself in that girl. I always used to wonder: would she turn out selfish and stupid like Claire, or brave and clever like me? Now that I know the answer, she's gone.

"I'll be right back," I tell him. "I'm going to pack the car."

He jerks against the cuffs, calling me a heinous name, but I don't have time to fight.

If Abby goes to the cops, or someone calls 911 after seeing her alone, the police could show up any minute.

Rob is yelling at me to let him go, but I ignore him as I grab the suitcase I've been prepping for days and haul it out to the car. At some point on the journey, we'll have to stop and buy him some essentials. It would be too risky to swing by his house in case the cops have already found her and brought her home.

Once my suitcase is in the trunk, I pack us a cooler of turkey sandwiches for the drive, even remembering to go easy on the mayo and add a sliced pickle the way he used to like. He has it *so* good with me. I wonder when he'll come to his senses. And stop yelling, for God's sake.

When everything's ready to go, a notification pings my phone from my GPS app. I almost ignore it because I'm so used to seeing the updates. Anytime Claire's car goes anywhere, my app lets me know her location within fifteen feet, thanks to advanced satellite data. The whole thing was ridiculously simple to set up. After I started working at the Garrison school, I accessed Abby's file for her address. Then one evening after midnight, I swung by their house and snapped a discreet two-inch magnetic tracking device under each car in the driveway. In less than sixty seconds, I was out of there.

From then on, I've been able to watch both her and Rob's movements from afar. It's come in quite handy. I'm about to silence the notification out of habit when I realize that Claire is at the mental hospital. I shouldn't be getting an alert about her movement at all.

I swipe open the app. CONNECTION LOST. BATTERY FAILURE.

Wait, what?

I checked the battery twice before installing it. The thing was brand spanking new, guaranteed to last for six months. It's only been a couple of weeks. Either the company is full of shit, or . . . someone disabled the device. Someone who noticed Rob and Abby were missing. *Fuck.*

Gun in hand, I rush to the basement to release him.

"Time to go!" I announce. He's about to yell again when he sees it and goes silent. I need him to get the message: we can't afford his belligerence. I unlock his cuffs with one hand while tightly gripping the gun in the other.

When the cuffs come loose, I aim the gun square at his chest.

"Hands up," I command.

He doesn't mess around.

"You first," I say. "I'll follow you."

He walks in front of me to the car, because I'm no idiot.

"What about Abby?" he demands, staring ahead.

"I told you, she'll be fine."

"You don't know that."

"I trust her to figure it out."

A siren wails in the distance. It could be an ambulance. Or a cop.

I open the passenger door for him. "Get in."

He obeys. I climb in the driver's side and place my gun in the pocket of the door. The siren grows louder. "Give me your wrists," I demand. "Hurry."

When he extends them, I quickly snap the cuffs into place.

"Oh, come on," he protests. "Is this really necessary?"

I peel out of the driveway without buckling my seat belt. "I think so."

"Whoa!" he exclaims as I careen down the winding road, throwing us against our seats. I don't breathe until we're clear out of the forest. We pass a shrieking cop car that flies by in the opposite direction. It doesn't slow down for us. It's going after someone else.

Once it's out of sight, I exhale.

"We made it."

I smile at him, but he's monitoring the window. His restrained hands move as one unit toward the door handle.

"What are you doing?"

"I need to find my daughter." He pulls on the handle; as we

accelerate toward the highway entrance, the door cracks open and wind roars in.

"Stop!" I crush the gas, merging onto the ramp. "You're going to want to stay."

He sticks one ankle out. "Never."

"Are you sure?" I glance over at him, wanting to see his face in this moment, a moment I will remember forever. "Because we have a son."

ABBY

The stranger who is my father approaches the glass door to his office. He's short, a little overweight, and a lot older than I expected, with graying hair, slouched shoulders, and wrinkles around his eyes. In his black suit and shiny black shoes, he looks like someone who is used to being in charge. But there's also something handsome and gentle about his face that reminds me of the good guys in old movies. I want to trust him, but I'm afraid.

When he pokes his head out, his confusion is clear. He looks up and down the hallway for my parents.

"Hi. Can I help you?"

"Um, hi." I wave awkwardly. "I'm Abigail."

"Hi, Abigail." His smile is polite, but impatient. "Are you lost, or . . . ?"

"I'myourdaughter." I say it fast like one long word, then squeeze my eyes shut.

When nothing happens, I open my eyes. He's staring at me as if I'm an alien making contact with Earth. I search his face for happiness, or hatred, or *some* sign of his feelings, but all I see is disbelief.

"You're . . . you're not . . . ?"

"The three-parent baby? Yeah, that's me."

"Oh my God." He stumbles backward into an armchair. "Oh my *God.*"

I walk into the office, even though he hasn't invited me in. "Um, yeah, my mom kept it a big secret. I actually just found out."

"You just . . . ?" He blinks several times. "I'm sorry, I wasn't expecting . . ."

"It's okay." I clear my throat. "I didn't know about you either."

I stand in the middle of the office while he continues to stare, his eyes traveling from my pink sneakers up to my cutoff shorts and dirty tank top. God, this is weird. What did I expect, that he'd tell me he regrets the mean things he said in the newspaper, that he tried to find me, that he's sorry for missing out on my life?

Yeah, I secretly hoped for all that—I did.

And now I feel like an idiot. Worse—an *unwanted* idiot. I should have known better. I start for the door.

"If you're busy, I can go."

"No, no!" He runs over to another armchair and clears a pile of paper off it. "Please, sit down. This is just such a surprise; I didn't think . . ." He shakes his head, slowly smiling for the first time.

I settle into the huge chair, my feet dangling above the floor. "Didn't think what?"

"Well, I didn't think you were even alive."

I gasp. "Really?"

"Things were such a mess back then. I figured the science wasn't ready, so you didn't make it."

My heart soars. He wouldn't search for me if he thought I was dead.

"Well . . ." I smile shyly. *Here I am.*

"And you're okay? You're . . . normal?"

I laugh. "I think so. I mean, unless you count my obsession with One Direction."

"Wow." He leans back, still keeping his eyes on me. "What about physically?"

"I haven't been sick in years."

"Really?" He frowns. "I guess that scoundrel knew what he was doing?" His voice rises like he doesn't trust the answer.

I puff up my chest. "That scoundrel raised me." For the moment, my anger melts away, because he's the only father I've ever known.

Ethan's mouth opens in surprise. "He *lives* with you? Where?"

"For my whole life, in Garrison. He and my mom are together."

This seems to shake him up. He gazes off into space, and his lips curve down.

"I came because I need your help," I tell him.

"What for?"

"He's in deep trouble, but I can't call the police, so I came here. I thought maybe you could help me? Since you're my real dad."

The word *dad* sends a jolt through me. I'm sure he feels it, too. We're two complete strangers but connected in the closest way. I want to find some physical proof of our relationship, so I can say *that's where I got it*, but so far nothing jumps out. His eyes are brown, not blue; his skin tone is olive, not pale; and he doesn't have a dimple like me.

"What kind of trouble?" he asks. "Can't your mom help?"

"No, she's in the hospital."

He sucks in a breath. "What happened?"

"She's having some mental issues and went to get treatment yesterday. Then, me and my dad were basically kidnapped by the woman who helped create me, Mrs. Mi—I mean, Jillian."

He mutters darkly, "I remember her well."

"She forced us to go to her house, and I snuck into the bathroom, but she stole my phone before I could call the police. Then she locked me in her basement all night."

"Are you serious? That's insane!"

"I know. But I got away and came here after I found out about you." I think back to the fight I heard last night. "He might be hurt. She has a gun."

"Jesus." He glances at the cuts on my arms and shoulders, which have already scabbed up. "Is that why you're all cut up?"

"Yeah. I broke a window. But could you help me rescue him? If I go to the police, he could be arrested." I swallow hard as I imagine him stuck in that horrible cottage with her. "I don't know who else to ask."

"You do realize that *I'm* the one who called for his arrest a long time ago, right?"

My neck gets hot. I wonder if I have made a terrible mistake.

"Please." A tear leaks out despite my effort not to cry. "He doesn't deserve to be punished for my birth. Does he?"

Ethan says nothing. His silence can mean only one thing.

"Thanks a lot." Angrily, I jump to my feet. "Never mind."

"Wait." He stops me by the door. "Let me get my car. I'll take you there."

"Just so you can turn him in?"

"No. To help."

"Why? You think I should never have been born."

I storm past him into the hallway, fighting a full-on sob.

"Abigail, wait."

"Why?" I snap. "Forget it."

"I'm sorry. Maybe I did think that once, a long time ago, but I don't anymore. Not after meeting you."

I hesitate; I want to believe him so badly.

"What's done is done," he says. "I'm not sure who's right or wrong anymore, but you're my kid, you need my help, and I don't want to turn my back on you again."

I'm still not sure whether to trust him, but I don't have a lot of options, so I accept his help. He cancels his afternoon class, citing a "family emergency," and ten minutes later we're on the road in a Toyota Camry he keeps parked in a garage for weekend trips. His phone's GPS says the drive to Jillian's address will take fifty-five minutes. I hope we won't be too late. My mind plays out awful scenes about what could be happening—what if he's bleeding out? Or being tortured and drugged, then stuffed into her car . . .

As Ethan merges onto the Palisades Parkway, I roll down my window for some fresh air. "Can you drive a little faster?" Luckily, traffic is light.

"This good?" He speeds up a bit, but not quite enough. It will be a miracle if I manage not to have a panic attack on this drive. Would he think I was a freak then? Would he change his mind?

I try to focus on the task ahead. "What will we do when we get there?"

"I was just thinking the same thing." Keeping his eyes on the road, he pops open the glovebox. "See in there?"

I pull out a black spray bottle with a red trigger.

"Pepper spray," he explains. "I carry it when I go hiking. It's a pretty decent weapon if the target isn't expecting it."

"So, you'll just, like, walk in and spray her?"

"I'll feel it out. But if I can disarm her quickly, then Nash can go free, and we can call the cops. This woman *kidnapped* you, after all. She's the one who should be arrested."

"Okay." My stomach relaxes a tiny bit. We have a plan. There's an adult on my side—I think. I don't have to do this all by myself.

I feel a sudden pang of loneliness for my mom. Thinking of her in the hospital reminds me of Colton . . . Ethan's kid, too. It's so weird to think about her being married to this guy, having a kid with him, a family before I ever existed.

I wonder if he was as broken about Colton's death as she was.

"What was my brother like?" I ask.

Ethan draws a fast breath. I've said something forbidden.

"Sorry, we don't have to talk about him."

"No, it's fine." He gives me the barest smile. "It's just that no one's asked me about him for years. Everyone else has moved on."

"Not my mom. That's why she's in the hospital now."

His smile disappears. "I'm sorry to hear that."

There's no ring on his left hand. I guess he's not remarried.

"Do you still hate her?" I ask.

I don't know why the answer matters, but it does.

He sighs, switching hands on the wheel. "It's complicated."

"What does that mean?"

"You really want to know?"

I shrug, but the truth is, I'm dying of curiosity.

"Your mother broke my heart," he says flatly. "I didn't expect to lose her too."

We sit in silence. It reminds me of being at a funeral. People are together, but no one talks because it would interrupt someone else's precious memories.

Eventually, he breathes out long and slow, forcing out some tired grief.

Then a slight smile tugs at his lips. "He was so full of life, your brother. That was the ironic part."

I perk up. "Like how?"

"He loved animals and nature. He loved to be outside, and he could tell you all about space. He read constantly. And he loved making up stories." Ethan pauses. "All his fantasies had one thing in common."

"What?"

"They were always about a kid discovering another world, like on some other planet, or under the sea, or in his own backyard."

"Did they have happy endings?"

"They did. They always ended with happily ever after."

"Not like in real life."

His voice goes quiet. "No."

"I'm sad I never got to meet him," I say, surprising myself. I've spent a long time being jealous that my mother would never let him go. I've always wondered why she loved him more. But hearing what he was like . . . I probably would have liked him.

"How old are you?" Ethan asks. "Around eleven?"

"Just turned eleven in February."

"Amazing. You've already lived three years longer than him."

Neither of us says it, but I bet we're both thinking the same thing: *Thanks to my dad.* The only one I knew before today.

* * *

When we turn onto the dirt lane leading to Jillian's cottage, my panic spikes again. The sun is high overhead and the air outside is warm, but I'm literally shivering as he pulls up her driveway. And then I realize: her car is gone.

"They already left." A sob rises in my throat. "We're too late."

"Are you sure?" He kills the engine and hops out with the pepper spray. "Stay here."

I watch him circle the house, peer in the windows, try the door handle. The place is dark. When he comes back, he mentions the broken window I smashed out. "That's the only opening. But there's a ton of glass."

"I'm not going back in there. They're obviously gone."

"Yep." He walks around to the driver's side. "Now what?"

I try to come up with another idea. The only other place I can think of is my house. She wouldn't go back to school, but maybe she would take him to get his stuff before running away somewhere else. I suggest it to Ethan, and he agrees. It's better than nothing.

I'm also starving and have been wearing the same clothes for two straight days. If nothing else, at least I'll take a quick shower and grab something to eat.

The ride home takes ten minutes, and when we pull up to the house, both cars are in the driveway, just like we left them. Everything looks so normal, it's hard to believe my life is totally out of control.

Ethan parks on the curb and we head to the garage, where I punch in the code on the security panel outside.

The door groans. I sneak underneath without waiting for it to open all the way.

In the pitch black, I hear a familiar creak.

The inside door is opening, too.

Oh my God. I immediately drop to the ground, sure that I'm about to come face-to-face with Jillian and her gun.

The lights flip on. And then I hear a shriek of joy.

It's my mom.

CLAIRE

At first, I'm terrified that my daughter is another fantasy conjured by my broken mind. How else to explain her sudden appearance?

But she's crouching in fear, shielding her face, and there are scratches all over her arms. None of my delusions have been this dark.

She winces, peeking through her hands. "Mom?"

I run over and lift her off the ground, cradling her head in my palm. "Oh honey." I stroke her hair. "It's okay, it's just me."

Rage flows hot through my veins. *That psycho hurt my little girl.*

She buries her face in my neck. "I thought you were in the hospital!"

"Not anymore. I was worried about you."

Before I can ask about her scrapes, someone nearby coughs. A man. I glance up, expecting to see my husband. Instead, this time, I *am* imagining things.

It's Ethan.

My vision distorts. I feel like I'm swimming upstream, my movements labored, my breathing stunted. The air is a rip current sucking me under. My pulse thunders in my ears.

I blink and set Abby down. He's still there. His presence is incomprehensible here in my garage, next to the stacked bins of her old schoolwork and scrapbooks—memories he knows nothing about. I size him up, unsure if we're still enemies at war, or merely two older and wearier people who once shared a tragic life.

It takes a minute to recover my voice.

"What are you doing here?"

"I found him," Abby says.

I whirl on her. "*What?*"

Ethan walks toward us but stops a few feet away and clasps his hands. It strikes me as a sign of respect.

"She showed up at my office this morning. It was quite the shock." He shakes his head with a faint smile that quells my fear: he apparently no longer resents her existence. His vengefulness of the past has given way to something softer, but maybe no less painful; he regards me with what seems like sadness.

"I told him what happened," says Abby. "And he agreed to help me, because, you know, he's my real dad." An edge creeps in her voice that sounds accusatory, but I ignore it.

"How did you know about him?" I demand.

"I found out last night."

"How? What *happened*?" A looming dread is gathering in the pit of my stomach. I quickly scan the garage and the driveway behind Ethan, but Rob is nowhere to be found.

Abby proceeds to tell me that Jillian kidnapped them both after posing as her art teacher at school and luring them to her house.

I am completely taken aback. Once again, Jillian has me beat. Breaking in like a regular criminal would be too straightforward. Her weapon of choice is manipulation. She's a virtuoso, and she played us all.

"It was really bad." Abby's voice quivers. "I wasn't sure I was ever going to get out."

"Oh, baby. I'm so sorry." My anger intensifies, if that is even possible. "Why didn't Daddy protect you?"

"She had a gun."

"Oh, no." My horror drags me to the ground. "No."

Ethan approaches me and bends down.

"Look, if there's anything I can do . . . ? I heard you're sick again."

"You don't have to stay. But thank you for bringing her home."

"I'm staying. You guys need help."

"But you hate us," I protest, unable to keep the suspicion out of my voice. "Why would you want to help?" The last I heard, nine or ten years ago, Ethan was still campaigning for our arrest, trying to reenergize the feds' abandoned witch hunt.

"That was a long time ago. A lot's changed. I could explain . . ."

I hesitate. There's so much unfinished business between us, I don't know where to start. But now is not the time to hash things out. The man I love is in harm's way, and nothing else matters until he is home safe and sound.

"Go get my phone," I tell Abby. "It's on the kitchen counter." When she runs into the house, I return my attention to Ethan and fold my arms.

"Give me one reason I should trust you."

"Because I've never stopped loving you."

I am speechless. He averts his gaze, waiting for me to end the silence.

"Um." I cough. "I wasn't expecting that."

"I know. But I've spent all these years wondering what happened to you, and now I know he was a big reason you ended up okay."

"He's the *only* reason," I correct him.

Ethan smiles. "I can't believe we have a daughter. A few hours ago, I thought that was literally impossible."

Abby dashes back into the garage with my cell. "Here. Are you gonna call the cops?"

"I have a better idea."

"Oh really?" Her face clouds with doubt. Given my recent struggles, I can understand. But she doesn't realize that before she was born, I was the best damn investigative reporter around. I still remember one trick of the trade: build on the trust you already have. Information will follow.

I call the school, thinking of Carla, the sweet, bubbly secretary I've known since Abby was in kindergarten. As the phone rings, I picture the messy watercolors taped up in her office like prized artworks. She is surrounded by a world of innocence that could work in my favor.

"Garrison Union Free School," she answers. "How may I help you?"

Her singsong tone contrasts with my somber one. "Carla, hi, it's Abby's mom."

"Oh, *hi*." Her voice lowers to match mine. "We were worried about Abby. Is she feeling any better?"

"No, unfortunately. As you know, I was out of town, but I came home when I heard she was sick."

"I'm sorry. Is there anything we can do?"

"Actually, yes. Last night, Abby had dinner with the new art teacher, Mrs. Miller, and it seems they both came down with food poisoning. They're both throwing up and dehydrated, and we might take them to the hospital."

"Oh no! Oh my gosh, that's terrible! In fact, Mrs. Miller did call in sick today, too. We had to scramble to get a substitute."

"Do you know if she has an emergency contact? Anyone we could call for her?"

"Let me check her file; hang on." The line switches to classical music. Abby and Ethan watch me pace around the garage with the phone on speaker. *Come on.*

Finally, Carla returns. "There is someone she listed: Sharon Hendricks at River Road Academy. Ready for the number?"

"Go ahead."

I repeat the digits aloud for Ethan to note on his phone.

"Good luck!" Carla says. "I hope they feel better soon!"

"Me too. Thanks so much."

After I hang up, Abby wrinkles her nose. "What's River Road Academy?"

"Isn't it that fancy prep school? Ethan, can you Google it?"

He reads aloud from the website, which pictures a sprawling colonial manor overlooking a vast lawn. "*A world-class educational institution dedicated to shaping the next generation of thinkers and leaders* . . . Maybe she has a sister who works there?"

"True." The woman Sharon does share her real last name.

"Call them." He hands me his iPhone, which is already primed with the number. I put it on speaker.

"Hi," I say when the receptionist answers. "Can I please speak with Sharon Hendricks?"

"Headmaster Hendricks is in a meeting right now. Can I take a message?"

"Um, can you tell her it's a family emergency?"

I'm swinging blindly, but my gambit appears to work.

"Hang on."

A full minute passes before a new voice catches me off guard.

"Hello?" It's husky and British, belonging to a much older woman. I mentally cross *sister* off the list. "Who's this?" she asks.

I clear my throat. "I'm a friend of Jillian's."

"My daughter doesn't have any friends."

Daughter catches me by surprise. Jillian's a lone wolf—a rabid one. I can't imagine her as someone's child.

"Well, unfortunately, she's missing," I explain. "And I really need to find her. Can you help?"

"There must be some misunderstanding. I just talked to her, and she's on her way here now."

"Oh. Okay. Sorry to bother you."

I end the call and hand Ethan back his phone.

"Let's go." I race into the house and grab my purse.

"It's in Rhinebeck about an hour away," Ethan calls. "Shouldn't we notify the authorities first?"

"No!" I rush back with the car keys. "If they get there before us, she might not even stop at all. She might just keep on driving."

"Then what?" Abby cries. "We have no idea where they could go next!"

"Come on!" I sprint to the car, brimming with more energy than I've felt in months.

"Wait." Ethan runs up behind me as I reach the car. "Should I—do you want me to—?" He points at my keys with concern. I get it. My relapse is not something we can ignore. If I suffer a delusion while driving, it could be disastrous.

Reluctantly, I hand him the keys. As we start out toward 9 North, I imagine Rob somewhere up ahead on the same highway, at Jillian's mercy, racing toward some nightmare fate without us.

"Hurry," I beg Ethan. "We could already be too far behind."

"What if we are?" Abby demands, thrusting herself between the two front seats.

"Put your seat belt on! We'll figure it out."

I don't tell her what I'm really thinking: we may never see him again.

JILLIAN

"What do you mean, *we have a son*?" Rob's face is sickly white.

I reach across the console and take his sweaty hand, which is still in the cuffs. "His name is Charlie. Charles Robert. After you."

"You were *pregnant* when I left?" His guilt is too enjoyable to deter, so I stay quiet. I let his horror mount, let him believe for a second that he skipped out on his own child when he abandoned me. I wish I had been pregnant back then: knocked up, left alone, and unjustly sent to prison. Who else would deserve more sympathy?

"Wait." He's cringing with remorse, taking my silence as a yes. "Seriously? You were pregnant, and I didn't even know?"

"No," I admit. Charlie's too young to pass for eleven. "I had him later, after."

Relief smooths his brow. "Then he's not mine. That's impossible."

"Actually, I think he is."

He rolls his eyes. "You really do live in a fantasy world, huh?"

I ignore the jab. "Remember when we found out that Claire's husband had shitty sperm? And the whole experiment was hinging on us creating viable embryos?"

He's confused by my pivot. "Yeah . . ."

At the speed I'm driving, I can't study his face, but that's okay. I don't want to make eye contact when he learns my biggest secret of all, the one thing in my past that's reframed the purpose of my existence.

"Did you ever stop to wonder why we got two perfect embryos?"

“The odds were low, but not impossible.”

“Well, that night, you came back to my apartment . . .” I wait to let his memory fill in the details. He shifts uncomfortably in his seat.

“So?” he says.

“So, I saved the condom and went back to the lab when you left. Your sperm was still fresh, and it was freaking good.”

I realize he’s going to puke the same time he does: too late. We’re both stupefied by the yellow bile that flies out of his mouth and saturates his lap, filling the car with a revolting stench.

“Goddamn it,” I mutter. The stink is unbearable. I spot an exit coming up and veer off the highway while he rolls down his window, hanging his head out as far as he can. On the side of the road, the golden arches of a McDonald’s beckon us. I pull into the drive-through and ask for a bunch of napkins, then park the car while I clean up the mess. He’s too dazed to move. He hasn’t yet said a word.

Despite his aversion to my touch, I can’t help noticing how intimate it feels to wipe his legs and dab his mouth. Plus, the bandage on his ear is still a bloody mess, since I never got around to changing it. I replace it carefully with the supplies in my first aid kit while he glares out the windshield.

“Better?” I say, after I finish my handiwork.

He opens his mouth, expelling not vomit this time, but fury. “You stole my *motherfucking sperm*.”

“I did it for you. I know it’s hard to believe, but it’s true.”

“Are you actually insane?”

“I get how it seems, but we’d worked too hard to let everything go to waste.” I’m desperate to make him understand; any hope of a reconnection depends on it. “If none of the embryos had made it, that would have been the end of the whole project. But you never would’ve done this—you’re too honest. So I did it for you. And it worked.”

His face is hard as stone. “And I banked the one left over.”

“Yep. After you disappeared but before I got locked up, I went to the cryobank and paid up front for a long-term storage plan. A couple years later, I returned and took the embryo in a thermos of liquid

nitrogen to a nearby fertility clinic for my transfer. Charlie was born eleven months after my release."

"Why?" He finally looks at me. "Why would you have a child?"

"It's complicated." How do I convey to him the certainty I felt all those years ago that I was meant to bring our one last embryo to life? That at first my conviction was rooted in ambition and rebellion—continuing the experiment I was punished for seemed like poetic justice—but the second I got pregnant, those feelings morphed into something deeper and purer—the fierce desire to be a mother. I was twenty-seven and alone—ghosted by him, blacklisted by my field, rejected by my own parents who couldn't tolerate my disgrace. I wanted someone to love, who loved me back. I wanted a new reason to live—someone who would never give up on me.

"He's a wonderful kid," is all I say. "It was the best decision I ever made."

This is an oversimplification, but it sounds better than the truth: yes, I love Charlie, of course I do, but there are times when his uncanny resemblance to Claire and her son turns my stomach. And the rocky ride of single motherhood has not been the cozy union I'd envisioned. Between those tedious early years and sleepless nights, the lack of help, and the relentless hustle to make ends meet as a former felon, relying on online tutoring gigs, I was running ragged on my best days.

When Charlie was two, my dad passed away from a massive heart attack, and my mom, alone with her grief, let go of her anger enough to let us live with her in Rhinebeck, where we've been for the last five years. As a perk, Charlie gets to attend my family's fancy private school for free. Without her support, we'd be lost—and she never lets us forget it.

Saying good-bye to her will be harder for Charlie, but I'm sure that an even better life awaits us once we make it to Canada. Then we can publicize our breakthrough without fear of retribution. Charlie's periodic scans, genetic testing, and tissue biopsies show that he is exceedingly healthy—living proof of our success.

"Wait," Rob suddenly starts. "Does this mean Abby is mine, too?"

My smile is triumphant. "You're welcome."

"But then why did you make me tell her about Ethan back there?"

I shrug. "The truth is, you'd have to test the kids to be sure. All I know is that I held back two of the hybrid eggs on the day of the protocol, just in case my plan to seduce you worked. I told you those eggs were damaged, but really I just set them aside so I could go back and fertilize them with your sperm from the condom that night. I had to try, because we suspected that Ethan's sperm would only make duds. To keep our numbers the same, I trashed two of the original specimens and replaced them in the incubator with yours. Then when you went in to test them all later, you moved the petri dishes around and I lost track of which was which. But lo and behold, we ended up with two perfect embryos. So I can't say both kids are yours for sure, but doesn't it seem likely?"

"This is outrageous." He's on the verge of tears. "We don't even know if Abby's okay."

"She will be. I wish she was coming to meet her brother, though."

"*That's* where we're going?"

"I've always told Charlie that one day, when I find his father, we'll start a new life together. He asks about you all the time."

Rob is dumbfounded. "He does?"

"Yeah." I feel a gush of nervous excitement, like a girl about to ask her crush on a date. "Ready to go meet your son?"

* * *

River Road Academy rests on an enormous plot of land made up of rolling hills, lush trees, and impeccably manicured fields. The school is the gem of the Hudson River Valley, the K–12 equivalent of Harvard, and my family's legacy for three generations. Since my father's death, my mother has run the place alone. Its name is synonymous across the Northeast with prestige, ambition, and success; as an alumna myself, it's no wonder I'm an overachiever. Anything less would be intolerable.

When we pull up to the entrance, the lower school is on recess. On the other side of the fence, about a hundred kids in navy uniforms and white sneakers are running around the vast field, kicking soccer balls and lounging at picnic tables.

I finally unlock Rob's handcuffs. "Don't try anything stupid," I tell him as we get out of the car. "There's a guard watching the whole campus on eight different video screens."

He nods and rubs his sore wrists.

In the fresh air, the bright notes of the children's laughter ring out like chimes. I spot Charlie right away. He's hovering near the net in scoring position, hollering at another kid to kick him the ball.

I point him out as we approach the gate. "There's our boy."

We both stand and watch as he receives the ball, maneuvers around a defensive player, and kicks it straight into the net. He pumps his fist with a grin, and his friends cheer him with high fives.

A stab of guilt pierces my pride. I'm about to wrench him out of this safe, sun-kissed life and hurl us straight into the unknown. But it's for the best. Rob and I have no career future otherwise. You can't be expected to sacrifice yourself for your child forever, can you?

"That's him?" Rob touches the chain-link fence. I sense him going weak in the knees. "That's my son?"

Instead of the joy I expected, he's breathing too hard. He backs away from the fence—from me.

"What's wrong?"

"He doesn't look like me at all." Rob squints, shading his eyes with his hand. "In fact, he looks exactly like Claire's first child."

"So?" I exhale irritably. This fact has never escaped me. "Why is everything always about Claire?"

He takes another step back, as though I'm a bear trapping him in a standoff.

"You deployed this kid to torment her, didn't you?" he says. "To make her think she was crazy?"

I cross my arms. "Okay, now *you* sound crazy."

"You wanted to move in on us without opposition. God, I literally drove her to the mental hospital. I *insisted*."

"Oh, please. Like Claire hasn't been a mental case from day one."

"How did you get him to taunt her and run away?" His voice is dripping with disdain. "Did you bribe him or something?"

I roll my eyes, although he isn't far off. Charlie loves hide-and-seek. Each time we played the game, I took him out for ice cream afterward.

Rob takes his eyes off me to search the grounds, possibly looking for an escape, but we are surrounded by acres of grass. Perched up on a hill sits the white school building. Like a castle, it encompasses multiple wings, domes, and upper levels. Behind us, the parking lot leads out through trees back to the highway along the Hudson.

"You have two choices," I tell him. "One, we go to Canada with Charlie, publish our work, resurrect our careers, and be free. Or things can get ugly. I'm sure you want to make it out of here alive. But it's up to you."

He falters. I can't stand his despair, so I march to the security booth at the entrance. I wave to Harold, the longtime guard, who recognizes me and opens the gate.

"That man is coming, too," I inform him, pointing to Rob. "Hurry up," I hiss.

He follows reluctantly as I stride onto the soccer field right up to Charlie, cutting off the kid who has the ball. The other boys freeze midplay.

"Mom?" Charlie says, embarrassed. It doesn't escape my notice that he no longer runs into my arms these days. Instead, he hangs back, with his friends. "Um, we're kinda busy . . ."

"It's time to go. Come on."

"Now?" His lower lip juts out. "Why? Recess isn't over yet!"

"We're going on a trip. I'm sorry, but we have to go."

His voice grows whiny. "In the middle of the day?"

"Yep. Say bye to everyone."

Charlie gives his friends a halfhearted wave, then grudgingly turns to me. That's when he notices Rob on the sidelines. Charlie's nose scrunches up when he asks, "Who's *that* guy?"

I understand my son's repulsion. Rob's white shirt and denim jeans are stained, his ear bandage is bloody yet again, and his greasy curls are sticking out in all directions, like a madman's. Not the best look for their first meeting. And yet, he's still handsome to me.

"He's my friend," I say. "I'll explain when we get in the car."

"He's coming?" Charlie asks, surprised. No one except my mother has ever gone on a trip with us before.

"Yes."

When we approach, Rob squints down at him. I can't tell whether the sun is simply in his eyes, or whether he's trying hard to contain his emotions.

"Hi," he says awkwardly, holding out his hand.

"Hi," Charlie replies, offering him a fist bump instead.

"Rob, Charlie. Charlie, Rob," I jump in.

Rob appears taken aback that I've used his first name instead of *dad*, but he doesn't object. Making a big, momentous introduction feels all wrong under these circumstances. It would surely disappoint Charlie, who's been told all his life that his father is a genius scientist. There will be time to tell him the truth later.

"Now, let's go say good-bye to Grandma," I announce. "Rob, come with us." I don't want to leave him alone in case he tries to make a run for it.

The three of us make our way through the field and up the fairly steep hill to the school building. Inside its marbled foyer, I lead the way to my mother's office, which overlooks the grounds. Charlie drags his feet. I snap at him to cut it out. Rob cooperates without protest, but I don't like the glint in his eyes. Disobedience lurks in his gait.

We enter my mother's waiting area, which consists of a black leather couch and several straight-backed wooden chairs. I instruct Rob to take a seat. I'll be able to watch him through my mother's glass wall. Also, her secretary, Denise, presides over the area from her desk. I call out a hello as we pass her. On second thought, I backtrack to her and lower my voice. "Would you mind making my friend some coffee while I talk to my mom?"

"Of course, honey," she replies. "You got it."

Now he won't be able to sneak out unnoticed.

My mother rises from her desk when Charlie and I walk in. Mature seven-year-old that he is, he still runs into *her* arms. She crouches to receive the full burst of his affection. Improbably, she has become one of Charlie's best friends. They play board games together, construct Lego towers, live-stream rocket launches, visit truck theme parks—you name it. If Charlie is into it, my mother's enthusiasm follows. From the first day they met, their bond was instant and uncomplicated. She doesn't know the truth about his origins; only that I had a romance with his father, who left me.

"What's going on?" she says to me now, in lieu of hello. With her high cheekbones, fine wrinkles, and graceful figure, she could pass for an aging dancer instead of a powerful headmaster. After I went to prison and my father died, she fell into a deep depression, but over the last five years, she's undergone a striking transformation. When Charlie came into the picture, she rediscovered joy.

My throat tightens. As much as my mother and I have clashed over the years, she and Charlie are everything to each other. And we're about to leave her for good.

"There's an opportunity up north," I tell her vaguely. "A big career thing. But we have to leave now."

She frowns. "*Right* now?"

"Yes."

Charlie burrows into her dress. "I don't wanna go!"

"Jillian, he needs to finish up second grade. Whatever it is can wait another few weeks until the summer."

"No, it can't."

"Then you go, and I'll take care of him until you come back, just like it's been. I don't mind."

"Yay!" he shouts, jumping up to rush back outside to recess.

I grab his arm as he whizzes past me. "No." Through the window, I spy Rob taking a cup of coffee from Denise. But he's also asking her something, and she's pointing down the hall, toward the bathrooms. I watch him walk out the door.

"Gotta go," I announce. "Sorry, Mom. I'll stop by the house to get his clothes."

"No!" he yells. "I'm not going!"

I hoist him into my arms, all fifty-one squirming pounds, and stomp out the door. "I'll call you!" I shout over my shoulder at her. My impending sadness is eclipsed by a much more pressing concern—where the hell did Rob go?

"You can't just leave!" my mom shouts at me. "Where are you taking him?"

In the foyer, I find Rob asking a teenage student to borrow her phone. I intercept them and pull him outside, as Charlie continues to whine and hit my chest and my mother screams at us to wait. She follows us outside, so I break into a run, dragging Rob along by the elbow.

"I'm sorry!" I call to her. Then I lower my voice to Rob. "Hurry, or she might recognize you. She still blames you for everything that happened to me."

With a groan, he sprints alongside me down the hill, past the field, toward the parking lot. Then, when we're far enough away that she's given up trailing us, he stops and flashes me a smile—the first I've seen.

"Hey," he says, like a brilliant idea has just occurred to him, "what if you publish the study by yourself? You don't need me! Just take full credit!"

I sigh as we pass Harold at the gate. "Don't you get it?"

"Get what?"

"We're meant to be a family."

Charlie, who's still been wriggling in my arms, abruptly goes limp. "Wait, is he . . . are you my *dad*?"

Rob flinches. "Um, I think so?"

Needless to say, it's not the tender moment I was envisioning.

But there's no time to finesse it, because a silver Honda Accord rolls into the parking lot. It has a slight dent on the front bumper, just like the one I've been tracking on GPS for weeks.

Claire's car.

CLAIRE

What I see on the curb is not possible. My first thought is to curse myself for leaving the hospital, because I have officially lost my mind. If I was in denial before, now I'm ready to surrender.

About twenty feet away, Rob appears to be standing on the sidewalk chatting with Jillian. I don't know whether to feel relief that he's alive, or skeptical of the entire mirage, because in her arms is the fantasy version of Colton.

I blink several times. The boy's golden hair shines in the sun and he's perched on her hip with one arm around her neck, like he belongs there. Rob's got a bandage on his ear and looks haggard, but otherwise seems unharmed. As our car approaches, we capture Jillian's attention first. She looks at me through the windshield with unmitigated horror, her mouth forming a silent *O*.

Abby rolls down her window with a shriek. "Dad!"

The second Ethan parks, she jumps out and makes a beeline for him. Never have I seen an expression of such elation on his face. Laughing, he scoops her up high. So he is real. He's alive. Thank God. He spots me in the car and grins in surprise.

Jillian shifts the boy to her other hip, or so it appears. I fixate on his plump cheeks, reveling in my familiar hallucination while also willing it to pass. But no matter how much I rub my eyes, he remains.

"Is it just me," Ethan says, "or is that kid the spitting image of our son?"

"What?"

"I mean, it's uncanny, right?"

Something clicks internally that compels me to rip off my seat belt and scramble out of the car. I'm overwhelmed by the desire to touch this bizarre doppelgänger, to verify his existence and my own sanity, even if it means coming face-to-face with the woman I've avoided for a decade.

"Back off!" she screams as I run toward them, but her voice sounds hollow and small. With my family safe, I have nothing left to fear.

The moment I make eye contact with the boy, I instantaneously realize two things: he is *not* Colton—his blue eyes are lighter, like Abby's—and he doesn't know me at all. As I reach the sidewalk, he flinches, and Jillian leaps back like I might try to snatch him.

She yells at me, but I barely hear her over my own pulse. How do I make sense of this new reality in which such a child exists? Seeing his face up close is like coming home—and I don't even know his name.

I turn to Rob in speechless confusion.

He nods, tight-lipped—an apology. I'm not crazy after all. But there's something else in his expression that I don't understand. A hesitation, some unspoken distress.

With Abby still clinging to him, he pulls me into a hug.

"My God," he mutters. "I thought I might never see you guys again."

Over his shoulder, I notice Jillian sneering at us. The boy asks to be put down, but instead she breaks into a sprint across the parking lot.

"Wait!" I cry, extricating myself from Rob and running after them. For some reason, I can't bear to let him slip away again.

"Harold!" she screams, waving one arm. "Help!" She motions frantically at me. "Hurry!"

I look around, unsure what's happening. A weathered security guard comes lumbering toward me from his post at the front gate. "Stop right there!" he shouts to me.

But I can't. I won't, because a short distance ahead, Jillian reaches her car and opens the passenger door. Let the guard shoot if he dares. I charge after her. She puts the boy in and fastens his belt, but before she can slam the door, I sidestep her and throw myself at his side.

She seizes a fistful of my hair and jerks my head back—hard.

"Get away from him!"

My neck cramps in pain. I teeter off-balance as two much larger hands grab me under the armpits and drag me away. I try to struggle and kick, but it's no use; the guard's strength dwarfs mine. He pins my arms and pushes me down to my knees. Cold metal handcuffs clamp down on my wrists. I feel them clicking into place when Rob's booming voice rises above the chaos: "Let her go!"

I see him rushing toward us with his hands up.

"No!" Jillian screams. "She's harassing my son!"

"He's *my* son," Rob says, incredibly. Then he points at Jillian. "And that's not his real mother."

The guard freezes, bewildered. "Then who is?"

Rob's eyes meet mine. "You are."

JILLIAN

I look over my shoulder as Claire wobbles on her knees. Behind her, Harold hesitates over the cuffs. "Uh, this doesn't sound like my business."

"Harold!" My heart is beating wildly. "You know me!"

Rob kneels in front of Claire. "He's yours. That's why he looks so much like Colton."

"I don't understand." She struggles against the cuffs, and Harold idiotically unlocks them. Rob helps her to her feet. Dazed, she staggers toward me. "You have to let me see him."

My first instinct is to take off, but when I turn my attention back to the car, Charlie is crawling across the driver's seat to escape out the other side.

"Get back here!" I grab his ankle as he grabs my door handle.

"I don't wanna go!" he cries, petrified.

Claire is encroaching, and this time, no one is stopping her. I tug him back by the leg, and that's when I notice a silver handle poking out the door's side pocket. My gun. I'd almost forgotten about it.

I lunge over Charlie to snatch it, then slide out, plant my feet, and turn it on her.

Several things happen at once. About ten feet away, she stutters to a stop, raising her hands. Protests erupt at different pitches: her yelp of surprise, Rob's shout, Abby's cry.

"Drop the weapon!" Harold yells, raising his own black revolver at me.

We make eye contact over the barrel. No one moves.

I lower my gun, letting him think I'm surrendering. Then I reach for Charlie, who's cowering against the seat, and scoop him up into my arms. He lets out a frightened cry and pushes me away. "Hold me," I say sternly. "I won't hurt you."

Whimpering, he wraps his legs around my hips and lays his head on my shoulder. "Good boy," I mutter. Against my chest, I feel him quivering like a hummingbird. But Harold wouldn't dare shoot a child. Poor old Harold. In his two decades with River Road, he's never faced a hostage crisis.

He bares his teeth in distress. Sweat drips down his temples. But he lowers his gun halfway. And I raise mine again at Claire.

I expect her to drop to her knees and beg. Instead, as if to provoke me, she stands taller. When she opens her mouth, her voice drips with scorn: "And you call yourself a mother."

Right as my finger curls around the trigger, Rob bursts into a run, raising his arms, heading straight for me. "Wait!" he yells. "I'll come with you!"

I keep the gun steady as he approaches.

"Let's go to Canada," he gasps. "Let's start over together."

"Fuck you." I tighten my arm around Charlie. "You're just protecting her."

He opens the back door of my car and sticks one leg inside. "This is how it was supposed to be. Our family"—he points at me and Charlie—"and their family." He nods toward Claire, who's still rooted to her spot on the asphalt, and Abby and Ethan, who are further away, huddled near their car in alarm.

"You don't mean that," I snap.

Charlie shudders with a quiet sob. My shoulder is wet with his tears.

"Give him to me," Rob demands. "Don't you see he's terrified?"

He reaches over the open back seat door, and Charlie, despite not knowing him, eagerly extends his hands to his father. The sight of them trying to embrace stirs a deep longing within me, and my grip on Charlie relaxes. In that second, he launches himself into Rob's open arms.

And I find myself unprotected. Harold springs into firing position. "Drop the gun!"

Watching him, I lower it to my side.

"All the way to the ground!" he commands.

I hesitate. What if, the instant I cede power, Rob delivers Charlie straight into Claire's waiting arms?

As though reading my mind, Rob puts him in the back seat and fastens his belt. "Let's go," he says to me, then climbs inside next to Charlie and shuts the door.

"No!" Over by the curb, Abby struggles against Ethan's efforts to restrain her. "Don't go!"

"Drop the weapon!" Harold shouts at me again. "You have five seconds!"

But Claire's not running or screaming. She's studying my license plate.

"Five—" Harold begins in desperation.

And that's when it dawns on me. If I get in the car and drive away, she'll call the cops, and they'll track us down. She'll claim I kidnapped her son, and a DNA test will give her more maternal credibility than me. The authorities will remove Charlie, and I'll be left with nothing.

"Four—"

No family, no comeback. Rob's surrender is a decoy. He must be willing to turn himself in if it means saving her.

"Three—" Harold gazes at me imploringly.

But for every action, there is an equal and opposite reaction.

"Two—"

Before I raise my gun for the last time, a sense of pure freedom washes over me: I have nothing left to fight for, nothing left to fear. I've been released from the prison of ambition, and all that remains is the will to destroy.

Claire cries out when my bullet flies.

* * *

CLAIRE

The shot discharges with a terrifying crack. I launch myself to the ground, but the shot burns my right hip. My breath catches in agony as I skid onto the asphalt. At almost the same moment, another blast goes off, but I barely notice, because the sting that explodes in my side is deeper than muscle, deeper than bone. The pain is gnawing me apart. When I clutch at the wound, my fingers sink into a gushing hole of raw nerves. Blood is pouring out. My shirt is already soaked, and a warm puddle is forming beneath me.

That's when I realize the second bullet never hit me. My ears are ringing; my eyelids are closing, but I don't want to let go. I struggle to focus through the black tunnel engulfing my vision, and in the last sliver of light, I glimpse Jillian crumpled on the pavement—facedown, limbs askew, and very, very still.

* * *

ABBY

"Mom!" I sprint to where she's collapsed. "Mom!"

I run as fast as I can, but in the time it takes me to reach her, she's already passed out—or worse, I don't know. The security guard, Ethan, and my dad all run over to her, too. The blood is terrifying; it's so dark red, it's almost black. But I can't look away. I want to touch her, but I'm afraid of what I might find out. Her cheek is pressed against the ground, her eyes are closed, and her lips are parted.

Dad touches a spot under her jaw. "She's alive. Call nine one one!"

The guard whips out his walkie-talkie and radios for help.

The next minutes are the longest of my life. Dad tries to stop the bleeding by ripping off his shirt and tying it around her waist, while Ethan strokes her forehead and I hold her limp hand. When the ambulance finally comes shrieking into the lot, the only thing I can do is stand out of the way while they load her onto a stretcher and carry her inside. As Dad starts to follow her, I grab his sleeve.

"Is she going to die?"

"No," he says firmly. "Not on my watch." Then he kisses the top of my head and hurries into the ambulance.

Ethan motions to me. "Come on, we'll follow to the hospital."

I'm about to go with him when I pass by Jillian's car and see the dark outline of the boy still hiding in the back seat. An older woman who ran down from the school building after the gunshots is now begging him to come out.

"Hang on," I tell Ethan.

As I make my way over to Jillian's car, I shield my face from her body on the ground. The guard's bullet went straight to her head, a clean single shot, and the last thing I can handle right now is seeing her brains all over the street.

Now the older woman is half inside the car, pleading with the boy. I tap her leg and she scoots out. Her face is covered in tears that she wipes with her sleeve. "He's too scared to move."

"Let me try."

I crawl inside. The boy is rocking back and forth next to the window hugging his knees. He looks at me with scared blue eyes, the same exact shade as mine.

"Hi," I say. "I'm Abby."

He stares at me silently.

"It's safe to come out now." I stretch out a hand. "Will you come with me?"

"I don't even know you."

"You will soon," I promise. "Turns out I'm your big sister."

CLAIRE

When I open my eyes, three shadows surround me.

I blink as their figures come into focus. There's my darling girl—pale but smiling. There's Rob, who's almost unrecognizable with a half-grown beard and puffy eyes. And standing further back, behind them, is Ethan, who's chewing his lip in his habitual way.

Abby picks up my hand, which is stuck with an IV. There's another needle inside my elbow, and several white bands around both wrists. A low beeping noise is coming from somewhere above my head, and a sheet is draped over my body. Everything feels heavy and stiff, like my body is made of tree stumps.

"Mom?" Abby says, a little too loudly. "Can you hear me?"

I realize that my throat is horribly dry, so I only nod. Something important is nagging at me, a thought I can't quite grasp.

"Hi, honey," Rob says, stroking my other hand. "You pulled through."

"What—happened?" My voice startles me; it's low and scratchy, like a first-thing-in-the-morning voice, but much worse.

"You had to have surgery," Abby blurts out.

Panic thumps in my chest, but Rob's expression is calm. "The bullet fractured your pelvis and perforated your small bowel," he explains matter-of-factly. "You had emergency surgery, which was successful, and two blood transfusions, but you're stable now. You're going to be just fine."

His words glide into my ears, but I don't really hear them. I still feel weak and foggy, unclear how I got here. The last thing I remember is—I'm not sure . . . we got to the school, and then Jillian was there with—

"Where's my son?" I search behind them for a blond head. *He's* what I'm missing.

"He's at home with Jillian's mother," Rob says. "While we sort out what to do."

"Jillian's *dead*," Abby announces. "The guard guy shot her."

Rob purses his lips. "We'll never have to think about her again."

A vivid image flashes into my memory: my boy being held hostage, like a human shield. The fear on his face—and my inability to rescue him—will forever haunt me.

"But he's okay?" I ask anxiously. "He's safe?"

"He's fine. His grandmother pretty much raised him, so he's in good hands."

"I still don't even know his name."

"Charlie," Rob says. "He's seven years old."

There's only one way he could be mine. "The leftover embryo?"

"Yep. She kept it in storage."

The implications of this bizarre situation slowly dawn on me. I lock eyes with Ethan. "So then he's also . . . yours?"

Ethan glances at Rob. "Um . . . do you want to . . . ?"

"Well." My husband clears his throat. "The day we created the embryos, we hit a bump in the road. And it turns out Jillian did something extremely manipulative to fix it, something I had no idea about until a few days ago." He draws a breath and addresses Abby. "I might very well be your father after all. It's not clear."

A gasp escapes me; I instantly piece together what must have happened. Long ago, I privately worried about Ethan's low sperm count due to his brief bout with prostatitis, so if that did prove to be a problem, Jillian must have schemed her way around it. In the midst of her affair with Rob, and devoid of a moral compass, she would have stopped at nothing to create viable embryos.

But Abby is frowning in confusion. Such adult machinations are way over her head. "I don't get it."

Rob's face is getting pinker by the minute. "Suffice it to say, she went behind my back during a very important time . . . so either of us"—he tilts his head at Ethan—"could be your father, and same for Charlie. The only way to know for sure is if we all take a test."

"I'm all for it," Ethan volunteers. "Why not?"

"Sweetie," Rob says to Abby, "are you comfortable with that?"

She nods. "I want to know the truth."

I say nothing, but the puzzle pieces fall into shocking place for me; Abby's mysterious red hair must have come from Rob's Irish ancestry, *not* from Jillian's tiny fraction of DNA. It's so obvious, seeing Abby beside her two possible dads, that she looks nothing like Ethan; that her fair complexion and high cheekbones in fact resemble the man who raised her as his own, not knowing that she really was.

"Then I'll arrange the tests," Rob says. "I've already explained the situation to Mrs. Hendricks, and she's agreed to have Charlie tested, too. She was completely taken aback about his origins, so now she wants to establish his paternity *and* maternity. I guess Jillian lied and told her she got pregnant from a one-night stand."

"Shocker," I mutter.

I try to push myself up to sit, but a stabbing pain in my lower right side cuts me off.

"Don't," Rob says. "What do you need?"

A new body, I think. *A lifetime of vacation.*

"A stiff drink," is all I reply.

He cracks a smile. "Well, your IV is full of Demerol, so that's even better."

"How long do I have to be here?"

"Another few days at least to monitor you for infection. My guess is we'll go home over the weekend."

I perk up. "That's not so bad!"

"But you'll need to be in a wheelchair for some time. I won't lie, it's going to be a long road to recovery. There will be lots of doctor's visits, physical therapy, a follow-up surgery . . . I just want you to prepare yourself."

My head sinks deeper into the pillow. It occurs to me that I've traded a mental affliction for a physical one; I'm not sure which kind is worse.

"But I'll walk again, right?" I ask. "I mean, eventually?"

"You totally will!" Abby declares, betraying a slight hysteria. "You're not going to be in a wheelchair forever!" She blinks at Rob. "*Right?*"

He smiles confidently at her. "Knowing your mother, she'll by running by Christmas."

Whatever it takes, I think. *Jillian will not steal my legs from me.*

"Consider it done," I declare.

Abby is satisfied. "And what about Charlie? When will we get to see him again?"

"I'm not sure." Rob shrugs, glancing at Ethan. "A lot will depend on the test."

"Can I call him? I want to see how he's doing."

"Let's not bother them. It's a tough time for their family."

"Please?" she begs. "Just for, like, five minutes? He's my *brother*, isn't he?"

"Oh, just let her," I tell Rob. Our poor girl has been through enough. I'd do anything to make her happy for a couple of minutes. "He might like to hear from her."

Rob considers. "All right. You can use my phone outside."

"Yay!" she squeals.

When they leave the room, Ethan and I find ourselves unexpectedly alone. Standing at the foot of the bed, he gestures to a chair nearby. "Should I . . . or do you want to . . . ?"

"Go ahead."

He pulls it up and sits. The silence looms heavy. We haven't been alone together since the day we broke up—another lifetime ago.

After a bit, the urge to fill the void is overwhelming.

"You could have gone back to the city," I tell him. "You didn't have to stay."

He shrugs. "The cops interviewed me, so I ended up sticking around. I wanted to make sure you'd be okay."

Again, I think of Charlie clinging to Jillian in terror while she brandished her gun. I can't imagine the trauma he's suffering now; and the fact that I can't comfort him, or even be with him, is its own form of torture.

Ethan seems wrapped up in his own disturbing memory. "I can't stop replaying it all."

"I know. At least no one else got hurt. I mean, aside from her."

"She doesn't count." He grimaces. "But let's not talk about her."

"Okay." On an impulse, I switch tracks. "How about the fact that you might have two kids?"

As soon as I say it, my worry spikes. If he *is* the father of one or both kids, will he try to take them away? I can't risk going to court and being exposed for who I really am, so he would have all the power.

"Let's wait and see," he says. "But don't get all worked up. I'm not in a position to raise a child anymore."

I try not to let my relief show. "Oh no?"

"I'm planning to retire next year and travel the world. Remember how we used to talk about living in Florence or Rome?"

"Yeah, but Colton was too sick . . ."

We both fall silent. The moment is strangely intimate.

Then he says, "I'd still want to be in their life to *some* degree. Like an uncle or something."

I smile. "That would be nice."

"And you . . ." He trails off. "You and Rob are . . . happy?"

I consider how to be truthful without hurting him. "It works."

"That's good." He swallows and looks away. "I'm sorry for the way things ended between us."

"Me too." Despite my desire to avoid a fight, my voice hardens. "All of a sudden, you're just, like, fine with him? After what you did to destroy us?"

"I didn't understand before," he admits. "I really didn't get it."

"Get what?" I want to hear him say it.

"The second I met Abby, everything changed." He gazes off into space. "I'd always stood by this absolute boundary of never engineering human embryos, but she wasn't created to be smarter or better than anyone else; just normal. Who knows if she'd still be alive otherwise?"

"Gee, I never tried to tell you that."

"Well, I had to see it with my own eyes. And now I'm going to have to rethink some of my positions. It's pretty confusing, to be honest."

I motion toward my sandbag legs. "I don't feel bad for you."

He cringes. "Fair enough. So, can we start over? Be friends?"

I sigh. "It's not that simple. You ruined us, and we're still paying the price."

"Because of the warrants?"

"You mentioned the cops . . ." My mouth goes dry. "I guess they haven't made any connections—yet."

"I actually gave them your fake names in my statement," he says, to my surprise. "Michael and Lisa Burke, right?"

It's a gesture of goodwill if I've ever seen one. "How did you know?"

"Abby told me."

"Thank you. For real, that means a lot."

"You know, I still think of you as family." He smiles sadly. "I think I always will."

* * *

A week later, I'm back at home with Abby and Rob, but life is nowhere near normal. Despite my new physical limitations, in some ways, it's better. I'm not fixated on Jillian invading our lives. I'm not worried about any delusions accosting me. And Rob's regained his confidence in my mental stability. Instead of his voice bristling with concern, he speaks to me again as his wife. He kisses me like he means it. The footing I thought we lost has been restored.

Best of all, the DNA test proved my hunch: he *is* Abby's real father after all. We were thrilled when we opened the letter from the hospital. Not that we needed the validation; we're a family and we always will be.

As for Charlie, his tests proved that he's my kid, and—remarkably—Ethan's. No wonder he looks so much like Colton. Ethan was thrilled; he told me he would consider moving upstate after his retirement next year to be closer to us.

But sadly, I still haven't set eyes on my boy again. Mrs. Hendricks and I have agreed to take things slow. We don't want to force a meeting on him before he's ready.

When I spoke to her on the phone, she reminded me that he had just lost his mother. "I mean . . ." She faltered. "Well, you know what I mean."

The anguish was plain in her voice; Jillian was her little girl, despite the disastrous person she became.

"I understand," I told her, "and I'm sorry for your loss." No matter the circumstances, the death of a child is a tragedy no parent should ever face.

"I appreciate that," she said. "And *I'm* sorry for what she did."

"Thank you." I tried not to let the desperation creep into my voice. "I would love to see Charlie when the time is right . . . but I agree that it's best not to push him."

So here we are, in a holding pattern that could last indefinitely.

In the meantime, I feel like an elderly woman with a litany of physical complaints. Confined to my wheelchair, my universe has shrunk to the few rooms of our house I can navigate without going upstairs. I'm sleeping on the pull-out couch in the living room. I need help going to the bathroom and taking a shower. I'm on opioids for the constant pain in my hip. And my stomach issues are severe: you've never experienced real bloating until your intestines have been operated on. All I can eat so far is applesauce and tofu.

Abby's been a champ about my limitations. Without my asking, she's been bringing me tea in the mornings and doing her homework beside me in the afternoons. While I know she's happy to be back at school with Riley and Tyler and to join the big end-of-year field trip, I think she's also eager to spend time at home. Now, she barely checks her phone around me, and she doesn't run to her room as much to be alone. The past few weeks have infused our relationship with a subtle gravity. Our time together is too precious to waste.

That's why this morning, a Saturday, I call her over to my couch-bed after she finishes her Cheerios in the kitchen. There are things that need to be said, and I'm done with hiding—if not from the world, then at least from my own daughter. Rob's out in his woodworking shed, so we have a window of privacy as she climbs up next to me and grabs the remote.

"Cartoons?" she asks. "Or a movie? We never finished *The Parent Trap.*"

"In a minute." I shift on my pillows to face her, wincing as the pain flares up in my hip. "We need to clear the air."

Her face scrunches up in dismay. "Am I in trouble?"

"No, nothing like that. The truth is, I owe you an apology. I should have told you sooner about your history. I'm sorry for keeping it a secret."

She scowls. "You never told me at all."

"I know. It was wrong to lie to you."

"Yeah." She broods in silence. "You know what sucks? If we're really being honest?"

"Tell me."

"That you go all the way to the city for Colton's birthday every year, but you won't even come to my soccer games."

"Oh honey." Her dejection fills me with an ache that no medication can relieve. "You've got it all wrong. Colton gets one day a year. The other three hundred sixty-four are for you."

She frowns. "How's that?"

"Getting seen at your school events runs the risk of someone putting two and two together—you know how the moms gossip. And then it would be bad news for all of us. Someone could call the cops . . ." I trail off, not wanting to animate this worry too much in her mind. "You have no idea how much it kills me not to come."

"But Dad does once in a while," she points out. "How come?"

"Because it was *my* face all over the news. I was the Frankenmom, the pregnant runaway." I roll my eyes. "Your dad was rarely pictured."

She gets very quiet. "Do you think I'm a freak? Or, like, some kind of monster?"

I gasp. "Of course not! How could you think that?"

"Because, remember that note? The one that called you crazy? I *told* you I didn't write it, but you didn't believe me."

I recall the incident with shame. "You're right. I didn't. And it's ridiculous to admit, but I was worried that maybe you inherited some mean streak of Jillian's. I promise I don't think that anymore."

"Oh my God." Her eyes widen. "It wasn't Sydney who wrote it. It was *her*."

"Are you serious?"

"The permission slip was given out in *art* class. And she was super jealous of you."

A familiar mix of disgust and shock overwhelms me. "I *knew* she was finding ways to cause trouble. This is exactly why I've been so overprotective."

And then my sage child articulates the real point. "But you didn't stop her, did you?"

"No," I agree. "I didn't."

"Well then?" She raises her eyebrows expectantly, and I catch a glimpse of the teenager she will soon become.

"Fine," I say. "I'll work on *chilling out*. I guess it's inevitable. One day you'll start driving, and then you'll go off to college, and eventually I won't even know what you're doing. You'll call home a few times a week if I'm lucky." I smile to show I'm joking, but it doesn't counteract my undertone of despair. My other fears surface, too—one day, the world will find out about her and Charlie. Will they be able to stand up to any bullies? To the press? To a lifetime of scrutiny? And what will happen when Abby wants to have children of her own—children who will inherit Jillian's mitochondrial DNA, too?

"Mo-*om*," she groans. "I'm not even in sixth grade yet. You won't even let me go on Instagram!"

I laugh. She's right. I can't problem-solve the future.

"Go ahead. Scroll your heart out. But don't talk to strangers!"

She extends her hand, businesslike. "Deal."

"You know," I say, shaking on it, "I always thought the hardest part of being a mother was protecting you. But I was wrong. The hardest part is letting go."

"I'll be *fine*." Her smile brims with the invincibility of youth. "Don't worry."

"I'll try." I blink back my tears. "I just never had a child grow up."

EPILOGUE

THREE MONTHS LATER

September has snuck up on us the way it always does. The brisk air and the back-to-school shopping are a reminder that the lazy days of summer are winding down. But this Labor Day weekend marks a clean break with our usual isolation. For the first time, we're hosting a family barbecue.

Abby, Ethan, and Rob are hanging out near the grill, and any minute, I hope, Charlie and his grandmother will be joining the festivities. I've waited out the entire summer without properly meeting my son, so I couldn't resist the opportunity to call Mrs. Hendricks and tell her about today's gathering. She said she would run it by Charlie—that he loved hot dogs—but that she couldn't guarantee their attendance.

Of course, just in case, I've bought three kinds of hot dogs and an Oreo ice cream cake, because what kid doesn't love Oreos? It seemed like a good bet in the store, but when I saw it this morning in the freezer, I realized I don't actually know my own kid at all. I have no clue what he likes for lunch, what his favorite book is, who his friends are. I'm greedy for the intimate knowledge that can only be acquired by raising him day in and day out.

The sun is arcing higher in the sky, a reminder that they're late—if they're even coming. Each time I steal a glance at the gate from my lounge chair, my desperation rises a notch. Meanwhile, Abby's now scarfing down her own hot dog on her way to the pool, and Ethan and Rob are eating burgers at the patio table, presumably talking business.

Last month, Ethan called us with some shocking news. In his capacity as head of the President's Bioethics Committee, he's privy to the highest level of discussions about national science policy. Turns out that the new president has been complaining to her staff about how the U.S. is lagging behind China and the U.K. on genetically engineering embryos to prevent heritable diseases. She has decided to not only dismantle the current restrictions but also dedicate a new center at the National Institutes of Health to incentivize research. Rob is interested in being a consultant, and Ethan is working on facilitating the connection for him. Best of all, Ethan's pulled a couple of strings with his old friends at the Justice Department, who are eager to ingratiate themselves with the new administration, so our arrest warrants have been thrown out.

We're no longer living a lie. No more hiding out in the house, no more skipping Abby's events, no more terror if a cop is driving behind us. When the Center for Embryonic Cell and Gene Therapy opens later this year, Rob may commute once a month to DC, and I plan to get involved with the PTA at Abby's school. I also want to take up my own writing projects again—maybe a memoir, to set the record straight.

A creak near the fence makes my heart leap.

They're here. Mrs. Hendricks is opening the gate for Charlie. Seeing him across the lawn is surreal—his scruffy blond hair, his tanned skin, his skinny body. I want to stop time and simply revel in the sight of him. He steps inside tentatively, wearing red swim trunks dotted with little sharks. Abby jumps out of the pool and rushes to greet them. I make my way across the grass, leaning heavily on my cane.

"Hey!" Abby squeals, offering him a high five.

He gives her a timid slap in return, but her exuberance is not diminished.

"Wanna try my Slip 'n Slide?" She points to the fifty-foot blue slide we set up on the hill at the edge of our yard. "It's really fun!"

He shrugs. "Sure."

"Yay, I'll go start the hose!"

She scampers away as I approach.

"I'm so glad you guys came." I resist reaching out to Charlie for a hug; it's not yet my place.

Mrs. Hendricks rewards my restraint with a smile.

"Glad we could make it," she says. "Actually, he's been asking about you guys. He wanted to come."

I kneel down in front of him, barely noticing the sting in my hip. It doesn't bother me that we're two strangers starting from scratch, or that it will take time—maybe years—to feel like a real family. In this moment, only joy registers.

"Hi, sweetheart. How are you?"

He regards me shyly. "Okay."

"Are you hungry? Can I make you a hot dog?"

He gazes across the yard at the grill, where Ethan and Rob are waving us over.

"That sounds good," he says. "Thanks."

"With ketchup and a pickle, no mustard?"

A grin lights up his face. "How did you know?"

I smile, thinking of the brother he never met. "Just a guess."

By the grill, I see Ethan slowly stand, his eyes glassy and his fingers clasped at his waist, as though a soldier has finally come home.

I extend my palm to Charlie. "Ready to go meet your dad?"

He slips his small hand into mine. "Let's go."

ACKNOWLEDGMENTS

I owe a great debt first and foremost to my agent, Erica Silverman at Trident Media Group. Erica leveled with me about an early version of the manuscript and suggested I undertake a thorough rewrite; her advice paved the way for a much-improved book. While Erica is a tough critic, she is also my fiercest advocate. I am extremely grateful to have her in my corner, along with her colleagues Robert Gottlieb, Nicole Robson, Caitlin O'Beirne, Kristin Cipolla, and Lucinda Karter.

Deepest thanks to Matt Martz and Jenny Chen at Crooked Lane for embracing the book and guiding me through yet another rewrite, and then—you guessed it—another one. Their tenacity carried me through to the finish line when my own stamina was waning, and their wise suggestions made all the difference. Thank you to the entire Crooked Lane team for putting together an amazing package and carrying it out into the world—Sarah Poppe, Melanie Sun, Jennifer Canzone, Ashley Di Dio, my copy editor, and the sales reps whom I will never meet but whose efforts I am no less grateful for. And to my publicist extraordinaire, Meryl Moss.

Thank you to the expert sources who provided me with inspiration and education in the area of fertility medicine—Dr. Mark Sauer and Dr. Eric J. Forman. And thank you to Robert Klitzman and my other professors in the Bioethics Master's Degree program at Columbia University for a world-class learning experience.

Thank you to my friends and family for the encouragement over the difficult years it took to finish this book, while I was also caring for my own new baby—specifically, to my parents, Leonard and Cynthia, for their unwavering belief in my writing ability, and to Rosalie and Alan Beilis for cheering me on and providing countless hours of loving childcare. It really does take a village to raise a kid—and to write a book.

My husband Matt takes the cake for the world's most supportive spouse. He tolerated my weekend and night writing schedule for many months and was often game to talk late into the night about my latest plot problem. His perceptive feedback pulled no punches, and the book is immeasurably better for it.

I could not have written about pregnancy, birth, and a mother's love for her child without having experienced those things for myself. I happened to start writing this book the week before I found out I was pregnant. I finished it when my son was two years old. The story may be fictitious, but the sentiment behind Claire's character is not; Zachary, I would do whatever it takes on this Earth to make sure you are healthy and happy—and one day, when you are much older, I will also try to let go. This book is for you.